Praise for *A SEAL at Heart*

"A romance with real heart, from a talented writer who has deep personal insight into what it takes—and what it means—to be a Navy SEAL."

—*New York Times* bestselling author
Suzanne Brockmann

"Two wounded souls find healing through love in Elizabeth's romance. Readers will find this book an accurate reflection of what's happening in the world today and perhaps be uplifted by its message of hope."

—*Booklist*

"Elizabeth's series starter is, like the title, filled with heart and action. Vivid descriptions of military missions, and the pain that can come from them, make this a page-turner."

—*RT Book Reviews*

"The connection between Jack and Laurie is instantaneous and combustible."

—*Publishers Weekly*

"An exciting and poignant read that gives insight into the dangerous and stressful life of a SEAL even as it shows the magnitude of the sacrifices and commitment of these amazing heroes."

—*Night Owl Reviews* Reviewer Top Pick

ONCE *a* SEAL

ANNE ELIZABETH

sourcebooks
casablanca

Published by Sourcebooks Casablanca, an imprint of Sourcebooks, Inc.
P.O. Box 4410, Naperville, Illinois 60567-4410
(630) 961-3900
FAX: (630) 961-2168
www.sourcebooks.com

Printed and bound in the United States of America
VP 10 9 8 7 6 5 4 3 2 1

This book is dedicated to our outstanding Navy SEALs,
our men and women in uniform, and their families.

Thank you for your tremendous dedication,
your sacrifice, and your service.

Chapter 1

DARK CLOUDS FILLED THE SKY ABOVE HER. *PLEASE don't rain.*

Aria rubbed her arms, hoping to chase away the chill. It didn't work. She shook the sand off the hem of her bridal gown and eyed the weather encroaching on her wedding day. It was impossible not to worry about a deluge, her not-present-and-accounted-for fiancé, and the guests who watched her like a hawk.

What would happen if Dan didn't show?

Her throat constricted. *Oh, God, I'd be mortified!*

The sun peeked momentarily from behind the clouds, briefly spreading a glittering cache of diamonds across the water. Shouldn't she relax? Coronado was known for its mild weather; though every now and then, nature kicked her heels, and a rainstorm became a tropical downpour that flooded everything and practically drowned those in its path.

Her hand touched her throat but it didn't stop the choking sensation from growing tighter.

"Are you okay?" asked a passing guest.

"Fine. Thanks." She pasted on a smile and dropped her hand, lacing her fingers together, hoping he believed her.

A class of BUD/S (Basic Underwater Demolition/ SEAL) trainees with numbers painted on their helmets ran by. Sweat dripped down their young faces as they shouldered giant packs on their backs. Several instructors nodded at her as the group sped by soundlessly.

"Dan. Where are you?" she murmured. Perhaps the white-knuckle look wasn't supporting the vision of a calm bride. She didn't want to be one of those monster brides. But with this completely crazy event—whose fiancé came to the wedding via helicopter? Didn't that count as understandably upsetting?

Waving back at the group gathered behind her, she said, "Just a few more minutes." She prayed that comment would be true.

Just then the wind picked up, making her curls fly askew and the white tulle tied to the backs of the folding chairs dance. The simple decorations of flowers and fabric felt right for getting married in God's biggest cathedral. Really, if it had been a regular sunny day, it would be beautiful.

Concentrate on something positive, she told herself. A memory splashed through her mind.

This spot, this exact spot, was where Dan had proposed.

She'd never forget that day. The sparkle of mischief in his eyes, the way his palms felt sweaty in hers, and the flourish with which he'd bent down on one knee and placed the diamond on her finger. Then he'd asked, "Will you be mine, forever? Please, say yes. I don't have the heart to take this off."

She remembered thinking, *We've known each other for such a short time, almost four weeks now, and yet it feels so right.* Tears had slid down her cheeks as she threw herself into his arms. "Yes, yes, yes!" she'd replied before she kissed him with every bit of happiness in her heart.

He'd scooped her up in his arms and found a secluded spot, where they made love.

Gooey warmth and giddiness filled her belly at the memory of their whirlwind romance. They had created memorable times together thus far, and she wondered what the future held for them. If Dan was as caring and loving as he'd been this first month, then it was going to be a wonderful forever.

"You look lovely," said the wife of one of Dan's teammates. She smiled kindly.

"Thank you," Aria replied. "I'm glad you could come."

Dan's friends and their wives made up most of the guest list. The only people on her side were her uncle, her brother, and her best friend, Mark. That was it. Friendship didn't come that easily to her, though she had a whole address book full of acquaintances and work contacts.

"I see the helos," shouted a tall man in a white uniform.

Oh, thank God.

Her brother Jimmy came running across the beach. All gangly limbs and fourteen years' worth of awkwardness, dressed in a tux and sneakers. "They're coming!" he shouted. "You should have seen them jump into the water. It was insane. Can I do that?"

She gave him a placating smile and brushed a strand of his wild hair behind his ear.

"We'll talk to Dan about it later, okay? Please, go tell Uncle David to come down. We have to take our places."

"Okay," he said, ducking out of her reach.

Under her breath, she added, "Heaven help us that this goes smoothly." She'd never been more stressed-out in her whole life.

The chaplain waved at her. Attired in his formal whites, he looked uncomfortably hot as he tugged at his collar. "Miss Kavanagh, I have another event at 1730. You have about thirty minutes before I need to leave."

The chaplain's tone wasn't judgmental, but she had a hard time not taking it to heart. It wasn't her fault that her fiancé had gotten called for an Op so close to the wedding ceremony. Of course, if she had her way, she'd have told the Navy to put their mission on hold so they could have their special day. When she had brought up that idea to Dan, he'd laughed out loud, telling her the CO would get a kick out of the statement. Unfortunately, things didn't always work in her favor, despite her best efforts.

"They're almost here. It will only be a few more minutes. Thank you for your patience and time, Chaplain O'Connor." He nodded and took his place under the small canopy that faced out toward the ocean.

She knew she shouldn't be nervous. Loving Dan was one of the best experiences in her life. She couldn't imagine life without him.

"It's time, Aria! Hurry! Go hide!" said Caty, Dan's sister, as she rushed over. Her future sister-in-law had a gorgeous tan and model-like slim figure. The dress she wore highlighted her generous cleavage and ensured Caty got plenty of attention. That kind of perfection could be intimidating.

"Caty, wait up." Naturally, her husband, Hank—an accountant—was never far behind, making sure that no one else was appreciating what was his.

"Aria, are you listening to me? I can see them coming onto the beach. Don't you want to hide yourself?" Caty demanded, hands on her hips.

Caty hadn't liked the idea of her brother marrying Aria so quickly, but eventually Dan had swayed her. His parents were another story. They had gone totally ballistic when they heard the news. It was even worse than when they had wanted Dan to go to Harvard and become a lawyer and he'd told them that "life was full of disappointments, and if he was one to them, then they could just choose to stay out of his future"…and thus far, they had. They hadn't even sent a card or a wedding present, preferring to not even acknowledge that the event was taking place today.

She admired his strength, though she would have liked to meet his mom and dad; to let them know she was a supportive part of Dan's world, and that although this was a very short courtship, it was going to be a very long marriage. Perhaps, by building a relationship with Caty, she could bridge the chasm between Dan and his family. If there were relatives to be had—to add to their lives—she wanted them in their future.

"I'm on it." Aria gave her soon-to-be sister-in-law a willing smile and then headed for the white changing tent they'd erected for this very moment.

"Is this the wedding you dreamed of? I think I would have opted for inside," said a woman in glasses, whose name escaped her.

Aria just nodded her head. What could she say? It didn't seem appropriate to mention the real reasons they were getting married on the beach—sentimental as well as financial. She just couldn't imagine spending money on a hall or hotel when this place was completely free and available whenever they wanted it. Of course, she'd opted to decorate the edges of the small canopy herself with real flowers—daisy chains interwoven with small hunks of Queen Anne's lace. Her mother had taught her to make them when she was a child.

A hand caught her elbow and she looked up, relieved. It was her best friend, Mark Anders. "Hey, there." His yellow tuxedo brought out his dark hair nicely and showed off the glimmer of gold in his eyes. She was so glad he had agreed to wear it. That was a good friend, one who'd wear her favorite color and act as man of honor.

"I thought you could use a break, or an out. We could keep walking and have you into my Hummer in about five minutes." He had an evil twinkle in his eyes and a smile playing on his lips. "Just kidding!"

"Ha, ha." Aria lightly punched his arm. "Some joke! You know Dan's the first man I've ever loved. He's my heart." She rubbed at the tickle under her nose. "For the record, he's going to be the last, too. I'm only marrying once."

"I'm sorry. Just trying to lighten the mood…you seem so tense." He brought his mouth close to her ear. "But in case you're worried…there *are* other men out there. You could postpone this and try others…make sure he's the one."

"I'm sure. Now, stop being a pain in the ass! I've got to go inside the tent before Dan sees me. Everything has to be perfect." She stopped in front of the small structure. Mark's teasing aside, she needed a moment or two alone. "Can you please make sure Jimmy looks decent?"

"Yes," he said as he kissed her cheek. "I'm available…anytime you need me."

"Thanks." She smiled up at him and then lifted the fabric of the tent entrance. She silently repeated words her mother used to say to her, "Happiness comes from a joyful heart." This was a place where she could be alone, get her thoughts together, and prepare for any last-minute touch-ups. Her hand released the material and the curtain fell into place. Laying her bouquet in a safe spot next to her makeup case, she let the tension ease of out of her body. The solitary moment brought calm as she sat down on the small stool, arranging her silk wedding dress so it didn't get dirty or too full of sand.

"Knock, knock," said a familiar voice from outside of the curtain. Her hands clenched together. There was just no "cone of quiet" for her today.

"Come in, Uncle David." When he didn't respond immediately, Aria repeated the words more loudly. "Uncle David, come in. I'm decent."

"I heard you, Aria. I was just watching your future husband get tackled on the sand by one of his friends and hauled off to the showers," replied David Kavanagh as he lifted the curtain and entered the small tent. "I didn't realize they would be arriving so late."

"Dan had a mission. With his job, he doesn't always have control of his schedule." She said it matter-of-factly. The last-minute entrance of her husband-to-be was stressing her out a bit. She knew he'd be there. Dan was a man of his word. But the Navy could sometimes be unpredictable. When Jimmy had said he saw them arrive, she'd let go of some of the stress. Now she had to contend with her own butterflies.

"Bunches of people are sitting out there already." Uncle David's black tuxedo was covered in places with clumps of sand and dried bits of seaweed. Obviously, he'd lost his footing and landed on his butt when coming down the dune.

"I saw them." She pointed at the mess, and he began brushing it off.

"I think I got it all," he said as he stopped fussing with the sand. Sitting on the stool across from her, he stared at her for several seconds as if he wanted to say something. Then two fingers touched his brow briefly before dropping to his lap.

"I'm not good at this." His hand landed abruptly on her shoulder—this was meant to be comforting—and then he thought better of it and placed both of his hands on his lap, mirroring her posture and position.

"It's okay, Uncle David." But it wasn't. She wanted him to share a morsel of wisdom. He was never a man of many words, though. What could he offer?

When at last he spoke, his voice traveled across the small expanse, sounding overly loud and very nervous. "M-m-must be a trick to walking on the sand. Why anyone would leave the pine needles and fertile earth of Vermont for the heat and sand of California is beyond me. Are you sure about this…wanting to get married… to Dan?"

"Yes, Uncle David. I love him. Be happy for me." Her mother's brother had been thrilled about her going across the country to college, getting a job, and staying here. He always said, "My Aria's a go-getter, and she cannot stifle her Scottish spirit for anyone." Secretly, though, she suspected it had been hard on him to watch her go and see her really move on from life in the small town of Dorset, Vermont. She couldn't stay a child or a theater rat forever. Now she was an advertising consultant with a thriving clientele and deeply in love with a man who made her life feel complete.

She could dream of adventures with Dan…or just revel in the warmth of him as he embraced her. He was the man she'd never realized could be real. So perfect!

"Right, right. Of course, I am. I'm very happy for you," he huffed. She wanted him to hold her gaze, to really be there, to tell her everything was great and that Dan was perfect for her. Instead, her uncle—her only living relative, besides her little brother—glanced around the small tent. "Not much of a space to prepare for your wedding. I could have contributed, gotten you something a little better."

"It's fine. I've never needed very much." She plucked a few grains of sand off her lap and dropped them on the ground next to her.

"It's important to be surrounded by people you care about on your wedding day." Uncle David finally stopped looking around and held her gaze. Color flushed in mottled tones on his pale cheeks. "I know this isn't really the time. Or maybe it is…and I should have prepared some words of wisdom." He scratched his bald scalp and then waved his hands in front of him as if shooing away a disruptive image. "I'm too nervous. I don't know what to say. Your parents should be here." He sighed. "Aria, they would have been so proud of you—for graduating with honors, for marrying someone you love, and for going out there and getting on with your life. They'd want me to tell you…that you did it…did it right."

Tears welled up in her eyes. That was the message she craved! She'd needed to hear his heartfelt words. She would have sacrificed anything for her parents to

be here right now. To have her father walk her down
the aisle and to have had her mother to help her plan the
wedding and to answer all the questions she had about
the union she was about to enter into. But none of that
could happen. Even after all these years, she hadn't fully
reconciled herself to their deaths.

Pulling the lace handkerchief out that she'd tucked
into her cleavage, she dabbed her eyes and nose. *Please,
God, don't let me bawl. I'll never stop…*

Aria swallowed the knot of emotion and gave him
a hearty nod. "Thanks, Uncle David. I appreciate the
sentiment." She could follow her heart. She could buck
up and get married. This was what she needed and
wanted…to be with Dan for now and always.

Awkwardly, she leaned over and hugged her Uncle
David. He smelled like almond soap and peanuts.

Drawing back, she resettled herself. She didn't want
to drop the train of her dress, and hers had never been
a very physical interaction with her uncle. David was
more the stoic type, one whose hugs were fierce and hurt
a little and who never held either her brother or her. "I'm
glad you're here."

"Me, too."

She turned away and lifted a round handheld mirror to
check her makeup. Everything pretty much looked okay.
Her eyes were a little red, but her mascara and eyeliner
were still in place. She freshened her satiny pink lipstick
and then stowed her small bag. "I'm ready."

"Okay." Her Uncle David stood and offered his arm.
"Let's go get 'em. Remember, I'm right here with you."

"Thanks." She took a deep breath and then stood. She
held her bouquet to her nose, drawing in the fresh scent.

Taking her place beside her uncle, she accepted his waiting arm. It was time to walk the path...to be with her future husband. This was the first step on the way to the rest of her life. Nothing after the next few moments would ever be the same for either of them.

Chapter 2

DAN HAD NEVER TAKEN A SHOWER SO FAST IN HIS LIFE. And his groomsmen weren't far behind. They knew how to muster quickly when the occasion called for it. His wedding to Aria definitely counted as Priority One.

They had completed a mission, been dropped in the ocean, and swum ashore. Even to him, it felt dramatic, but it was impossible to change the fact that this was who he was: a SEAL. For now, the Navy had the final say on his duty list, though he was pretty sure his wife-to-be would have something to say about that in the future. He grinned at the thought as he stood now looking out over the people gathered here for his wedding.

"How are you doing?" asked JC as he rubbed his shoe on the back of his pant leg. The speck of dirt that had been there disappeared. Those shoes were shiny enough to be used for scoping out single girls, if JC had been at that point in his life. Instead, he was Joe—the family man with a penchant for dependability and bad jokes. He was just as much of a wiseass as the rest of them, though they rarely shared their unusual brand of humor outside their small circle.

"Peachy. Ducky. Yeah, I'm okay." Dan nodded, letting air out slowly and breathing in the same way. He was prepped for this…that nerves might sock him in the gut at the last minute. None of it was going to change his plans. Building a life with Aria was right. He couldn't wait another day to get this mission under way. "How's my uniform?"

"Ya look like a train wreck, Mr. Peachy Ducky Okay," commented Hammer with a cheesy grin. He turned away and slapped Dirks on the back with his meaty hands, nearly bowling his swim buddy over. "Christ, I wish I had a chance to meet Aria first. She's a looker. Don't you think, Dirks? You're a lucky dawg, McCullum."

"Bet your wife would disagree, Hammerhead," said Dirks, glancing at a willowy blond who sent a questioning glance Hammer's way. Her eyebrows were almost to her hairline, and she didn't look pleased.

"Shit! What kind of radar does Hannah have that she can always catch me in the middle of my crap?" Hammer waved at his wife, who responded with a smile, lowering her eyebrows and going back to her conversation with the woman next to her.

"Man, I can't believe I put on tighty-whities for you," said Joe.

"Appreciated," said Dan, relieved his guys had gone the whole nine yards in their uniforms. Nothing was worse than wearing whites commando style and having everyone see the size of their worlds through the cloth.

The guys continued to peck at each other as if it were just another day at work. Nerves nibbled at Dan's ability to be calm. Some guys hadn't been so lucky at marriage, but he knew in his soul that Aria was the woman he wanted to spend the rest of his life with.

He paced his breathing again, using slow inhalations and exhalations. There was so much she didn't know, though. So much she could never know, because of his job. Parts of him that it didn't seem possible she'd ever be able to understand. There were so many more advantages to keeping the darker parts of his world separate, and yet...

Dirks noticed. "Listen, McCullum, Aria's a keeper. I know you'll have better luck than I did. So chill out."

Dan bounced on the balls of his feet. He hadn't been this wound up since the first day of BUD/S and the last day of Hell Week. Only when it really mattered did his gut tie up in a bowline. His stomach had been doing flips, trying to unknot, ever since they exited the helo.

To distract himself, his eyes searched the beach. That spot, down there, right where the riptide split the current, was where he'd gone through Hell Week. It was fitting he had brought Aria to this place, and now they were joining their lives on this spot. He was relieved she wasn't a luxury lady who had to have everything prim and proper and mostly five-star rated. He needed a partner who could rough it and could make the best of what life would give them.

"Aria did a decent job decorating," commented JC. "Anyone help her?"

"No, she did it all herself. Aria's sort of a solo act. I'm hoping the other wives will help her out a bit. Get closer, once we're married." Dan shook his arms out as if they were covered in red ants. In truth, adrenaline was still coursing through his body. The way things were looking, he might be running on that energy all day.

"On it," added Hammer. "I'll have Hannah give her a call next week. Help ease the culture shock."

"Thanks." Dan was eager to get this wedding under way. He could imagine all the reasons Aria wouldn't want to marry a SEAL, and he wanted her to commit before she changed her mind. His life was not an easy one.

Looking in the direction of the small white tent, he momentarily stopped breathing. There she was.

Bagpipes sounded. The notes screeched louder than the seagulls and then became a melodic song as the wedding march began.

Aria. She was a vision in white.

The sun peeked through the clouds at just that moment, making gold light dance in her red hair like some kind of heavenly being. She practically glowed. The wedding dress highlighted her gorgeous body, with ample lace decorating her bust and going all the way down to her delicate wrists.

"Breathe," whispered Joe.

Dan let out a whoosh of air he hadn't realized he was holding. When her emerald-green eyes met his brown ones, he almost dropped to his knees and begged for mercy. *God, she's the most beautiful woman I've ever seen. Please don't let me screw this up!*

She was holding a bouquet of white daisies with yellow roses, and her movements were poetic and peaceful as she walked in time to the crashing waves.

Mine. It was the one word that chased through his mind.

She smiled and he grinned back. He couldn't take his eyes off her.

The wind kicked up, plastering the dress even tighter to her body. Her every curve was discernible. He swallowed.

—⁂—

Uncle David escorted Aria to her spot next to Dan. Taking her hand in his, Dan nodded at David and then kissed

Aria's fingertips. She squeezed his hand tight, as if afraid that the wind could take her away at any moment.

Aria handed her large bouquet to Dan's sister, who immediately tucked it next to her smaller one. Then Aria nodded at Mark, a strange dude who was standing next to Caty as man of honor. Seemed weird to him—a male bridal participant—but it was impossible to argue with Aria, and it was such a small concession. She asked for so little, and this made her happy, so he got on board with it.

Aria squeezed Dan's fingers again, and his eyes went immediately back to her.

Together, they stepped forward and faced the chaplain.

Small grains of sand pelted them, and he wrapped his arm around her, trying to shelter her from the wind.

The chaplain cleared his throat and shouted, "Please be seated." In a softer tone, he began the ceremony. "We are gathered here today to witness the union between Daniel Gregg McCullum and Aria Ruth Kavanagh. The sacrament of marriage is a solemn and joyful occasion, not to be entered into lightly. Rather, marriage is the happy pronouncement of what God has brought together. Let no man or woman put asunder this union, lest he or she be guilty of sinning against the consecrated bond blessed by our Lord. Instead, let us celebrate this day as the first step of two souls joined on a journey. May it bring them their greatest desires, and exultation through the Lord's name, Amen.

"Do you, Daniel, take Aria to be your wife, to have and to hold in triumph and in trial, to love and to cherish for now and forever?" The words held in the air like a mythical pronouncement. Would he? Could he?

"I do," said Dan, gently squeezing Aria's delicate hands as they rested in his own. He took the ring from Joe and slid the simple gold band onto her finger. Emotion welled up inside of him. This was his wife, the one person on the face of this earth he was intentionally taking on as his partner in life, his swim buddy, his best friend, and his one and only lover. Commitment for a SEAL was a do-or-die proposition, and he did not do anything lightly.

"Do you, Aria, take Daniel to be your husband, to have and to hold in triumph and in trial, to love and to cherish for now and forever?" The Chaplain stared at Aria as he waited for her answer.

Aria's hand shook. She dropped the ring in the sand before she could get it on Dan's finger. Bending down at the same time, they bumped heads.

God, I hope I didn't dent her skull.

"Let me," he said, righting her and then digging around in the sand. His fingers finally connected with it. He handed it to her and stood.

She smiled at him and then slid the matching band onto Dan's finger. "I do," said Aria, smiling up into his eyes.

The wind snatched the copious tears off her cheeks and splattered them on his face. He didn't care about the wetness, just her.

"I love you." Those words, said with such strength and conviction, stirred something primal in him. He'd give his life for her.

"I love you, too," he said back, cupping his hands

protectively around both of hers. Unfortunately, those thick strands of red hair whipped against his face and he had to lean in—touching his forehead to hers—to avoid the attack.

The chaplain lifted his hand. "Let us pray. Lord, please bless this marriage and protect Daniel and Aria as they live their lives together. Let them have patience, understanding, and the ability to communicate through all their experiences. Amen." He nodded at Dan. "You may kiss the bride."

Dan brought his lips to hers. His heart beat a cadence so fast, his brain could barely stand the pace. As his lips tenderly met hers, a pulse of electric heat zipped through him. What had started out as a chaste kiss suddenly felt much more intimate.

"Cool it, man. You've got onlookers," Joe whispered to him, and when he didn't immediately disengage, he felt a hand signal against his back.

Yeah. Yeah. I get it. Reluctantly, he pulled back from his bride. Aria's eyes were glazed with passion.

The chaplain shouted as the wind picked up. "I'd like to introduce Petty Officer Second Class Daniel Gregg McCullum and his wife, Aria McCullum. Congratulations!"

"Hooyah!" yelled his brethren from next to him. A chorus of congratulations rang out from the audience, as well as a smattering of applause.

Dan scooped Aria into his arms and carried her down the aisle. He wanted to escape to their hotel room right then and block out the whole world for weeks on end. His body was primed. Unfortunately, there were duties to attend to. This first one…was something he'd antici-pated since she accepted his proposal.

"Dan?" she asked him tentatively as he paused at the very last chair.

The audience quieted. He continued to wait, holding her in his arms.

Aria's words were a breathless whisper. "Dan, everyone is staring. Please put me down."

"No way. I'm not letting you go until we finish the tradition." The sword ceremony was usually reserved for officers, but SEALs tended to break the rules.

She was adorable when she was angry. She began squirming, but he held tight.

Officers from their platoon had quickly assembled into a double line with raised swords for them to cross under. A few of them had looks of mischief on their faces, and Dan knew why. One of them would swat his new bride on the ass with the flat of his sword. He hoped Mrs. McCullum wasn't going to flip out. Maybe he should have prepared her...

He whispered in Aria's ear. "You have to answer their questions." Lowering her feet to the ground, he helped her right her dress and then he tucked her hand into his arm.

The clouds took that moment to open their faucet. As the sprinkle descended, he nodded at a couple of other guys, who opened umbrellas over them. "Come on, it's just a little water...and in the South, that's a blessing."

"I should have asked about what I was getting into." She looked at him and then nodded.

"It's not going to be that bad."

"You're worth it. Husband." The emphasis on the last word held enough sarcasm to grease an exit strategy.

He caught her drift and stepped up alongside her, placing his right hand on her elbow.

"Onward," she sighed, willingly stepping up to the swordsmen.

The first question was posed by Bender James. "Do you promise to be faithful, even when your mind is filled with doubt?"

"Yes," she answered breathlessly. "Of course." They walked beneath the first set of swords.

They made it through the next sets and then stopped at the two swords crossed before them. She looked up at him questioningly, and he touched her chin and then kissed her tenderly. The swords moved out of the way and they passed through. Unfortunately, no one had warned her when the last swordsman swatted her soundly on the tush.

"What the…!" She tried to reel on the man, but Dan held tightly to her.

"Welcome to the Navy," said the last swordsman, LT Duke Hanson, nicknamed Handsome, with a grin.

———〰———

He hustled Aria past the waiting crowds with the cheers, laughter, and all of the applause, and got her over the sand at hyperspeed. He didn't stop until they were inside a waiting stretch limo.

"Dan!" Aria squealed as he laid her down on the seat in the back of the luxury ride, between the bouquet of American Beauty roses and the cooler of Moët & Chandon champagne, and quickly secured the privacy divider between the driver and them. "What are you doing? Whose vehicle is this?"

"Ours! Actually, it's my buddy Pete's. Wedding prez from Hammer and JC. Don't worry, no one will ever know."

"Know what?" she protested.

"That I'm going to make you squeal with delight before we go to the reception!" He flipped the silk wedding dress over his wife's head and trailed his fingers along the inside of her leg.

"Stop! People will see," she protested, pushing the fabric off of her face.

"Not possible. Those are Grade A privacy windows. All your secrets are safe with me." He looked into her big green eyes and grinned. "Trust me, my love. I would never hurt you and never embarrass you."

His fingers connected with the undergarments. "Dan," she sighed, sinking into the plushness and pulling her dress back up over her face with a throaty laugh.

He tugged the tiny scrap of fabric gently out of the way and then gave her his full attention. His lips rained kisses, caressing the tender flesh until she was pushing into him, and then his tongue was diving into the depths of her, making her squirm and pant.

Hands tugged at his hair, trying to bring him closer. He wouldn't be rushed. He wanted to bring her again and again until her body was drenched with satisfaction.

His lips wrapped around the delicate bud of her clitoris, and with his tongue he lazily lapped the tip until she came in a flourish of convulsions. Then he made his way to her honey and lapped up the sweetness, bringing her again with his lips and tongue.

When his own body could take no more delicious delight, he shifted away from her, reached up, and pulled the hem of her dress down, smoothing her curls and smiling into her flushed face. This was his bride, and she was the most beautiful woman on the face of this earth, and they belonged to each other.

———∼∼∼———

The meal had been incredible.

"I raise my glass to Dan and Aria. Cheers!" JC toasted the happy couple and then downed the shot of tequila.

Dan resisted the urge to join in the drunkenness, wanting to remember every minute of tonight. He was really married. He'd really done it. He would be loyal to her until the day he died. He was a SEAL through and through, and they took commitment seriously. As the saying goes, "Once a SEAL, Always a SEAL."

"Hooyah!" shouted the men of the wedding party. Having the Team guys and their female companions there made for a festive time.

There were empty plates piling up on the table. They'd begun with appetizers of shrimp and crab, then had eaten steak and lobster, grilled asparagus and steamed broccoli, mashed potatoes with gravy and garlic, and three baskets of freshly baked bread with an assortment of cheese and fruit. For dessert they'd dined on a special dark-chocolate mousse with layers of white mousse and freshly whipped cream and shavings of mint candy on top and plates of chocolate-dipped strawberries. The food was satisfying and abundant, and they'd all eaten until they were about to burst.

"To frogmen everywhere and their families," said Liam Keith, who sat at the end of the table with several Team FIVE SEALs, including Hayes Johnson, Miller Roth, Declan Swifton, and Harvey Wilson. They'd all gone through training around the same time and spent their free time on various gun ranges scattered up and down the West Coast. Now that Dan was married, he knew most of his days off would be spent with Aria. Maybe he'd be able to sneak off with the guys now and then...or even teach his new wife to enjoy this favorite hobby.

"And to the Hotel del Coronado and its fine grub," added Hammer as he lifted his third shot and slammed it home. "Mmmm-my, that's good."

His wife, Hannah, placed her hand on his arm. She did not look pleased. "I think it's time we headed home, Michael."

"Not until we finish the toasts," his LT broke in and took the floor. "May your head and heart work as one, and never a cross word separate them." He threw back his drink and cleared his throat. "I first met McCullum when he visited the Team to provide weapons training. The new toys were brilliant! It could bring the enemy down in less than two seconds flat. I liked him then and even more so when they decided to transfer him as permanent part of Team THREE. Here's to Dan—one of our new Chiefs—his lovely new bride Aria, and Platoon 1-Bravo, Team THREE."

"And his visits to ST1," said Jack Roaker of Team ONE as he and his wife, Laurie, stood, raised their glasses—one filled with beer and the other with milk— and toasted the happy couple. Her belly was just beginning to show. It had been more than a year since their marriage, and it was obvious how happy they were as Jack doted on his wife, helping her sit down again and quietly asking if she needed anything.

Commander Charles Gich added, "To the Teams.

We are all one." He downed the whiskey in one gulp, then smoothed his thick chevron mustache back into place and scratched his long sideburns. He was known as one of the best instructors in the Teams and was a legend in his own right. Gich was always there to support Teammates. Meeting him through Roaker had been a solid gift.

"Hear, hear!" echoed the sailors as they slammed their shot glasses on the table.

A couple at the table across the room frowned at them. Their displeasure wasn't going to stop the wedding celebration.

Mark stood and then held his water glass and tapped a knife on the rim. He waited until everyone had quieted down. "I've been Aria's best friend through college. We've faced tough times, we've celebrated good ones, and throughout it all, I know how loyal and dedicated she can be... You're a lucky man, Dan. She's quite a catch, and I hope you'll be very happy together. Congratulations!"

This time the women joined in, too. "Congratulations!"

"On that note..." said Dan, who was receiving some rather overt body language from the wives. He looked at his wife and she nodded. "Perhaps we should..."

"Yes," said Aria, catching the same wave and joining in. "I think it's time to say good night. I'd like to spend some quality time with my husband."

Hannah grabbed her husband's hand and practically dragged Hammer from the table. "Thanks for a wonderful dinner. Congratulations! Good night, everyone." He went willingly, though his grumbling voice was heard until they exited the restaurant.

A round of "Sleep tight" and "Score one for the

Team" rained down on them as the partygoers departed. Dan had enjoyed having his closest friends feast with them. The men at this table would go to the mat for him, and it felt good to know it. Besides, if the smiles on their faces were any indication, most of them had had a good time, he decided.

Aria tugged his sleeve. She seemed to be studying her husband, running her eyes up and down his body and then locking onto his. He didn't have to be a mind reader to guess what she wanted.

Grabbing her hand, he turned to lead his new bride away for some wedding-night fun and games and bumped straight into a busboy carrying a tray, which crashed noisily to the floor. He tried to help the young guy, but was waved off. Dan was relieved that the havoc was only silverware and not dishes; otherwise he'd have felt obligated to pay for anything damaged.

"Dan?" asked Aria with raised eyebrows.

"I'm not drunk. I only had one shot. I dumped the rest into the planter behind me. Don't give me that look. I didn't commit planticide, I checked—they're silk." Dan signaled the waiter for the bill. Reaching into his pocket, he withdrew his wallet and laid several bills inside of the leather folio. He'd already slated a certain amount for the pricey dinner and knew what the tally would be. "Keep the tip."

"Yes, sir. Thank you, sir," replied the waiter as he took the folio full of money away.

Dan smiled. "I want to remember every detail of tonight. I wouldn't have gotten drunk and disrespected you that way. Give me a little credit."

"I give you a lot. Really!"

As they stepped through the double doors, cool night air hit their skins. The sting was invigorating, clearing away the cloying heat of the restaurant. The choice was…head straight back to the room or enjoy the cool evening first.

Music drifted up, coming in on the ocean breeze, down from on the beach. Someone was playing a guitar and another person was singing. Dan could hear the ocean like a siren's song, calling to him.

He wanted to feel the sand and see the waves, to hold Aria in his arms and connect with the rhythms of the world. If he could live on the beach with her, it would be ideal. A little hut or a house somewhere, a hammock, and each other was all they needed.

"Shall we take the long way to our room?" he asked with a raised eyebrow. Either way, they'd have to walk outside for a bit to get to it. The Del was designed that way…like a giant plantation house.

"Yes." She laughed suddenly, acting giddy and seeming a little nervous about being alone with him. "Let's go explore. Maybe we can dance." She tugged on his arm, encouraging him to hurry as they made their way down the path and toward the beach. Aria looked as if she belonged in another era, with her old-style wedding dress and her buoyant curls.

A woman's soulful voice made the melody haunting as she sang "The Very Thought of You."

Several people were already dancing to the ballad.

Aria pulled off her shoes and spun away from Dan, turning in a circle with her arms wide and her head tilted toward the stars. She looked like a little girl dancing under the glittering stars, and he fell in love with her a little bit more in that moment for embracing that freedom and living that happiness out loud. He wholeheartedly reveled in her sense of release and joy.

"Dan, come dance with me."

His hands caught her and brought her body against his. He held her tightly against him as he rained kisses down her neck. He would do anything to protect the life that fluttered through those veins. Then he laid his cheek against hers and waltzed her around as if they were in a fancy ballroom.

When the song ended, several people clapped.

Aria blushed, realizing so many eyes watched them.

His lips nuzzled her ear. Softly, he said, "You look beautiful, Aria. Don't worry. I'll always help you shine. Enjoy this time, this moment. Us. Let the rest of the world disappear."

She looked up at him. "When I'm with you, it does. And I do." Her green eyes twinkled and tears welled up in her eyes. "You make me feel brave. Capable. And better at things than I am, like I'm living up to what I want for myself and for us." Blinking her eyes quickly, the extra wetness moved away. "I love you, Dan."

"I love you, Aria. How did I get so lucky to find you?" She often challenged him. This woman intrigued him like no other. That's what it took to be with him. Her mind could change in a blink of an eye, and yet she was in command of her emotions.

"The same way I was blessed to find you?" She wrapped her arms around his neck and brought his head closer for a kiss. Then she murmured, "I'm ready for bed."

"Aye, aye, ma'am." Dan scooped her up in his arms

and carried her off the beach and toward their room. "Your wish is my command."

"Then you better prepare, because I have a lot of commands to give."

"Try the word...*orders*," he suggested.

"Wow, I get to order you around. Priceless. I think I'm going to like marriage," she said with a wicked grin.

"What have I gotten myself into?" He laughed.

She smiled up at him and then laid her head against his shoulder. "Hey. Thank you...for my perfect day." Her hands stroked the side of his neck and then his jaw.

Lightning streaked across the sky. The storm was finally coming. A series of bright flashes showed the anticipation and eagerness in her eyes. That openness was a quality he admired. Aria was his fierce adventuress. Even better, he adored the way she fit into his arms as if she was meant to be there. She was a multifaceted creature, and he looked forward to spending the rest of his life discovering new things about her.

"My pleasure," he murmured against her hair as he laid a kiss on the top of her head. She was all his, and his body ached to lay claim to her. "There's so much more to come, my sweet Aria. Just you wait and see."

⁓

It had been a real trick, getting the door open using the card key and keeping her right where he wanted her, snug in his grasp. The lighting was subdued and the maid had turned down the bed, leaving mints on the pillow. He gently laid her down in the center of the bed. Her hair was downright messy from the dancing, the wind, and the trip from the beach, as if he'd already bedded her. He liked that look on her.

"You are so gorgeous." His compliment made the color on her cheeks darken. Her silk dress was radiant and oh, so beautiful on her. His eyes ate their way over her and he was eager for both of them to be naked.

"Do you need help?" He didn't know where to begin.

"Yes." She rolled onto her stomach. There were at least a hundred tiny little buttons with small loops.

He swore under his breath, and then asked, "How did you get into this thing?"

"One foot at a time, and then I wiggled."

"Ha, ha!"

"Seriously, Jimmy spent an hour buttoning it." She shimmied, obviously ready to be out of the silk cocoon. "I told him it was his duty as my brother. Did he do a good job? I tried to check using a hand mirror, but it wasn't that great a view."

"I beg to differ on that. From where I sit, the view is awesome." His hands swept down the back of the dress, caressing the flawless silk. "He deserves a gold star." Then his fingers moved to the top of the dress. "Are you sure you want to take it off using the buttons? There's a lot we could do that…"

"Danny! Don't you dare! Our daughter or daughter-in-law might want to wear it one day." She swatted the mattress for emphasis.

Oh, yes, I married a very fiery vixen! He grinned broadly. "Okay. But I'm taking off my uniform first. Then, I'll help you. I want to be comfortable, so I can enjoy my work."

"Okay. Thanks." She arched her neck toward him.

The scowl that had been on her lips melted away as her eyes became transfixed to his movements. He made a show of disrobing using his very best sexy manner, bending and flexing appropriately. He wasn't shy about showing her how turned on he was. That's just the kind of guy he was.

"My…we are excited about our wedding night." A pleasant blush reddened her cheeks.

"I would hope so," he teased back. Standing naked before her, he grabbed first one of her feet and then the other, pulling off her shoes. Then he reached underneath the dress and ran his hands along her stockings.

"Wait, I want to show you my underthings. Please."

His hands stilled. How could he deny her? He had been planning to strip her from the waist down and begin their lovemaking. Plan A was if Aria hadn't wanted to keep the dress, he would have ripped the silk off her and made it a thrilling part of the night. Understanding her wish to keep it, though, he acquiesced. Plan B was sex with the dress on, playing with the silk to both of their advantages. Plan C was…get the dress off. She was adamant. "Fine, I'll begin at your tailbone and work my way up. But you might have to get me inspired when I finish this task—just letting you know."

Her voice sounded incredulous. "If me standing before you in my sexy underwear doesn't get your motor started, I don't know who you are or what you've done with my other half."

He laughed. "A challenge. Well, let's see how fast my fingers can work." True to his statement, he released the tiny loops in record time, helping her ease out of the silk dress, with its lacy highlights.

As he was about to place his arms around her, Aria's phone started buzzing.

She picked it up and started reading. "Just Mark." She turned the phone off and tossed it to the side. "Now, where were we?"

She stood before him in a white demi bra with her nipples peeking through the sheer fabric. They were begging for his touch. Her panties were made up of tiny bits of sheer white silk mesh in the front and back. The white satin garters holding her stockings showed a teasing, tantalizing glimpse of her creamy thighs. His cock hardened.

A guttural sound came from his throat, part agreement and the rest pure need. He laid her on the bed and rubbed his face between her breasts. His head moved to the side and he sucked her nipples through the sheer fabric before releasing them fully from the bra's captivity. He took his time as he kissed his way down her stomach, running his tongue along the lines of smooth muscle on either side and into her belly button before going all the way down.

Reaching her panty line, he used his teeth and tongue to toy with the silky mesh fabric, making her buck and move as she urged him lower. He adored the panties, with its little hidey-hole just for him, and it fit his mouth and tongue perfectly.

Her hands gripped his hair as he tongued her clit. Soft moans came from her throat as he brought her again and again until she was panting and glazed with sweat. Only then did he strip the panties and stockings from her.

Pulling her into his arms, he kissed her long and deep. Waves of passion rolled over her senses as she ran her fingers down the muscles of his neck, shoulders, and back. His lean, hard body drove away every thought until she became primal, a wild woman, and their love was on some kind of prehistoric dimensional plane.

"Aria, open your eyes. See me."

It took a few minutes…to come back to him.

Responding to the request, she slowly opened her eyes. She shared her hunger…for him, for them. This want…to be together and make their two souls into one being…was the force that drew them back to each other's arms again and again.

"Dan…" His name was a whispered plea.

"I can take it. Give me all of you. Your love. Your fears. Your wants and desires. I'm yours, and I'll never judge you." He sat upright, pulled her over him and held her poised.

Need beckoned. "I need to see you, to watch you… as we make love for the first time as husband and wife." His words were a lure, whispering into the ache.

"Yes," Aria replied. She shivered with anticipation. She was so small against his body.

Slowly he lowered her until their skin connected. When he was fully sheathed, her body convulsed over his. She couldn't stop the waves of pleasure, and he was glad. It fed him. "Danny!" she cried out as she came, throwing her head back in pure abandon.

As the climaxes squeezed his cock, she lowered her head and sought his eyes again. Connected as they were, and with the edge off, it was evident what was on her mind. She wanted to take control…to feed him.

He nodded and watched her place her hands on the back of the headboard for balance, and then she raised herself up and down, riding him. His eyes rolled back and then focused in on her again. It was sheer nirvana as his cock slid in and out of her silken hold. He wanted to close his eyes and just enjoy the sensation, but her green gaze sparkled with fire and he wouldn't look away. "Give me your best, my mermaid."

She threw back her head and laughed, which made her sheath contract and his breath catch. He basked in the intense pleasure-pain. This chemistry, the way their minds and bodies linked and so much more, drove him…to make her his.

"Dan." She wiggled, getting his attention again.

He struggled to get words out. "What was that?"

"Just the beginning." She smiled slyly as she set yet another rhythm, making small circles with every pulse up and down.

"Aria. Damn… I'm not sure I can take much more." The strain was tightening the features of his face. Finally, his hands caught her hips.

She brushed them away. "No. No. No. It's my turn. To inspire you."

He nodded. Reaching behind him, he grabbed the top of the bed frame. He needed to do something with his hands.

"No fair," she said as her hands moved to his muscles. Her fingers ran up and down the taut six-pack. She became distracted…and lost her rhythm.

He was dying here… "Aria."

"Touch me, Dan, like I'm touching you."

That was all he needed. He was a doer. Cupping her breasts, he teased her nipples with the pads of his fingers, sending her to the brink but not over the edge.

She was watching him again, her back arching slightly with every move upward. "Please. Come with me."

His hands settled on her hips, setting the pace and bringing her over the edge right along with him.

"Danny!" she shouted. His wife was never quiet. That was another thing that he liked about her.

She collapsed against him. "It's official."

His hands rubbed up and down the smooth skin of her back. "It was official when we signed the marriage license. What we just did…was consummate it."

"Want to do it again?" she said against his chest as she nuzzled his pectoral muscles and her nails swirled a design into his dark chest hair.

"Can you give me ten minutes? Maybe twenty?" He chuckled. He felt as if he'd just run a marathon.

"If I must." She sighed melodramatically. Then she ran her fingers down his chest and toyed with the muscles of his stomach…making the six-pack dance now and then.

He unseated her and rolled her onto the bed, laying himself alongside her. "I can think of many ways to keep you occupied while my body recovers its strength, my dear," he said, putting his most wicked intentions into his wagging eyebrows.

She giggled at him. "Do your best." Pointing to the basket of goodies on the table near the door, he spied champagne, chocolate-covered strawberries, and what looked like different types of oil.

"Who gave us that?"

"I did." She smiled up at him. "It's not every day we have a luxurious hotel room, and I wanted to have some…fun. Isn't that what honeymoons are for?"

"Yes, and the obvious, of course, to make my honey moan." Rolling off the bed in one motion, he freed the champagne, popped the cork, and drizzled the bubbles and liquid over her body, which had her squealing with delight. "Mmmm, I'm ready for a little bubbly. Want to help me quench my thirst?"

"Only if I get to do the same. We're married. Equals. And you, my SEAL man, are fair game." She grabbed the bottle and sprayed him. Then she launched herself at him, and they rolled and played until each of them melted into the other…captivated by the pressing matters at hand.

Chapter 3

AT DAWN THE NEXT MORNING, ARIA FOUND HERSELF wide awake. Their room at the Hotel del Coronado was lovely, and lying next to Dan was pure bliss. She didn't want to miss one minute of it. His body radiated warmth, and he smelled so good, as if he'd been rubbed in spice and vanilla. Of course, she'd been the one to rub oil all over him and relish the experience. They'd made love until just before dawn, and overnight the oil had soaked into the sheets. All that remained was the scent and the luscious memory.

Placing tiny kisses over his back, she wiggled against his backside. She was pleasantly sore in all sorts of places, and yet she still craved him, wanted him inside of her. Every time they made love, it was as if the connection deepened and made each of them a greater part of each other.

The sunrise streamed in through an open window, bathing the wall and a glass-framed picture of a seascape with stripes of yellow and pinky orange. The springtime air was rich with a blend of tree blossoms and flowers, and the sea breeze was mild and light.

Her fingernails scraped along his back. This time, she felt his whole body tense. He held his breath. Aria knew she needed to speak so he could orient himself. Sudden movements were akin to attacks, for SEALs. Her lips moved along his skin. "Good morning, handsome."

He exhaled slowly. His body relaxed in stages.

Her hand caressed his back with small round circles. He would know that touch.

"Ah, the sexy woman who is now my wife." His hands stroked hers as it moved to his chest. "Aria, right?"

She smacked her other hand on his back. "You'd better believe it."

Turning over, Dan pulled her into his arms and kissed her. She was eager to hold him closer, to join together as one.

Slowly he rolled her onto her back. His eyes held hers captive even as her arms wrapped possessively around his neck. "Good morning, Mrs. McCullum."

She laughed outright. "It sounds strange, doesn't it? Mrs. McCullum. I wonder if I'll ever get used to it."

"Probably by our fiftieth anniversary." Lowering his mouth to hers, he kissed her slowly, seductively, exploring all of the sweet succulent nooks of her mouth until their tongues began to dance the very primal war of hunger.

"Danny…" She sighed. Her hands wrapped intimately around him.

"You could call me John-Boy, and it'd sound great to me right now." He laughed. "Just kidding. What do you want, my love?"

"You." Aria laughed and then caught his lower lip in her mouth.

"Dare I move?" he slurred out.

She relinquished her prize. "You better. Your wife is in need of your attention."

Trailing his fingers along her skin, he stroked the center of her hand with small circles and then moved upward to the sensitive crook of her elbow. He kissed her there and at her shoulder before he stroked his way along her neck. Teasing the tips of his fingers over the slim column of throat, he caught her gaze and held it. Those green eyes, so full of passion and fire—she was one of a kind. He would protect this precious soul with his life.

He kissed her lips and then trailed his fingers lower to capture one of her taut nipples. Gently he squeezed, making her squirm and push her body against him. Torturing the plum-colored jewel, he kissed his way to it, wrapped his lips around it, and drew.

"Danny, please…"

Lifting his head, he looked at her. Holding the worried piece of flesh oh, so tenderly with his teeth, he said, "Please, what?"

Aria's fingers laced into his hair and tugged him away from his sweet treasure, bringing their faces level. "Make love to me, Dan."

He kissed her. "Your wish is my pleasure, Aria. But perhaps it's time for you to take charge. Wives are always a rank above their husbands in the military. We're a logical bunch. So consider this your opening gambit."

"I don't believe in logic. I believe in instinct." A wicked spark gleamed in her eyes as she wrapped her legs around him and rocked to the side.

More than happy to acquiesce to his bride, he helped her flip them over and settled her on top. From this position, she looked like a temptress leading him astray. Wherever she wanted to go, he would follow.

His body was rock hard beneath her. He was rapt as Aria's fingers traced along the six-pack of his abs down to his manhood, where she wrapped her fingers tight. The breath caught in his throat as she slid her fingers slowly up and down.

He watched her until the sensation was so consuming he had to close his eyes and just revel in the pleasure coursing through his body. That's when he felt her shift, and he had to see her lower her body onto his. One of the most erotic moments of his life was feeling his cock enveloped by her heavenly warmth.

"Yes," he growled, pulling her down to his chest and rolling her beneath him. "Showing off your horseback-riding experience, huh? Well, I do not need to be tamed. It's my turn." Her legs squeezed tightly, making other parts of her clench. Sensation battered through his brain as his body claimed his bride. He'd wanted to go slow, to play and enjoy the bliss of their wedding morning. But the need to feel her body convulse around his, to climax as many times as possible, had him taking control and driving her to the brink of exhaustion. When she begged for release, he finally gave in and came, planting his seed deep within her.

Sweat glistened on his skin as he rolled her back on top of him. His cock slid out of her and lay pleasantly spent as she clung to him.

He could feel her heart beating and the rapid in and out of her breathing.

"I have to admit, when you give someone your total concentration, you give one hundred percent." Aria sighed. The compliment was meant to stick, and she liked the look on his face her praise brought. If only she could freeze this moment in time and that expression, she'd bottle it.

"Yes, ma'am. That's my job." He pushed the hair off her forehead and kissed it. "Let me know when you'd like my focus again."

Lifting her head, she placed her elbow on his chest. It dug in pleasantly, as if his 120-pound wife could really physically hurt him. Fixing her gaze on him, she gave him a weighty stare. "Give me an hour and a decent breakfast, and perhaps I'll rally."

"Smart-ass," he said, slapping her bottom playfully. "If that's your way of saying 'Feed me now,' then the point has been made."

She laughed as she propped up the other elbow. "Yes, it is. I'll have the eggs Benedict and fresh-squeezed orange juice, or whatever they have that's close to that." Rolling off of him, she slid off the bed and walked slowly to the bathroom. Before she went in, she turned. "I knew you'd be watching. If you'd like, I could always use someone to wash my back."

He was out of bed and by her side before she'd finished her statement. "I've got your six, Mrs. McCullum."

"Good to know, Mr. McCullum. I have a few places that, uh, could use your special attention. A couple of… hard-to-reach places." She threw him a wicked look before sashaying into the bathroom.

The shower was short-lived. A ringing cell phone sent Dan dashing out of the shower and into the bedroom. He had ears like a bat! If it had been her choice, she would have let that work phone ring all day long. But she wasn't "on call" to the Navy, and that, of course, changed things in terms of his availability.

Rinsing the soap off her body, she contemplated washing her hair, when Dan shouted from the bedroom. "Aria, come here. It's important!"

Shutting off the water, she grabbed a towel, blotted her skin dry quickly, and then wrapped it around her body.

"Aria, are you coming?"

"Yes, I'm on my way."

Her bare feet padded from the tile to the soft bedroom carpet. The spring breeze from the open window made the room chilly, and she shivered.

"Great news! That was the housing office. There's a house on Silver Strand! Granted, it's not guarded—open to the public to drive through anytime they want—but it's less than two minutes from the Amphibious Base. I have to go the housing office right now to secure it, but other than that, we are set. Damn, I love the Navy!" He picked her up and spun her around. Placing her on her feet, he kissed her lustily and then said, "Can you handle packing everything up in here, and I'll meet you in the lobby in an hour?"

"It's our honeymoon." Her stomach tightened. She wanted more time—to talk, to be together, and to just relax without rushing off somewhere. This wasn't how she pictured their romantic getaway.

She sighed. She was fighting her own expectations and fantasies. It wasn't him. Mentally, she agreed this was a great opportunity. The best thing she could do was join in the excitement and let go of her wish for control.

"Please don't look at me like that. Aria, this is about our new home." The expression in his eyes was candid and earnest. "We're being given a great opportunity. Call this a gift. The best one we could ever receive.

There are sailors who would move the pillars of hell for an opportunity to be in this housing area."

My apartment is uber-small. It would be nice to have a bigger place.

"Aria, what do you say…can you handle it? I promise to make it up to you, the honeymoon part."

She looked away, taking in the clutter and chaos of the room. There was stuff everywhere: her wedding gown, his uniform, and all their discarded accessories. She supposed it could be worse. Pasting a smile on her face, she said, "Absolutely." Besides, she liked the idea of a new home, particularly when it made him this happy. Perhaps it would make him more excited to come home every night, not that he'd ever needed prodding to visit her apartment before.

"Thanks. You're a great wife. I promise, you'll love it." His hands squeezed her arms affectionately, and then he practically sprinted to his overnight bag and dug out a pair of faded jeans and a navy blue Tommy Bahama short-sleeve shirt. He pulled them on quickly, slid his feet into deck shoes, and walked around as he buttoned the shirt. Grabbing his watch, cell phone, and wallet off the nightstand, he was out the door with a wave. "See you in sixty with our new keys."

The door slammed shut with a bang. She stared at it for a few seconds. "Ah, married life." The words rang hollow in the room.

Now, where to begin? She pulled out a polka-dot sundress, a matching peach-colored bra-and-panty set, and sandals. After getting dressed, she wound her long hair into a bun and then began packing.

She found a granola bar in his bag and ate it as she

worked. "For the record, I would have liked breakfast in bed."

Finding the phone, she thumbed through the messages. There were thirty-seven from Mark. Nothing important…just chitchat. She deleted most of them, laughed at a couple, and then stuffed the phone into her purse so she didn't forget it.

Catching sight of the clock, she rushed around the room, gathering their stuff.

Laying the last wrinkled article of clothing into her bag, she sat on it, trying to squish all of the air out and squeeze the sides of the L.L. Bean duffel closed. She wrinkled her nose as she looked at the piles on the bed. *How did we get so much stuff already?*

His uniform and her wedding dress had to be hung up, and they needed to be in protective bags. She contemplated calling Dan, asking him to stop at her apartment and pick up something to help her cause. Yet she didn't want to give in to the temptation. She was a SEAL wife; she could handle this…come up with a creative solution. She could be just as ingenious or resourceful as Dan bragged about the Team guys being.

Grabbing the card key, she headed down to the gift shop and found exactly what she needed: one long and one short garment bag with brightly colored beach umbrellas decorating them. They weren't the exact item she would have preferred, but the selection was limited. Regardless, it would be a memory of their honeymoon, even if this jaunt felt somewhat brief.

Too bad they hadn't sat together on the balcony. Or made love on the beach in front of the Del—not that it would have been private. Or swum in the pool. Or gone to the spa. Dozens of wonderful options to make them both feel pampered, relaxed, and refreshed. Instead their world was go, go, go! "God, I hope we can slow down and enjoy each other at some point."

———∿∿∿———

True to his word, Dan pulled his Mustang up to the front door of the Hotel del Coronado precisely one hour from the time he left. She was waiting exactly where he'd asked her to be.

He easily hauled the bags into the trunk before he came around, kissed her cheek, and opened the car door for her.

"I noticed you added to our luggage collection. Those beach umbrellas are just my style," he said with a wink.

She adored his smile. "I think all our bags should be decked out in rainbow colors."

"Very chic." He opened his car door and slid behind the wheel. Putting the car in drive, he sped out of the semicircle, down the drive, and across Orange Avenue. "By the way, a few things I forgot about. The first is about…your ID. We need to do that now, and then go back to the housing office. I went to your apartment and picked up your passport and social-security card. I think between that, your driver's license, and our marriage certificate, we should be able to get the job done."

"Does that require a picture?" She bit her lip, hoping that wouldn't be the case. Between buying the garment bags and doing the packing, she hadn't been able to put on any makeup.

"Yes. Why?" He didn't get it. Men never did.

Flipping the visor down, she studied her face in the mirror. "I wish I had more time. I look sixteen."

"Are you kidding me?" He seemed shocked. "Aria, you're gorgeous."

"I have freckles. There are lines around my mouth and eyes, and my lips are too pale." She had more criticisms, a laundry list of them actually, but she kept those to herself. She wasn't prepared to take the bloom off the rose quite yet. Dan would see her faults soon enough, and there was little she could do about them physically, other than work out more. On the other hand, if she felt herself perfect, wouldn't that be an issue, too? Letting out a long slow sigh, she decided it really didn't matter. Who wanted to look like a magazine ad?

"Shall I kiss each freckle to make you feel better? Besides, aren't those laugh lines? I like those." He was so sweet. How did she find such an adorable man?

Fanning herself, she laughed as she said, "Fine. Kiss them later." Glancing over at him, she could feel anticipation coming out of him like waves. "Okay, okay, I'll give it up. I'm game. Let's go get my ID."

Undoing the knot at the top of her head, she shook out her red hair. The frizzy curls clung to each other as she attempted to comb her fingers through them and free the more stubborn strands.

As they neared the gate, Dan reached into his back pocket, pulled out his wallet, and fought the small plastic holder to remove his military ID.

She didn't understand why. "Why are you taking it out? Can't you just leave it in there? Isn't that why wallets are designed in that manner, for easy display?"

"It's required. At the gate, they need to be able to

check—verify the hologram on the front and flip it to the back and make sure it's authentic. Also, if you have your car lights on, turn them off. This is a must, and you'll usually see a sign posted about it. Regardless, it is proper etiquette to do it." Dan's voice had slipped into instructor mode. She wasn't fond of the tone, though she was mostly used to it. "FYI, if you present your DOD— Department of Defense—ID upside down, this is a sign of distress. Your car will immediately be searched at gunpoint for a threat."

She gulped. She hadn't known that. "What else do I need to know? Are there a lot of rules?"

"Use a hands-free device to talk on the phone. Keep in mind that you're on base. If you're caught holding your cell phone and speaking on it, it's serious...a federal offense. Take it to heart, okay?" He glanced at her. "I know how you like to chat on that thing."

The guard at the gate examined Dan's ID, returned it, and then waved him on. Aria gulped. Their guns looked pretty lethal.

"Yes, there are a lot of rules, but you'll figure it out. Also, you can always ask me...if I'm around." Dan drove the car through the gate and past a small building and then said, "Over there on the right is the commissary for groceries and the exchange for household items, clothes, and such. Naval Air Station North Island has some good resources. You'll need to check it out." He caught her eye. "I'm serious. We'll need to keep to a budget."

"I've made my own money my whole life, Dan. I'm pretty prudent, if you haven't figured that out already."

Silence sat between them. They hadn't talked too much about money matters before.

"Aria, I just want to make sure we're in agreement, in terms of my salary. We're using that for the rent, bills, et cetera. Your money is yours. If you want to contribute it, that's fine." Dan slowed for a light and then stopped. "Let's clarify the issue and move on. I don't want to dwell on this."

"Dan, I get it. But I disagree with you. This isn't the Dark Ages. Unless something changes, we'll split the bills. I don't want your whole paycheck to go to living expenses, where I have expendable cash and you don't. Either we're partners, or we aren't. Tell me now, which is it?" Her temper was climbing up a notch.

He thought about it for a minute, reassessing his thoughts. He'd been trained to be flexible, and he could roll with this new info.

"I understand." His hand reached for hers. He held it tenderly, entwining his fingers with hers. "In all ways, we share. I agree with you, with my partner."

"Good," she said, adding a silent harrumph.

"We're almost there." Dan flipped on the blinker and turned. They pulled up in front of a building with a door that was propped wide open by a couple of phone books, and Aria quickly got out of the car by herself. Though she enjoyed Dan opening the car door on occasion, it would drive her crazy if he did it every time they left a vehicle.

They climbed the steps and entered an office with several desks. Televisions were set up at odd angles, and there were chairs positioned in front of them. Posters were hung in the wider spaces: messages of security, health, and family wellness issued from the faded faces. A few signs spoke about etiquette and waiting patiently for *your* turn.

An odor of acrid cleaners and popcorn permeated the office. A coffeepot sat empty in the corner, and a water cooler bubbled up with glugging sounds now and then. Discarded newspapers and magazines were open on the seats before the television, and several puzzles and plastic toys sat on a low shelf underneath the giant screen.

"This is a first. We're the only ones here. I can't ever remember that happening. It's usually hurry up and wait…and be patient, when it comes to the military." Dan spoke softly. He seemed to be waiting for one of the people behind the desks to notice them. When no one did, he cleared his throat and then all of the office workers looked up at once. Aria almost laughed out loud at her mental image of a family of meerkats in white cotton shirts and ties, staring at them in surprise.

The person closest to them gestured for them to sit in the seats in front of his desk. He was an older man of Hawaiian descent, and his eyes were the color of buttery toffee. "I'm Mr. Saba. How can I help you today?" His voice was heavily accented, and the baritone sound rumbled in their direction.

"Mr. Saba, I need to get an ID for my wife. This is Aria." Handing him the envelope full of credentials, Dan added, "I apologize in advance for this, but we need to be back at the housing office within the hour."

"You have a red-hot housing prospect. I understand." Checking the clock, Mr. Saba nodded. "Happens more than you think around here." He perused the papers and then slowly pronounced, "We will make your deadline in plenty of time, young man. Now, let's see to your bride."

Saba's fingers flew over the keyboard like magic as the information was entered into the system in record time. In less than five minutes he was flipping the screen toward them. "Please confirm that all of this information is correct. Sign this and I will take Mrs. McCullum's picture, print your ID, and you'll be on your way."

"Great," Dan said. "Thanks."

Aria's eyebrows rose. This was it. This was the way everyone was going to see her from now on. She was Aria McCullum, Dependent. But she had never been dependent on anyone—not ever—in her whole life.

"Yes, it's all correct." She nodded her head and then felt the flash as the camera took her picture. There it was...documented, filed, and frozen in time forever. Her identity.

—◇◇◇—

After visiting the housing office and securing their key, they stopped at the commissary and picked up sandwiches, chips, and a container of sliced fresh fruit. Then he drove her across the base and over to an empty parking lot, where they could watch the planes take off and land.

Someday soon she would be dropping him off at the terminal on the other side of the strip and saying goodbye for an unknown period of time. He felt she'd handle it okay. Nothing could be as bad as Dirks's first wife, who had almost banged down the CO's door, demanding answers as to where her new husband was. Christ, he hoped Aria would never do that. From what he knew of her, she was pretty levelheaded. Regardless, he'd brief her on the ins and outs and introduce her to the Ombudsman, who would provide info and act as liaison.

"You're pretty quiet," she said, opening her sandwich and taking a bite.

"Just thinking." He smiled at her. "There are details I need to share with you on Navy life. After we move into the house, I'll fill you in. Okay?" One step at a time, chunk by chunk, he'd help her get assimilated. No sense in freaking her out within twenty-four hours of getting married.

He took off the sandwich's wrapper and took a giant bite. God, it tasted good. His stomach ached from the lack of food. Wolfing the first half of the turkey on wheat bread, he washed it down with a quart of milk, then popped the top on the container of fruit and scarfed down four slices of melon.

"What's that?" she asked, pointing over her shoulder.

"Behind us is the old O Club—the Officer's Club—which they use for weddings and events now. There's a three-quarter view of the island from up there. I've been to a few celebrations there. Next to it, that's the Base Commander's house, and next to that is a house where Admirals might stay." Pointing across the airfield, he said, "Over there, you can see a large plane. Those are sea lions being loaded into the back. I've met several of the trainers who work in that program. Pretty cool stuff! They teach the creatures to find everything from enemy subs, swimmers, and even bombs. I've got a lot of respect for them."

Dan stuffed a handful of chips into his mouth with each bite of the second half of his sandwich. He was like a vacuum cleaner.

Aria watched him demolish his food in record time. She was still working on the first half of her sandwich when he opened his second one. After visiting the commissary, she was thinking about the grocery list she was making in her head. "How much do you eat in a day?"

"About four thousand calories. I carbo-load as we prep for Ops. I tend to burn a lot of energy quickly." His teeth ripped off a large chunk of the sandwich, and he made a grunting noise with it.

"Animal!" she retaliated.

He chewed and swallowed. "Is that a label or a request?" Waggling his eyebrows at her, he continued to speak between mouthfuls. "What can I say, I'm starved. If someone hadn't eaten my emergency granola bar, I might have more control."

"Uh-huh." She lightly punched his arm and went back to her sandwich. "So why didn't I know this about you?"

He shrugged. "It's natural that there are things we're going to learn about each other, right?"

"Sure," she replied uncomfortably. What other surprises were in store for her…in terms of his life? Maybe she should stick to the basics: food, clothing, and shelter. "What should I stock in the refrigerator—or cupboards, for that matter? I assume I'll be doing most of the grocery shopping on my own."

"I'll help when I can. Just know, whatever you get will be fine. Fish, fruits and vegetables, pasta, and lean meats are my favorites. I eat it all, though." He made a face. "Wait, I'm not fond of liver. Please don't get that."

Holding up a hand, she waved it in front of herself. Forcing the bite in her throat to go down, she added, "No problem. It's not my favorite either." She took a sip of her cranberry juice and then asked, "When do we move in?"

Digging into his pocket, he removed the brand-new keys. He jingled them. "What a terrific sound." He smiled at her. "How about today? When we finish eating."

Wrapping up the rest of her sandwich, she placed it in the bag and drank down the rest of her juice. She stowed the bottle and turned to him. "I'm done. Let's go."

He laughed. "Anxious, much?"

"Hey, I gave up my honeymoon and a pretty killer breakfast for this. Let's get to it." Crossing her arms over her chest, she smiled. It was hard to be serious when he was staring at her like that. Her phone beeped and she checked it. A client wanted to talk to her about his advertising materials. She would have to get back to consultant work soon enough. Sending a quick message, she told him she'd talk to him next week.

"Work?"

"Yeah. Sorry."

"No worries." Dan saluted her. "Onward, ma'am. Your pleasure is my duty." With that, he stuffed the rest of his second sandwich into his mouth, started the car, and put it in gear. They drove out of the parking lot, onto the road, and underneath a giant plane as it flew above them, preparing to land.

"Wow!" She held her breath. It was an awesome sight. She wondered if she would have been able to touch it if she'd reached out a hand.

"Yes, indeed," he said. "That's why I brought you here. Someday we're going to fly on one of those C-130s, and we're going to travel to wherever it takes us—Australia, Spain, and Italy. We'll explore the planet, just my partner and me on an adventure. How does that sound?"

"Exciting. Scary. And wonderful." She loved the idea of visiting those countries and seeing everything through his eyes. Sometimes his wishes sounded too good to be true. Yet she longed to incorporate his optimistic beliefs into her own and lived to make his dreams become theirs. Did he know she was often uncertain, not about herself, but about others? She knew it was a conflict—an optimistic person who also worried, always waiting for the other shoe to drop and some kind of chaos or upset to come her way. Maybe she could let go of her old habits and become like him. She wanted the life he talked about, and she wanted to be the person she was with him. Even though it wasn't easy, he made her better.

Dan grinned at her. "Good. Because I want to take you places that are mind-blowing, whose beauty takes your breath away, and whose people touch your heart in a manner you never imagined…"

Reaching across the small distance, she took his hand. Their fingers entwined. "With you by my side, I'm ready. Bring it on."

Chapter 4

September 15, Operation White Pigeon, an undisclosed location in Asia

BULLETS STRUCK THE WATER ONLY INCHES FROM HIS face, forcing columns of vertical spray to rise as high as a foot. He resisted the urge to take the bait and to expose himself to the enemy.

Less than a week ago he'd been on his honeymoon, and now he was surrounded by water, over a continent away. His wife was packing her apartment and preparing to move into their new home, and he was hidden among the reeds. He was practically invisible to the naked eye, and he was damned well going to stay that way.

Gunfire peppered around him, so familiar from training that he'd become almost immune to the sound. But he wouldn't be immune if he got hit…he had to remind himself of that at times. Remaining hidden wasn't just a matter of his survival, but the Team's, too.

Abruptly, the firing stopped. The display had been routine. The soldiers were moving away from the bank of the river now. If anyone had truly seen the SEALs, there would have been grenades and a more aggressive exchange. It was imperative the Team remain invisible.

The rustling of foliage signaled the departure of their foes. Bastards barely had any protocol—they sounded like elephants.

Cocking his head to the side, Chief Dan McCullum caught the signal from the point man and the LT. Zankin and Dirks were bringing up the rear, and the rest of them were in the middle. It was an eight-man mission. They would wait for twenty minutes—in case the enemy's retreat was a trick—and then it would be time to move. If they heard one twig break or strange leaf rustle, they'd sit there longer. Their ability to be still was part of their training, often forcing the enemy to give themselves away.

Time clicked by. Nothing happened.

Then, like cottonmouths in a swamp, they ghosted forward, swimming soundlessly through the water. They'd trained for this type of mission, going over the sequence on a similar terrain, for months. Peacetime was for practice so war was a reflex. Either they'd achieve their goal or die trying.

Their Intel, confirmed by several sources, was that Ru Ryuk Kang had become an enemy of the United States of America while stationed abroad. Ru had begun his career in the U.S. Diplomatic Corps and then "defected" to his ancestral homeland to pursue his real job as a double agent. In truth, his job had been to spy for the U.S.

Ru had been making significant headway, but one day the flow of information stopped. It was now believed he'd been turned again and that he'd directly led to the death of fourteen agents.

The problem with spies was that sometimes agents began to believe their "surrogate" country's propaganda—that bullshit they wallowed in each and every day. That's when a turned agent became dangerous. Just because an operative was vetted for a covert assignment didn't mean he had the brains and balls to keep his mind-set together and stay on mission.

In Ru's case, it didn't seem that he had been planted long enough to go nuts. But within only a couple of years, the hidden agenda had come to light and the body count could not be denied.

The U.S. had planted him. Now it was SEAL Team's job to take him out.

Dan's head emerged briefly. He slowly drew in air and slid back below the water. The last time he had been in this country, it was to gather Intel from a different person. A mission had gone horribly wrong when the enemy shot Sandra Niang as she reached out for him. Dan had been tasked with keeping her safe. Even now the memory was seared into his senses: The crack of the shot being fired. The way it impacted her body...and the blood. Her lips moved...providing the urgent Intel. Even in death she'd been loyal.

The memory slipped through his mind and out again without causing his focus to waver.

When the orders had come down that they needed a Team to go in-country on a covert jaunt and that the repercussions of being discovered included torture and possibly the next world war, SEAL Team THREE's Platoon 1-Bravo—nicknamed the Ghosts of the Teams—was tagged for the job.

He was grateful to be back. Maybe this time he would get a hint of who had ordered Sandra's death, and they could avenge her. Not that a vendetta was part of their mission, but it would feel great to him. He wanted to protect those who fought and sacrificed for the USA, and revenge seemed to honor that memory. It was one of the reasons he had been given this task, aside from the fact that he abhorred traitors.

In sync, the Team emerged from the water, guns held at the ready. Everything was clear.

One by one they left the wet depths and moved in the forest, taking up positions prior to infiltration. Moving soundlessly, they headed forward like an oddly shaped serpent. Their path took them deep into a forest and finally toward a small vine-covered house.

A sweep of the area showed that no other soldiers or guards were lurking in the shadows as Dan, JC, and Hammer slipped inside. Being the first into the room, JC found Ru asleep in a chair, listening to a recording of some kind of discordant symphony. Next to him was an empty bottle of Irish whiskey and a crystal glass. On his wrist was a shiny new Rolex encrusted in diamonds, and a large opal in a gold setting gleamed on his forefinger.

To Dan, it didn't seem like enough to betray the USA. But what did he know? He was just as happy eating Spam as he was eating steak. What luxury could fill the void, when you gave away your integrity and your honor for it? That soul-sucking forfeit had the means to torture you forever.

The room was lushly decorated in silk fabrics and what looked like original art and antiques.

On the couch across from Ru was a sleeping woman. She was short of stature, native to the country, and her long white robe gaped open, revealing her naked body. There were marks around her throat and wrists, most likely from recent rough interactions. White powder clung to her nostrils, and more cocaine was laid out in rows on the table next to her.

JC signaled him and then moved ahead, pulling from his belt a locally crafted, traceable blade specially garnered for this mission. He clamped his hand over Ru's mouth and slid the knife swiftly and efficiently across his neck, severing the carotid. When the body stopped its spasms and the life had drained free, JC tossed the knife gently to a spot on the carpet near the woman.

Dan glanced briefly at the traitor. This turncoat wouldn't be sharing any more secrets...with anyone.

The betrayer's eyes were open and his mouth was wide. No sound came out. Blood had sprayed dramatically along the wall and chair, turning the room into a macabre painting. So much for the museum-quality art.

Dan checked back at the couch where the woman slept. Must have been some marathon she and Ru had had. At the very least, the drugs had been effective, because her breathing was even and there was rapid eye movement. She was still out cold.

JC nodded at Dan and they started to backtrack out of the room. The frame job looked authentic enough to point the finger at the right person. Her.

Suddenly, soundlessly, without warning, the woman attacked. She was on JC like a leech, trying to draw blood and sucking in air as if she were going to summon the wrath of God in a bloodcurdling scream.

Dan plucked her from JC's back, wrapped his arm around her windpipe, and applied pressure. He felt her struggle...the beat of her heart...the anger of her movements...and the last shudders of her life. The choice was black-and-white, her life or theirs. This was reality.

Laying her down, he noticed a small mark inside her arm. It was from the same group that Sandra had infiltrated, the group that had eventually killed her. Perhaps there was greater purpose to killing Ru's woman—one member fewer of this well-known terrorist organization.

Pulling the sash free from her white robe, Dan fashioned it into a rough-looking noose using ordinary knots, tied the end to the beam above Ru's chair, and hoisted...as if this were a remorseful act. The scenario was plausible, though not very pretty.

JC tapped his shoulder. They had to go.

With everything in place, the men exited the house. Brock and Thomas emerged from the bushes as LT and the rest of the Team fell in behind, protecting their six.

Swift steps moved the SEALs into the trees and back into the thick of the forest. The Team disappeared into the shadowy night, melting into the darkness like the ghosts they were.

Chapter 5

September 18, Coronado, California

As Dan arrived back at NAS, the Naval Air Station North Island, the day was cold and dreary. The marine layer hid the sun, and he craved the warmth on his skin. Standing in the middle of Aria's old apartment, he could barely believe how little she had gotten done. Guess it was up to him to wrangle this mess.

Even on only a few hours of rest on the plane, his adrenaline was pumping joy juice through his bloodstream. He was married and they were moving into their first home. Putting his mind and body into hypergear, he moved like lightning, getting back to Aria's apartment. He snuck in and gazed at his wife, peacefully sleeping. *This place is a mess.* There were half-packed open boxes and stacks of stuff everywhere. She had dark circles under eyes and there were files from work surrounding her on the couch. *Let her sleep.*

Within two hours, he'd packed everything and had carried all the boxes out to the truck. The apartment looked bare, but it was good to go.

"Dan?" Aria called. He walked in to find her stretching across the bed. Lord, was there anything sexier? "Where did all the boxes go? This place looks amazing."

"I'm magic," he said as he scooped her up in his arms.

"Hold on. What about my office and my files?"

"All set. I even swept the floors." He kissed her lips, so soft and sweet. He wanted more, but not here. They were done with the place, a furnished apartment where she had been single. Their needs were bigger than this place. "C'mon, let's get moving. It's time for…our new home to welcome us. Somewhere that can fit us both."

―――

Aria was stuck in chatterbox mode. She gushed about her work and everything that had happened over the past few days. He liked it. Her voice was easy on his ears and psyche.

Checking the rearview mirror, he let out a silent sigh. He could have done without Mark following them in his truck, but the man refused to let anyone else drive. Granted, it was useful to have all of Aria's boxes piled in there. It would have taken them at least ten trips in his Mustang otherwise. Selfishly, he preferred to have this moment be just theirs.

"Are you listening to me?" She poked his thigh with her finger.

"Yes," he answered automatically. He'd heard her. There wasn't a lot for him to add, especially when she complained about her job. Of course, whenever he brought up her giving up the occupation that drove her batty, she threw a fit. His salary could support them both. Maybe at some point she'd want to quit her job. If not, that was fine, too. The only requirement in his mind was that Aria be happy.

"Good, because I have a lot more to say. I couldn't believe Josh hated the proposal. He's a longtime client, but he hadn't really told us what he truly wanted until I badgered the answer out of him. So I had to stay up all night and do it and sent the info at 3:00 a.m. and then crashed out." Aria threw her hands up in the air. "You understand, right?"

"Sure. I don't rile easily. You'll find I'm pretty basic. All I need is you…and food." He winked at her.

"You're right. Stick to the basics. I'll let the work stuff go. We're moving into our first home. Yay!" Her hands fluttered in the air before her face. "After we finish, let's grab my car and some takeout. Okay?"

"Fine with me. But is it for us or him, too?" He gestured to Mark's truck. "You know I could have had a few buddies help us out. We wouldn't have needed Mark's help at all."

"Don't start that again. He wanted to help, and I want him here."

He shelved the food discussion as his Mustang rounded the corner. He didn't want their first meal in their new home to be overshadowed by an argument; this experience needed to be celebrated. Maybe they'd pick up something later…just the two of them.

They pulled up in front of their first house, the one that would be theirs together. His. With his wife. This was pretty freaking cool. It was as if his childhood dream had come true—a normal family—and it was happening.

Of course, carrying Aria over the threshold might have been a tad much for his wife to put up with, and yet he enjoyed every second of it. He knew she was a bit of a control freak. Thus, holding the squirming bundle of redheaded womanhood with her ire up and her body pressed against his chest for even a few extra minutes pretty much made his day.

"Put me down! Daniel Gregg McCullum, let me go… now!" she chided through gritted teeth, kicking her legs in the air and punching his arms like a five-year-old. "People are watching."

Looking over his shoulder, he didn't see anyone special staring at them. Sure, there were neighbors outside tending their lawns or walking their dogs, but it wasn't as if they were having sex on the front lawn. "The only person out there is your 'bestie,' Mark, and he's pulling boxes out of the back of his macho truck, the one with the humongous tires."

"Shush, he'll hear you!" she whispered.

"Oh, please, a man who has giant tires is compensating for something, and it's not a small ego. It's usually another part of the anatomy that…" He didn't get to finish that sentence, as Aria finally wiggled free and elbowed him in the diaphragm, relieving him of his air supply.

"Low blow," he finally got out when he got his wind back.

"Not yet, but it could be, if you don't let up. I promise I'll make it an even lower blow, if you upset my friend," she said, eyeing him and tapping her left foot. He knew from experience the action was a precursor to some well-intentioned and yet unpleasant tirade, so he disengaged while he was still ahead. But he was still thinking about it.

The house was a basic single-story, one-bedroom/one-bath unit attached to another, supposedly of a similar design. There was a separate dining room that Aria immediately called dibs on for her office, a living room, a kitchen, and a fenced-in backyard. He had learned from the housing office that the Silver Strand neighborhood was constructed mainly of single and double housing units.

There was a bike path that would bring him to the base in under a couple of minutes; they'd save a fortune in gas. Also, he could take a shortcut to get to the ocean side, or he could take his time and kayak all the way around Coronado, which was—actually—a peninsula, but everyone referred to it as an island. Whichever way he decided to go, he'd use the opportunity to train.

"There's no refrigerator. No washer and dryer. Only hookups. We're still going to have to buy a lot of stuff." She sounded worried.

"That's military life. There are rarely appliances in the housing units." He added, "We'll make it work. Just relax."

They were lucky there was a stove, an unremarkable electric one, but they could make coffee and cook. That was handy.

"Did you see this view?" Somehow Aria always managed to find a silver lining. It was one of the many things he loved about her.

The outside patio was situated right on the edge of Glorietta Bay. A gated path ran around the whole neighborhood, and it was ideal for evening walks, or they could slide over the fence and skinny-dip. Of course, most of their neighbors' houses faced out, too, but on a foggy night, as long as they stayed close to shore, it could be fun. She turned to grin at Dan.

"Yeah, pretty choice, huh? Glad you like it. Now you know why I was so excited to get a house here. There are an endless amount of options. Maybe you'll finally learn to stand up on the paddleboard." He made a mental note to pick up his double kayak and surfboards from Hammer's house. His buddy's father-in-law had built them a place in Ocean Beach, and the garage was insanely huge. Half the Team stored beach equipment there. Maybe he'd even snag JC's canoe.

"I did a pretty good job last time I was on one. I sat and I kneeled. The standing part's just a little tricky." She mocked herself, showing the expression she made the last time she hit the drink.

He laughed. Dropping the last box of books in the living-room area, he picked up the last bag of his gear and headed toward the bedroom. The place was a nice size, with ample closet space, and he believed it would suit them well. Unless, of course, his bride decided to set up the entire contents of her past bedroom in here; then they would probably have to stand up while they slept. Maybe he could convince her to spread her treasures throughout the new house.

He hung up his uniforms on the left side of the closet. Behind that, he placed his small collection of blazers, Brooks Brothers shirts and pants, and his tie rack. After high school and before he joined the Navy, he'd lucked into a position working in an office designing logistics programs, something he had a knack for. He'd met the owner through an internist at a rival company, who'd been hired away. It padded his bank account nicely and gave him time to figure out what he wanted before he committed to training for his real dream…the Teams. Using triathlons to help improve his times, he worked out six hours a day in addition to his office job. All in all, by the time he joined the Navy and made it through boot camp and into BUD/S, he'd known he was in the best shape of his life. None of that stopped him from making it even better. Every day he tried to beat his best time, willing to laugh at himself and work harder when he didn't and able to enjoy the achievement when he did.

His stomach rumbled, pulling his mind back to the present and its vast emptiness. They'd worked all day on the coffee and donuts they scarfed down for breakfast. He was starved. Grabbing a power bar out of his pack's new stash, he downed it in three bites.

Dan checked his watch—it was 1830. He had ten hours until he had to be on base. He set the timer on his watch. The alarm would sound tomorrow morning at 0400.

Looking around the room, he sighed. They had completed the majority of the work, but there was still a lot to do. Amazingly enough, they'd managed to move the contents of Aria's entire apartment and his clothes, footlockers, and gear into the house. His possessions were paltry compared to hers, not that it mattered very much. What was hers was hers, and if the rumors were true from his married friends, what was his was hers. He was fine with that, too. If he didn't want someone in his stuff, it wouldn't be in the house and he wouldn't have joined his life to another's. As it was, he was more concerned about the darker details of his life—never being able to explain what he did or where he was going.

The only question he had now was...where to stash his guns. He'd been collecting them since he joined the Navy, and there were at least thirty of them. Someday he'd share the reason for their presence in his life. For now he just needed to make sure they were safely stored.

"Aria, I know I must have asked you this before, but how much training have you had with firearms?"

He opened a case, extracted one of his favorites, pulled the slide back, and inspected the barrel of the 9 mm Sig Sauer. Empty and clean as a whistle. He held the sweet weight in his hand, then wiped it off and laid it back in its case. Securing the latch, he tucked it among the others. "Aria, did you hear me?"

"Yes." Her voice carried from the kitchen, where she was unpacking dishes. "I told you before, I can shoot single and double-barreled shotguns. I used to hunt with my dad. We have deer, bear, and a ton of other game in Vermont. I think I ate game before I ate cow for the first time, which was when I was seven."

He nodded his head. *Right.* "We definitely have a lot of work to do, and we most certainly need a gun safe." Looking in the master-bedroom closet, he saw the perfect place for one. It was hidden enough not to be obvious to strangers, yet an easy spot to access if necessary. Tucking the collection of guns and cases into his semi empty duffel, he zipped it up and slapped a combination lock on it. It wasn't much protection, but it'd have to do for now.

"What did you say?" she shouted. The sound of pots and pans clanging together was an annoying cacophony. "Speak up or come in here."

When she didn't get an immediate response, she yelled, "Dan!"

"Yes," he said softly, standing behind her.

Startled, she leaped into the air, dropping the pans she was holding onto the floor with a loud bang, and then reeled on him. "Don't do that."

Pulling her into his arms, he kissed her soundly on the lips. "Don't do what?" His arms wrapped tightly around her.

"That," she said, rubbing her nose against his and responding to his touch. "You scared me. Don't do that Spec Ops sneak thing." She wound her arms around his neck and rubbed her lips on his.

"Oh, but I enjoy watching your body move so quickly."

"Jerk!" She pushed her hands against his chest.

He refused to let her go. "I'd never hurt you."

"I know. I just…don't do well with surprises." She laid her head on his shoulder. "My first surprise ever wasn't pleasant. Remember, I told you…when my parents died."

Of course he remembered. She'd been nine years old, about to turn ten. Her mom and dad had gone to buy "special" Ben & Jerry's ice cream from the store. They'd been expecting Jimmy any day, so her mother's pregnancy cravings ruled the house. A drunk driver had hit them head-on. Her father had been killed instantly, and her mom had gone into labor. She had survived long enough to give birth before she died too.

Aria drew in a ragged breath. "It was the worst day of my life."

He could feel silent tears soaking through his shirt. With one hand, he gently rubbed small circles on her back, and with the other, he held her tight.

"It was up to me after that to keep the family together." She sniffed a few times.

"I'm sorry." He hugged her.

"I know. Thanks for the apology." She rubbed her face on his shirt and then groped in vain for a tissue.

Giving up, she blew her nose on a piece of discarded wrapping paper.

She pressed her body along the line of his and kissed him back. "I have so much to do. Let's get it done so we can relax."

"It can wait until tomorrow. There's no rush, Aria. Our life together has already begun. How it unfolds…is literally up to us." His lips were raining caresses across her chin and down her neck. Sliding his hands past her waist, he reached around and cupped her bottom, tipping her toward him. "Let's enjoy it."

Against his mouth she murmured, "We don't even have a bed. I shouldn't have rented my apartment furnished. I could have been acquiring stuff." Her bottom lip pouted slightly.

He caught it between his teeth and bit it playfully before letting it go. "Picking furniture that is new to both of us is better. It's a fresh start."

"Agreed, but tonight…" she began.

"Ah, my lady hasn't seen our outdoor bedroom yet. Follow me." He escorted her through the glass doors onto the patio, pointing at the concrete slab, where an air mattress and two sleeping bags—zipped together—awaited them. "Your royal chamber for the evening, m'lady." It wasn't the Del, but after a whole afternoon of moving stuff, he knew it'd beat the floor.

"When did you do this?" She sounded incredulous. There it was…her natural spark of happiness sneaking through the pain. Good. He'd stoke it, help it burn brighter…and bring his bride a smile. He'd ease her out of her habit of worrying.

"While you were bitching Mark out for breaking

your favorite lamp. He must really like you to put up with that tone. I'm not sure I would have dealt with it so easily." He hadn't meant for the comment to come out so harshly, but he'd wanted to broach the topic ever since it happened. She had been really unkind to someone who was helping her out; that didn't seem right. Besides, Team guys called each other on their shit. If she couldn't hack his forthrightness, he'd need to know. It was an indicator for how she'd deal with bigger issues.

"Dan!" There was a moment of shocked silence. "I...I don't bitch!"

"What would you call it?" He tilted his head to the side, curious about what she was going to call her terse display.

"Guidance."

He laughed. Yeah, she'd hack it. He was proud of her. There were no tears, recriminations, or denials. She'd do just fine. Humor worked well to lighten the weight of misspoken words, and problems too.

"Ha, ha." She smiled and then began to laugh, too. "I guess it is funny. Crap, I'm such a pack rat. I hate losing anything. I'll call Mark tomorrow and apologize." She looked up at him from under her lashes. "You're right, by the way. Damn, I just wasn't thinking. I was in reaction mode. I hate hurting anyone and...letting anyone down."

Wrapping his hands around her shoulders, he drew her toward him and kissed the top of her head. "Won't happen. Let go of the fear. Aria, we're in it for the long haul. There will be ups and downs, yet I promise I will always listen, and together we'll figure out the rough patches. We're partners." He gave her a squeeze. "Besides, if a friend cannot forgive you, is he really a friend?"

"No. You're right. Thanks…for being even-keeled and for being you." Placing her hand over his heart, she rose up on tiptoe and kissed him. "I feel better." Walking her fingers up his chest, she asked, "Now, what's this about bedtime?" She stroked her fingers down his chest, aiming lower.

He chuckled, and then he helped her down onto the mattress. Using his teeth, he opened her shirt one button at a time. His lips, tongue, and teeth tantalized and teased her flesh until she was pulling the rest of her clothes off herself and tugging at his.

"Dan, am I ever going to get enough of you?" Her hands were struggling with his pants, trying to pull them off of him.

Lifting his hips, he helped her slide them off, and then they were both naked, stretched out on the air mattress on the patio. The foliage on either side of their yard, courtesy of past residents, hid them. "I hope not… though I imagine you'll get used to me."

Her finger stroked his flesh. "I want it to always be like this…new. Can we make a promise to be perpetually in heat for each other?"

"I'm in," he said. "Though that type of promise will mean both us will have to be very imaginative."

"Oh, I can do that." She rolled off the mattress and extended her hand.

His eyebrows drew down. "What's up?"

"Trust me." He shrugged and took her hand. Getting to his feet, he followed her into the house. When she sat down on the living-room floor, surrounded by boxes of books, he didn't know what to make of it. As she began unpacking them, he opened his mouth to comment and she shushed him.

"Give me a few minutes." Watching his bride, he saw her dig out some large tomes, which she laid out in a rather peculiar design. Draping herself onto them, she beckoned him with open arms. "This is a fantasy of mine. Help me…make it come true."

Slowly, he lowered himself to her. He held his body in a push-up style, not wanting to crush her. It seemed strange, the way her hips were elevated and the rest of her body was lower. What was he supposed to do? "Aria…"

She beckoned him toward her. "Make love to me. I promise, you'll like it. This is a great position, too, for me."

Pushing up to his knees, he lightly touched her between her legs. Dampness bathed his fingers as she arched into his caress. He adored how free and uninhibited she was. Bringing his head down between her legs, he sought her clit with his tongue. When he touched the tiny nub with the tip of his tongue, she practically lifted off of her perch.

"Yes!" She drew the word into one thrilled, guttural sound, arching into his strokes.

God, she's so sexy!

"Dan," she sighed softly.

Hearing his name uttered in such abandon delighted him and made his pace swifter.

She sucked in a deep breath, raking her fingers along his scalp.

He held his rhythm, waiting, anticipating the moment when she—

"Dan!"

Slipping two fingers inside, he could feel her body shimmering with delight. Aria could give Aphrodite herself a run for her money.

Breathing in, a primal part of him screamed with possession. Her scent drove him wild…and this undeniable sweetness was his Aria. She was his.

His body ached for release. His craving for her would never be sated. Using his whole face, he scraped his beard tenderly and intimately and oh, so gently over her private parts before he went back to teasing her tasty clit. Little noises of pleasure were coming from the back of her throat, and he wrapped his lips around the small bud and suckled.

"Dan…" Fingernails scratched his shoulders as she tried to get a hold of him—either to stop him or hold him in place, he couldn't tell—but the books prevented her from bending toward him and grabbing him. Again and again he brought her until he couldn't take it any longer and she was begging for mercy. "Please, Dan. Please."

Only then, kneeling before her, did he enter her. In one stroke, he slid into her and felt her body spasm with release. Guttural moans came from her throat. Again and again he moved in and out of her body until she was weeping for yet another release. Using his finger to rub over her clit, he brought her in sync with his motion.

He let go…released…and the sensation washed over him in a full body spasm.

Her body drank in his seed more deeply than it had ever drunk before.

They both stilled, letting the peacefulness and

oneness wrap them in an afterglow embrace. Wanting to hold her, he reached for her.

She gave him her hands and he lifted her up and cuddled her to him. Holding her tight was special to him, indescribable in its value to him.

With her still in his arms, he climbed to his feet and carried her outside to their waiting bed.

"Aria?" He studied her face. It was bathed in moonlight. Her eyes were closed and her breathing was even. He laid her within their makeshift blind. She didn't even roll over to her usual position. His wife was sound asleep before he could even crawl in next to her. Wrapping his body around hers, he spooned her and tucked the covers around them both.

"You are the love of my life," he whispered in her ear. He doubted she heard him. The power of the statement felt right, and it warmed him down to his toes better than any blanket. Closing his eyes, he willed himself to sleep.

The smell of roses and lavender, leftovers planted by the house's last residents, drifted in, carried by the gentle bay breeze. His nostrils flared as he breathed in the sweet scents.

He opened his eyes to see it was still dark out. Checking his watch, he could see only two hours had passed.

Stretching his arms above his head, he pulled the kinks out of his body and noticed the marine layer had drifted in while they slept, adding another level of shielding from any neighbor's prying eyes even more effective than the foliage and darkness.

Lying on the air mattress, sandwiched in between the sleeping bags, was warm and relaxing, keeping any chill far away, but something was missing.

His eyes scanned the area. Where was his wife? Being out here was nice but not much fun without her. "Hey, Aria, what are you doing in there?"

"Trying to find stuff." Her voice sounded annoyed. It was followed by a loud bang. "Ouch! There it is!" A light came on over the stove. "I knew that light was somewhere in here."

"Do you need some help?"

"No, my stomach woke me. I'm hungry." Aria banged around for a few more minutes, and then she appeared in the doorway. Standing naked and looking like some kind of warrior woman, she held a tray at her waist. The bounty she carried consisted of a bottle of red wine, two glasses, a package of dried fruit, and a plastic-wrapped salami that sat alongside a box of wheat crackers. "Dinner?"

"Looks great," he said, getting out of their makeshift bed and taking the tray from her. He laid it down next to their nest and watched his sexy wife wiggle down between the covers. Damn, she was beautiful! He was hungry in more ways than one. "So you're starved?"

"Yes, for food. Though I was also concerned about you. If you get any skinnier, I might have to divorce you. My husband has to have a bigger butt than me," she teased and turned to the side so she could show him her behind. "At least for now. After a couple of kids, I reserve the right to change my mind."

"Duly noted." He grinned, taking advantage of the opportunity and swatting her playfully. "For the record, your size doesn't matter to me one bit. It's happiness and health and pleasure I care about, got it?"

"Yes." She licked her lips. "Thanks for saying that. I want you to always find me sexy."

"I will." It seemed strange for her to be unsure. Aria was one of the most confident women he knew. Little unknown elements tripped her sometimes, but he knew she'd pick herself up. She was unstoppable when she wanted to be.

He used the mini corkscrew on his key ring to open the wine and poured her a glass. Then he broke into the salami, sliced it, and made her a sandwich with the crackers.

"A little dry, but it will do." She leaned over and gave him a kiss. "Thanks for making me breakfast."

After stuffing a few salami-cracker sandwiches in his mouth, he brushed off his hands and stood. "What do you say we scope out what we're going to need for the kitchen?"

The room was littered with packing materials and partially emptied boxes. He pushed a few of the bigger boxes aside, creating a better pathway, and then he stuffed hunks of empty wrapping paper into a half-filled trash bag.

He eyed the largest clear space, obviously outfitted for a refrigerator with a water hose and electric hookups behind it. He had a ten-inch hand span from thumb to pinky, and he used it to measure the approximate width, depth, and height. "We can do a width of about thirty-six inches with a height of up to…let's say seventy-three or seventy-four inches and a depth of about twenty-five, but no longer than twenty-six, inches."

Aria was behind him with her cell phone browser already open to a page that showed a range of fridges. "That'll work," she said. He looked over his shoulder, and he could see her expanding the description and double-checking. The look of concentration was so intense, he had to stop himself from chuckling at her. His wife did not make decisions lightly. She could ponder and examine something so long, all the newness was squeezed out. "Promise me that you won't analyze everything to death, okay? Otherwise, it'll take forever to buy furniture."

She frowned. "I just don't want to rush into a mistake." She glared at him for a moment or two and then shook her head. Her eyes were soft and filled with a glint of laughter. "How is it that you know me so well?"

"I'm intuitive."

"Well, what am I thinking now?"

"That I should order the fridge before I ravish you again."

"You're so smart. Imagine me getting turned on by an appliance." She winked at him.

Coming back onto the patio, he sat on the bed, took the phone and logged in some information, and then pressed Send. He leaned over and kissed her. "Well, the refrigerator is done. It will be here in two days. They have your cell phone for the main contact. Don't book anything for that day, or they'll leave it outside the door. FYI, those things are a pain to move inside without a dolly."

"Oh! Ah! I'm so hot for you." She teasingly tapped his nose with her finger. When he didn't immediately reply, she said, "I got it!"

He grinned at her. She looked so sweet—her hair was messy from their lovemaking, and her lips were red from his kisses. Aria made him hungry...all over again.

Putting her hand up against his chest, she stopped him. "And the bed?"

"Really? You want to talk about *that* now?" Pushing the tray away, he laid his body down next to her.

"Yes." She rubbed her nose against his. "Remember my 'Oh! Ah!'" Laughter bubbled out of her.

"That, my love, we'll have to go pick out in person. Sounds like an interesting experience to me, bouncing around from bed to bed. Testing them. Seeing which one works for us. Too bad we have to be in a store." He reached for her, pulling her on top of him. He looked into her eyes. "Everything's okay?"

"Definitely." Her lips came down on his, claiming him and expressing her wish, a craving and hankering... for him, too.

From deep in his throat came a noise too primal and possessive for words. With her wrapped around him, he was content.

Chapter 6

THE NEXT DAY, A FEATHERY-LIGHT CARESS TOUCHED her cheek. Dan's voice drifted into her senses. "See you tonight."

She tried to dig her way up from her dreams, moving toward him, but she was so tired…sleep was hard to deny.

Hearing his car engine turn over brought her half-awake, and then she fell deeply asleep again.

A strange voice jerked her out of her dreams several hours later.

Having a neighbor yell over the fence, "Welcome to the neighborhood!" while she was lying naked, covered only by an edge of the sleeping bag, in their marvelous outside makeshift bed…made her eyes snap wide open.

"Hi, I'm Stan." Staring at the balding man who was holding a cup of coffee and watering his tomato plants as he overtly looked right at her made her want to scream. The fence was high enough. Either this guy was standing on a box or he was very, very tall. Whatever way she judged it…this neighbor was creeping her out!

"Oh, hi." She wrapped the cocoon of sleeping bags tighter around her body and rolled off the air mattress and into the secluded enclosure of the doorway. From there she ditched the sleeping bag and sprinted for the bedroom naked.

Of course, there were no shades to block the view of passersby, but it wasn't quite bright enough to see into the bedroom, either. According to her watch, it was seven thirty in the morning. She must have missed Dan leaving. Pulling on one of his sweatshirts and digging around until she located a pair of her sweatpants, she finally emerged feeling a little better.

She headed for the bathroom and tripped over two boxes blocking the door. "If that isn't a call for organization, I don't know what is." She washed up and then got to work, unpacking boxes and setting up their house.

The list of things they needed felt endless: coverings for the windows and a bedroom set, including night tables, dressers, and a bed frame, as well as a mattress set. "Can I pick it out for myself? Do I need to wait for him?" She sighed. "I don't want to wait to do all of this, I just want it done."

Going back into the kitchen, she unearthed a stainless-steel pot, a mug that Mark had given her saying "I'm grrrrrreat!" and her stash of tea. While she waited for the water to boil, she made a grocery list. It felt as though her tasks would never be done. And it was doubly hard having to take care of it all by herself. "How do military wives do all of this?" Pack, unpack, move, put everything away, stock the house, and then do it again a few months or years later. All she knew was that they'd better stay put.

Making a cup of tea was therapeutic for her—opening the tea bag and smelling the burst of English breakfast tea, dunking the bag until it was the perfect color, and then waiting for it to cool so she could take that first steamy sip. The calming effect was immediate.

It seriously made life easier as she looked around the living room and counted the rest of the unpacked boxes. "I guess I better get to it."

She missed the days when Mark used to stop by her apartment with breakfast. He'd surely make her laugh if he were there now. She was searching for the phone to give him a call when she found a granola bar with a note on it.

"Eat me. Xoxo."

Damn, Dan was adorable! Next to it was her phone. *Yay!*

The line rang several times before Mark answered. "Hello."

"Mark, it's Aria. Listen I'm so sorry…"

"To be calling me before I finished my workout routine and it was time for coffee?"

"Well, I knew you'd be up." She smiled and knew he'd hear it in her voice. "Listen, I'm sorry for being such a bee-itch. I didn't mean to take you for granted that way. I really appreciate all of the help you gave us in hauling stuff into the house."

"No worries. I was happy to do it." He had happiness in his voice. "Hey, want to get together soon? Just you and me… You can leave the ball and chain at home."

She laughed. "Sure. I'll call you after I get my world sorted. Have a great day!"

"It already is one…I talked to you. Bye, Aria Angel."

"Bye, Mark." She hugged her phone and then immediately located her purse and placed it into its depths so she wouldn't lose it again.

Her stomach growled, so she made her way back to the tea. Picking up the granola bar, she ripped open the wrapper and sunk her teeth in, pulling off a chunk of the espresso-infused, chocolate-chunk, chewy granola. "I must seriously be starved for this thing to taste good."

Sitting down on one of the boxes, she stared at her breakfast and then sighed.

Lifting the bar in the air, she said, "To new beginnings. It better get easier."

———————

By late afternoon, she'd set up what she could of the living room and dining room and some semblance of a home office. The desk had not been fun to assemble alone, but she'd managed, and without using the hammer, too. There were no awkward angles and overall it looked usable. *Yay, me!*

As soon as she booted up her laptop, email messages filled her screen. She opened the latest project and saw that one of the commercials she'd written needed an immediate rewrite for tomorrow's filming. She reread the last version and then wrote three different options. Sending them to the client, she asked for feedback and then went on to the next issue.

Her cell phone rang, jarring her out of her writing. She had answered most of her emails, handling three emergencies for a very needy client, adding new scripts to his television and radio campaigns, as well as sending two quotes to potential clients. Overall, she had caught up nicely and only needed another hour before she was ahead of the due dates on her project schedule.

The cell stopped clamoring and then rang back. It was Dan's signal for "Urgent, pick me up now."

She dashed over to her purse, fished out her cell phone, and answered immediately. "Dan, hi."

"Hi, Aria. Sorry to bother…you sound distracted… like you're working."

"I am. No worries, though. What's up?"

"Ah, I forgot to tell you... I ran into our neighbor on the right side this morning, and she invited you to a tea this afternoon. I told her you'd be happy to go with her." He sounded a little apologetic, but not nearly enough for having committed her to something without her agreement.

"Dan, why would you do that?" She looked down at her attire. Could she look any grubbier? She shook her head. She wasn't thrilled about going anywhere, especially with all the work she had to do. "Can I get out of it? What if you call her and tell her I'm busy?"

"Sorry, I don't have her info on me. Listen, I have to go in a minute." There were voices in the background; someone was telling Dan to hurry up. It sounded like Hammer.

Blast, blast, blast! She hadn't washed her hair. Her dresses were still wrinkled from the move, and she had tossed her old battered ironing board, planning on buying a new one. *Nuts!* She didn't have anything to bring with her, either. A hostess gift was required, wasn't it?

Dan's voice came back on the line. "It's a neighborhood thing. You'll get to meet more of the military wives." There was a short pause. "Just go. You don't have to stay long. Please? Do it for me."

She drew in a long deep breath. "Fine. When will she be here?"

The doorbell rang. *No way! This can't be happening.*

"I think I've answered my own question." As she walked to the door, she said, "Call me before you leave the base—you're picking up dinner." Hanging up before he could protest, she flipped the bolt and yanked open the door.

"Hello." There was a tall, slim woman dressed in a purple flowered dress with a small lace collar. A strand of pearls hugged her neck, with matching bobs in her ears. Her brunette hair was piled on top of her head. It was difficult not to stare at the tiny curls perfectly spaced around her updo. "I'm Eve Louise Lockwood. It's nice to meet you. Welcome to the Silver Strand."

"Hi, Eve. I'm Aria McCullum. Would you like to come in? Sorry for the mess. We're still getting settled in." She couldn't even offer the woman a seat, unless they went into her office and she relinquished her privacy and her desk chair. That was her special spot, and she didn't want anyone in there. Guess she'd have to forgo manners this time.

"Are you ready?" The woman looked her up and down. "I mean…is that what you're wearing to the tea? The attire is more elaborate, on the dressy side. Of course, if this is all you have… Um, I could loan you something, though our sizes might be off by a few inches." Eve was almost six feet tall and could have been a supermodel. Anything that Aria borrowed would drag on the ground and make her look as if she were playing dress-up in mother's clothes. She knew the woman was trying to be helpful, but how could she communicate politely that she didn't even want to leave the house?

Was it appropriate to say that she was nesting? Or rather, she'd prefer to live in sweats and pajamas for the next two weeks while she worked the kinks out of the new living space and her life in general, how about that?

Aria shook her head. Her husband had asked her to go. She knew she should at least try. "Thank you for the offer, but I'm fine. I have other things to wear." The woman didn't look as if she believed Aria. Her expression, with its raised eyebrows and turned-down nose, was dubious, to say the least. "I wasn't expecting you. My husband just called, literally two minutes before you arrived, to tell me about the tea."

"Oh, I see." She was very polite, but her tone grew a little chilly. "Well, we need to be at Caybreena Hinnell's house in fifteen minutes. She doesn't like her guests to be tardy. If you don't mind, I'd rather not be branded and stuck on her bad side. So, ahem, should I leave you the address, or are you coming with—"

"Give me a minute and I'll be good to go." Aria hurried into the bedroom.

Digging through the closet, she knew what she wanted to wear. Withdrawing an Armani blue silk dress, which was probably too dressy but fit her like a glove, she knew it would work. Carefully she pulled it on, then wedged herself into a pair of nude stockings and stuffed her feet into a pair of sparkly heels.

Unearthing her makeup bag, she quickly powdered her face, slapped on blush and mascara, went without eyeliner, but added a dash of her signature pink lipstick. She fluffed her hair so the curls were a wild mass of springy red gorgeousness.

Briskly, she left her bedroom and grabbed her keys off the kitchen counter. Stopping in front of her neighbor, whose eyes were wide, she asked, "Shall we go?"

Eve nodded, her chin practically on the floor and her mouth wide open. "Y-y-you look gorgeous."

"Thanks." Locking the house behind them, Aria walked down the street with her neighbor. "So tell me about yourself. What do you do? And the people I'm about to meet, what are they like?"

"Well, I'm a mom of triplets…Reggie, Ryan, and Rickie. You'll hear them before you see them. Our last neighbors didn't like them very much, but the military seems to change things up quickly enough that no one gets too annoyed. What rank is your husband?" The woman rattled on at a brisk pace.

"Uh, he just made Chief. I think. I don't know too much about military stuff."

Eve looked shocked. "Oh, you'll need to learn ASAP. Everything is about rank in this neighborhood. My husband is a Senior Chief Petty Officer and—Caybreena Hinnell's house that we're on our way to—her husband is up for Command Master Chief Petty Officer. She's the point person for the neighborhood, the one who sort of runs things."

"Are all of the people in this neighborhood associated with the Teams?" Aria was curious.

"SEAL Team? Oh, goodness, no." Her laughter was a titter, sounding like a little high-pitched bell. "You really are new, aren't you? Most of us are Navy, of course, but there are some other branches here. Air Force and Marine Corps. But there are no Army families that I am aware of. This neighborhood mainly houses enlisted Marines or sailors and their families." She stopped abruptly in front of a house with a mani-cured lawn and an insane amount of flowers planted so uniformly, Aria wondered if someone came out with a measuring stick to confirm they were all the same height, size, and width apart, ripping out the ones that did not fit.

The door opened before they made it even halfway up the walk. A tiny blond stood there with her hands on her hips.

Aria plastered a smile on her face and put out her hand. "Hi, Caybreena. I'm Aria McCullum. It's nice to meet you. Thank you for inviting me to your tea."

Her hostess gave her a cold look. "You may call me Mrs. Hinnell. And honestly, I had no idea Eve was bringing a guest."

Aria barely knew what to say, and Eve was shifting uncomfortably beside her. But Aria refused to be cowed. She straightened her shoulders and looked Caybreena—or Mrs. Hiney, as Aria now thought of her—directly in the eyes. "Well, how kind of you to allow me into your home." With no choice left to her, their hostess stepped aside.

"Well, if you insist on staying, Aria…" Caybreena's voice dropped to a whisper. "Though I think it's a mistake. It's never too early to learn that rank and privilege go hand in hand." A false bravado lifted her voice higher. "Then, come meet my neighbors."

Mrs. Hiney led the way into heavily scented room, as if potpourri had been mashed into every fiber and thread of furniture and carpet. Aria wrinkled her nose and then sneezed, bringing another sour look from Caybreena.

Yep, like hell Aria would offer to leave now. She'd rather be the thorn in this woman's paw then back down, and she wanted to know what she was up against. If a fight was what this tiny blond termagant wanted, then Aria could give it to her.

Oh, Dan, you should have let me stick to my plan and stay home. This tea is going to be awful.

She was right! The tea had been an unmitigated disaster. Especially after she'd accidently spilled tea on Caybreena's new carpet. Aria was sure the spot would come out without much effort, but of course Mrs. Hinnell had to throw a hissy about it. If her husband hadn't asked her to go to this event, she would never have attended. She cringed thinking about it.

Aria didn't think things could get much worse until she saw her front lawn.

There was a refrigerator in front of the door to her house and furniture filling their yard. Digging into her pocket, she looked for her phone. It was in the house. Someone had probably called, but she had been in such a rush when she left that she had neglected to bring her cell phone with her.

Tears filled her eyes. How was she going to get the door open, with the refrigerator blocking it? Worse yet, what was she going to say to Dan?

Sitting down on the couch, which was actually pretty comfortable, she gave in to the day's stresses, exhaustion from unpacking, and all the work she had to catch up on, and cried. She wept until there was nothing left inside of her, and then a thought occurred to her. She hadn't closed the back door to the patio.

Getting up from her comfortable spot, she walked down the block to the gate that let her onto the path that went around the whole neighborhood and walked down to her house. Sure enough, the door was open. She took off her shoes, tossed them into the yard, and then hiked up her dress and climbed over the fence. She was relieved to be home. Grabbing her shoes, she went inside. There she found a six-pack of beer on the counter from her neighbor Stan and his wife, Julie. Had he climbed over the fence, too? The thought of his being in her house gave her uncomfortable chills, yet more than anything she wanted to crack one of them open and drown out the afternoon's event.

"Nice." They were still cold. She opened a drawer, found the bottle opener, popped the top, and drank a sip. It burned her throat a little—she wasn't a beer drinker, just had an occasional glass of wine or champagne—but today she didn't care. She took another sip and put it aside to go change into more comfortable clothes.

She knew Dan wouldn't be able to answer his phone, but after such an awful afternoon, she just wanted to hear his voice. Even the way he asked to leave a message seemed deeply sexy, and she couldn't wait for him to get home.

"Hey, babe. Just wanted to give you a heads-up, we have a furniture situation in our front yard. Can't wait to see you tonight!"

She took a deep breath and tried not to let tears overwhelm her. She could get through this. *They* could get through this.

Her heart leaped as her phone rang. Maybe Dan had found a minute to call her back after all!

But it was Jimmy on the line—and he was crying.

"What's wrong? Where are you?" she asked.

"I'm…in San Diego. At the h-h-hospital."

"Jimmy, slow down. What hospital? Are you hurt? You were supposed to fly out a week ago." Panic clawed through her. She was the adult, though, and always had to be. Making her voice calm and firm, she hoped he would hear her stability and slow down his breathing before he had an asthma attack. When he didn't, she said, "Come on, Jimmy, draw your air in slowly. Do it with me. That's right. Now let it out slowly. Good, just breathe with me." Aria walked him through it for several minutes, getting her teenage brother calm, and then she asked the question that was on the tip of her tongue through the entire phone call. "Jimmy, where is Uncle David?"

Her brother took in a ragged breath. "He's dead. Uncle David was killed in the crash." The weeping began again as Aria put the cell phone on speaker and stared at it.

A police officer came on the line. The details came out slowly. Instead of going back to Vermont so Jimmy could catch the first week of school, her uncle and brother had driven up the coast to visit her uncle's friends. Today they were on their way back to San Diego. On Interstate 5, just past the exit for the Marine base, they'd been in a crash.

Uncle David went through the windshield and was killed instantly. Her brother was completely unharmed but needed to be picked up from the hospital.

She told the officer she would be there in twenty minutes.

She sent Dan a quick text before she allowed herself to give in to the grief. Flashes of her parents' death ripped her heart apart. But Jimmy needed her. "Get it together, Aria."

Swallowing the lump in her throat, she pushed her sorrow to the recesses of her brain as she made her way to the hospital. She knew delaying the grief would cost her later on, take a greater toll, but she told herself she needed to do it…for Jimmy. He must have felt so adrift. What would it be like to raise a teenager? She didn't know. She had been away from home for five years. Regardless, she'd make it work, because family was what mattered.

"All we have is each other."

As she entered the hospital, the smell of the antiseptic assaulted her nose. She coughed and then cleared her throat. Stopping at the water fountain, she took a quick sip.

Police officers were waiting for her in the small ER lobby area. "I'm Aria McCullum."

"I'm Officer Kendrik and this is Officer Rosa. Thank you for coming so quickly."

"Where is my little brother?"

The taller one, Officer Kendrik, said, "We'll take you to him shortly. Only a couple of things. First I need to see your ID."

"Yes, of course." She took her new military ID out of her wallet and presented it to them.

"We're very sorry for your loss. The doctor should be done checking your brother out by now. Let's go find him."

He handed her a business card as they walked toward a double-locked door that said Doctors and Registered Patients Only. "Someone will be in touch…you know, for the arrangements you would like to have made for your uncle."

Oh, God! Aria's stomach churned. Simultaneously, she put one hand on her stomach and the other on her head. She wanted to throw up or pass out. Her body was fighting both responses.

"Mrs. McCullum, you look pale. Why don't you sit down?" The police officer sat next to her. To his partner, he said, "Go get the brother. It's time for them to go home." He picked up a magazine and fanned her with it. "Do you want us to call someone for you?"

"No, I'll be fine. Just give me a minute." Aria counted slowly in her head, using a yoga technique to get control of her breathing. When she heard the door open, she looked up and saw her brother.

She rushed toward him and pulled him into her arms. Holding him as he cried, she patted his back the way she had when he was younger. She couldn't imagine what he was thinking or how afraid he must be.

"Aria," he sobbed.

"It'll be okay." She willed her own sense of calm into him, trying to ease him. But everything had changed. Nothing she could do would ever take back the horror of her brother experiencing the accident and witnessing his uncle's death. All she could do was make the present work. She would, too. Jimmy was her only blood kin on this planet, and she'd move mountains to protect him.

Closing her eyes to block out her own emotion, she said, "I'm here. I will always be here for you. I promise."

Chapter 7

THAT EVENING DAN JUMPED THE BACKYARD FENCE, jogged across the small green expanse, and entered the house. The only light came from the bathroom. As he headed toward it, he saw Aria's curvy figure in the doorway, standing guard as she watched her brother sleep.

He wrapped his arms around his wife, and together they watched Jimmy sleep—his gangly arms and legs completely tangled in the sheets on the air mattress. A protective, paternal instinct swept through him.

Aria turned toward him, her eyes swimming with tears. He pulled her to his chest, his hand brushing back her curls, and held her. There was so much they needed to say, but right now he knew physical comfort was the best thing he could give her. After a moment, he took her hand and led her to the patio. Once there, he brought her into his arms again. She seemed so tiny and fragile.

"Dan…" She tried to wiggle away, but he wouldn't let go.

"I'm here for you, hon. Whatever you need, we're one unit." He heard her choke as he spoke that last word.

She hid her head against his chest. "I know what he feels…some of it. When I lost my parents, I was so alone and had to be strong for everyone. I don't want him to have to go through the same stuff."

He nodded. "I know. But you can't protect him from

his own emotions. The best thing you can do is…to be there for him. Talk to him."

"Maybe if I had…"

"No, don't go down that road. There's nothing you could have done to prevent this." He held her as she wept. "Let it out. I'm here. I'll help, too."

She wiped her face on her sleeve and her eyes lifted to his. The wealth of pain reflected in her gaze nearly broke his heart. She swallowed hard and he listened to her cough. Finally, she spoke. "Let me just say this. Someone else I loved…died, and I wasn't there to stop it." Her eyes searched his, begging for a response… some kind of balm to ease the pain. There was nothing that could ease that kind of pain. But he could try to cut the burden in half…bring part of the work onto himself when he was home. Maybe some of the wisdom his grandfather taught him would help Jimmy.

Moving his hands to her shoulders, he held her and said in a firm tone, "Listen to me, you didn't do this, Aria."

Her lips trembled. "But my parents—" Tears rolled down her face, dripping off her cheeks and disappearing into the darkness.

"Aria, your parents were in the wrong place at the wrong time. If you had been in the car with them, you would be dead now, too." He drew her toward him and kissed the top of her head. "You are the kindest, sweetest, strongest, and most caring woman on the planet. You gave up a lot to care for your brother and uncle. I know I don't know everything you did, but I can imagine some of it." He placed a kiss on her lips. "I am here to help you with your brother and with everything. We're teammates. I am a part of this and want to be here."

His wife shook. He could feel the emotion bubbling up inside of her, and then it burst out in loud, wracking sobs. He held tightly to her, being her safety line in the storm of her emotions. "That's it. Let it out." *Maybe this time my message sunk in. She can't continue to make herself responsible.*

Aria wept until her tears ran dry, and still he held fast to her. Hiccups replaced the sobs, and her rapid breathing slowed to a more even pace. As her body seemed to lose its strength, she sagged against him. Before she completely gave in to the exhaustion, he picked her up in his arms.

"I love you," she whispered.

"I love you too," he replied as he carried her through the darkened house and tucked her into the bed next to Jimmy. He grabbed a towel from the bathroom and draped it over the window, then closed the door quietly behind him.

Stepping back out on the patio, he sent a text to his buds. Hopping over the fence railing, he walked down the pathway, to the road, and around to the front of his house. He stared at the furniture littering the lawn. "You've been a busy lady, Aria. Now, let's see if I can be the one to bring you some ease and comfort."

By the light of the streetlamps, JC and Hammer helped Dan survey the yard.

Taking a deep breath, Dan let it out slowly. "What a mess."

"We can make quick work of it," said Hammer, scratching his neck.

Dan didn't want to think about the day's events. It was much easier to tackle the project at hand. "Minimal talking once we're inside the house. Aria and Jimmy are finally asleep."

JC nodded. "Roger that."

Hammer slapped Dan on the back and moved toward the refrigerator. Dan and JC had to double-time it to catch up to him. At the front door, Hammer said, "I'll tip. Dan, you open the door, and JC, you catch the other end of the refrigerator and help me move it inside." The choreography was timed perfectly, and the refrigerator was soon in place, connected properly, humming along, and beginning to cool down. Of course, they put several six-packs of beer inside before they went to the front lawn for the next load.

"Who has a knife?" asked Dan as he wrestled with a large box that had fifteen plastic straps crisscrossing it. A Ka-Bar was placed in his hand, and Dan smiled as he recognized the feel of it. "Aw, JC, you're lending me Sally." Sliding the blade over the straps, in one movement he severed all of the restraints and even slit the box for good measure. Tossing the blade at JC's foot, the man caught it by the handle before it even touched the soil.

"Come to me, my precious." JC slipped the knife into the sheath attached to his belt and went back to wrestling with the couch. "Dan, I'm not confident about our ability to fit this baby through the front door."

"Is there another option?" Hammer did a quick measurement using his arms. "Unless you'd like me to get the ax out of my emergency tool locker and cut it down into three smaller pieces, this pup either has to go back or…"

Dan nodded. "Yeah, I was worried about that when I saw the size of it." Ripping open another of the boxes, he smiled. "Great choice, Aria." He pulled out the barstools and examined them. He liked them. "Let's bring these inside. We'll put them against the island in the kitchen. I think the back door, through the patio, will be our best option for the couch."

They brought them in and agreed that it was time for a boat drill. Going back outside, they picked up the couch, hefted it over their heads, and trotted down the street as if it were one of the water-filled boats from their BUD/S training. Humping it along the path until they got to Dan and Aria's place, they hefted it over the fence and through the patio into the open back door. As they placed it in the only spot available, it was clear the size completely overwhelmed the room.

JC waited until they were outside before he whispered, "Trying to compensate for something with that *huge* couch? You could've just gotten some tight shorts, you know."

"At least I have some size," retorted Dan.

"Too bad I have to put both of you to shame," added Hammer as he headed back in with the side table. "Where you want this?"

"Against the far wall, facing the bay," instructed Dan.

JC picked up one side of the recliner. "Are you going to stand there or help me?"

"Aw, can't I just admire your muscles?" Dan grinned.

"Only if you must," said JC as they lifted the chair and brought it into the house.

"Keep going. There's no room in the house. Take it to the patio," said Dan in a hushed voice. They took it out back and faced it toward the water. It would be protected somewhat by the patio overhang. Too bad they couldn't fit it in the house. This chair would have been perfect for relaxing in front of the television.

Lastly they tackled the outdoor furniture. Dragging the lot of it to the back of the house, they locked the front door and used some of Hammer's tools to screw the damn pieces together. It was midnight by the time they finished.

"Thanks," Dan said as they slapped hands and parted ways. They hopped the fence and raced each other to their cars. "Maniacs."

Looking out into the night, he wondered what was in store for him and his new wife. He knew Aria was being bombarded with a lot of newness, but now that they had a fourteen-year-old boy to watch over, it was doubled. He didn't doubt the experience was going to be a handful. Heading back inside, he locked the patio door, picked up his keys and a piece of paper he'd taken note of on the counter, and went out the front.

Opening the car door, he slid inside and started the ignition. He had to be on base in four hours. There was still plenty of time to stock the refrigerator. He'd find a 24/7 grocery. It was the least he could do to help.

Morning came too quickly. The alarm on his watch beeped and Dan saw he'd been able to catch about two hours of sleep. "I've functioned on less."

Rolling off the couch, he decided it was pretty comfortable.

He traced a path into the kitchen in the dark. Pulling

open the refrigerator, he withdrew three eggs, cracked them into a cup, added some Tabasco sauce, and downed it. Next he filled up his glass with milk, drank it down in several gulps, and took an apple from the crisper.

He scrawled a quick note to Aria, grabbed his keys, and ate the apple on the way to his Mustang. He resisted the urge to open the bedroom door and check on his sleeping wife and her brother. He'd talk to the XO and see if he could get a few days off. There were several weeks of time coming to him. Thoughts of taking Aria on a whirlwind vacation would have to wait…possibly years.

———

Dan flashed his ID at the ocean entrance and drove around the buildings until he reached the far side of Team THREE's Quarterdeck. He parked the car and then pulled off his sweatshirt. After tucking his car keys into his pocket, he placed his ID into a holder and secured it to his arm.

He didn't want to take the time to change into his PT clothes. He often ran in whatever he was wearing. This was going to be one of those times, because right now he just wanted to feel the wind in his face.

Heading toward the path, his feet picked up the pace. The rhythmic slap of his feet lulled him. Images flashed through his brain: Aria with her haunted eyes; Jimmy, who looked so small tucked in their bed; and himself, long ago.

He wasn't an ordinary kid. The son of the district attorney, he was the kid who had been required to take karate since he was three years old and experience home-invasion drills since he was five. How could someone strike so much fear into a child, making him constantly afraid?

Nothing comforted him in the dark. He'd go three or four nights without sleeping, and then exhaustion would take its toll and he would lock himself in his bathroom, where he would sleep for three or four hours, tucked into a corner under the window. He'd been taught to always have an escape route. He dreamed of someone breaking in and his having to yank open the window, do a high-wire act on the big branch outside, and climb down the tree. It didn't matter that he wasn't a fan of heights or that the window weighed almost as much as he did. That was the plan.

Just thinking about it made sweat burst out in thick drops on his brow. Quickly, he whisked it away with his fingers.

When his sister was born, he started sleeping on the floor of her room. Armed with a heavy toy train engine—that was his weapon to fend off the bad guys—he guarded her.

Those bad men… Like a warped cartoon reel, the faces scampered through his mind, the ones plastered on the nightly news, often vowing horrific revenge on his father and his family. Undefined violence, those unknown possibilities, sent dreadful images dancing before his eyes.

On that fated day, the one that changed everything, Dan was walking home from school. His mother had been late picking him up. Sometimes, if she had been at lunch with her friends, she was too "sick" on pickling juice to meet him.

Home was only a quarter of a mile away, and he decided to hoof it that day instead of waiting for the nanny. Next year he'd be entering the sixth grade, and it made him feel older, wiser.

Rounding the corner, he saw the door to his home wide open. He dropped his books on the lawn and sprinted inside the house.

He found a man in their kitchen, looming over his mother and sister. Their faces were tearstained, and a red mark was outlined on his mother's cheek. The intruder lifted his hand to hit Caty.

"Stop!" yelled Dan.

The intruder spun on him. "Well, well, well…you must be the son. I'm sure Daddy wouldn't want to see you hurt." The man grabbed his arm and twisted it.

Pain spread through his shoulder, but Dan just gritted his teeth. "What do you want?"

"I want to make sure your father knows that there are consequences when you mess with my friends." He picked up a knife from the kitchen counter.

Time seemed to slow and a sense of quiet calm surged through Dan's mind. Just as he'd learned in class, he twisted out of his captor's grasp, then took him out at the knees with a well-placed kick. A sharp jab while the man was down snapped his head back. It bounced off their floor and he was out cold.

"Caty, run upstairs and lock the door," he ordered, then moved to the phone and called the police. By the time the officers arrived, he was upstairs with his sister, holding her close.

No one asked who hurt the intruder. Everyone assumed it was his mother.

His father knew the truth. The reason this criminal was in their home was his fault. But his father neither said anything nor confronted the fact that his son's life would never be the same. All he cared about were appearances and that his son turned out like him. Being an uncompromising dictator was not what Dan wanted. He needed someone to know what his soul dreamed of and to love him for it.

The next morning, he called his grandfather, asked him to come get him. Then he went downstairs and told his dad he was going to live with his grandfather. He was determined to bring his sister out of this nightmare, too. One thing was for sure, he vowed, no one would ever hurt him or what was his, and he would do everything in his power to protect his family and those who could not protect themselves.

Dan shook himself out of the memory. A cold sweat chilled his skin. He took in his surroundings, noticing he had already run ten miles. Dawn was stretching its fingers toward the ocean.

Making a tight circle, he turned around. It was time to head back to the base.

Aria only knew part of the story, that he had been threatened as a kid. She didn't know about the horrible relationship he'd had with his father or why he had gone to live with his grandfather. How it all started with an intruder and a vow that led to him wanting to join the military—this was stuff he needed to tell her. He had eventually brought his sister with him, too, and then sued for emancipation when his grandfather died of a heart attack, and together they had finished growing up. Maybe that was why he felt as if he understood Aria. She'd had to do a lot of self-raising on her own.

Self-defense and weapons were a part of that world. They were as dangerous or safe as the person that wielded them. He knew how easily they could kill, and he also knew how his training had saved his life and those of his sister and mother.

After all that, there was still all the crap with his parents and how they had tried to buy Caty and him back again with the lure of paying for college, but it didn't work. He and Caty were capable of figuring it out on their own…and they had.

These were some of his secrets…the darkness and light that dueled in his soul. He'd lost his childhood in that one event. And his self-consumed jerk of a father—what would his wife say to that and his promise to be nothing like his own parents?

Aria had been lucky to like and love her parents. When she talked about them, their attributes and values were a lot like his. He'd be thrilled to be similar with his kids.

Damn, kids were a lot to think about, but they both wanted them.

A book he'd read as a teenager about UDTs—Underwater Demolition Teams—had led him to SEAL Team. When he joined up and made it through boot camp and BUD/S, they helped him, taught him, and forced him to work within an ethos. That healed a part of him. He honored that with his life and soul. His duty wasn't just a set of responsibilities, it was his reason to exist. Fighting for liberty and happiness…he would do anything to maintain those freedoms, and no one needed know what it cost him. As long as he could do his job, he would.

Taking the well-worn path onto the base, he double-timed it to the Platoon Building. Keying in the correct code, he opened the door wide and took the stairs two at a time until he reached the landing. Then he keyed in another set of security codes and let himself into the locker room. He unlaced his shoes, stripped off his clothes, and dropped them in front of the cage that housed his stuff. He could hear other guys in the showers already, preparing for the day ahead.

—∿∿—

Dressed in the Spec Op digitals, Dan checked his appearance in the window's reflection before he opened the door and entered the Team THREE Quarterdeck. He was determined to touch base with the XO before he joined his Team in the conference room.

In the hallway, he ran into Admiral Josh Winters, CO Commander Brian "Duckie" Diggins, and XO Chuck "Ox" Parker. He acknowledged them formally. "Admiral Winters, good to see you again, sir. Commander. XO."

"Mac, how's married life?" asked the CO. "Sorry we missed the wedding. My girls had a dance recital. You'll learn how that goes soon enough."

The XO grinned. "Yeah, me, too. We were at the boys' baseball game. They did a great job—six and zero this season, thus far."

The Admiral cleared his throat. "McCullum, congratulations on making Chief. I heard your last mission went well. When can we expect that After Action Report?"

The other men looked at him, and the casual banter separated like whiskey and water.

"I submitted mine yesterday, Admiral." Dan didn't mind being put on the spot—he was notorious for dotting his i's and crossing his t's—and as far as Dan knew, everyone on the Op had completed their required reports.

The Commander spoke up, taking charge of the conversation. "We'll make sure it's on your desk today, Admiral."

The Admiral gave a brief nod and walked away.

The Commander and XO exchanged glances and then turned their attention back to Dan. A lot was said in that look, and Dan didn't need a decoder ring to know that the Admiral was concerned about something critical.

"Good job in identifying that woman in Ru's presence as being part of the terrorism cell that killed Sandra Niang," Duckie commented.

"Yeah, I'd like to be part of the Op that takes the root down." Dan's jaw clenched. They'd nailed the man who shot her, but it didn't stop the group's poisonous effects from spreading.

"Duly noted," replied Duckie.

Unfortunately, Dan had to broach another topic. "May I speak briefly? My wife's uncle died in an automobile crash yesterday, and we are now charged with raising her fourteen-year-old brother. I'd like to take some time off to help her out and get things settled."

The Navy took the family unit very seriously. They needed their sailors on task, and at times that meant they only had a short intense period of time to concentrate on family-unit issues.

"Condolences. When is the funeral?" asked Ox.

"I don't know." Dan wondered if Aria would need to go back to the mountains. "I'll find out if Aria wants to go back to Dorset to have a wake with his friends there."

"Vermont?" asked the CO. Dan nodded.

"The Ombudsman, uh, Crocker, can lend a hand. Help you sort through the details and provide support. Make sure you contact him."

Dan watched his CO and XO closely. Finally, the XO spoke. "We need you on tomorrow's training mission. It shouldn't be too lengthy. We're reviewing and practicing the tactics for the next mission. Your particular skill set, Mac, will be crucial."

The CO picked up the thread from there. "If you can hold off on your plans, go on this jaunt and the upcoming jump, then we can give you some time off afterward. Would that work for you and your family?"

"Yes, sir. Thank you." He felt the phone vibrate at his hip. It was JC's code. He needed to hightail it to another briefing. The session had already started and he was late.

The CO patted him on the back. "Our condolences to Aria, Mac. I'll be talking to you." That was polite speak for "You're all set, so get going."

Dan didn't need a kick in the ass to move. He set his course for JC and the briefing.

His eyes tracked the CO and XO who'd began talking before the door even was closed. "This is going to be a dicey one," said Ox. "We need to verify the Intel again, before they—" As the heavy door clicked shut, their voices became an indecipherable and steady drone.

Dan would have given anything to be in there. He wasn't sure exactly what was going on, but he knew it was hot. Because it had brought the Admiral onto Team THREE's Quarterdeck, and usually the world went to him.

Chapter 8

THE PAST WEEK HAD BEEN A BLUR. GRIEF AND ANGER consumed her, but Aria was more focused today. Jimmy had started school, and she had been able to throw herself into her work.

Dan had been gone for several days. It was becoming the norm: sporadically home and then without warning gone again. She had been reluctant to talk to anyone else about her real feelings… Maybe she was *too* private for her own good.

Phone calls had flooded the new landline. Her message machine logged calls from several of the SEAL Team wives—women she had met for the first time at her wedding—in addition to the Ombudsman and many of Uncle David's friends from Vermont. She hadn't returned any of the calls, not even to Mark, who had loaded her cell phone with text messages. She was too overwhelmed…trying to keep her emotions locked tight in their mental-construct containers.

Uncle David's friends back east had taken care of the funeral arrangements. At some point she would have to go deal with his house, now hers and Jimmy's, but not now.

Dan's ringtone chimed from her cell, and she lunged for the phone. Clicking the answer button, she said breathlessly, "Hello."

"Hey, babe. I just wanted to share a morning squeeze with you and wish you a great day. I miss ya and love ya." Dan's voice cut off and the phone went dead. It had been a voice mail.

She played it again and then wished she hadn't. Regardless, she clicked Save on her phone and placed her head in her hands and wept.

I need to get out of this rut or I'm going to go crazy! I miss that man way too much. Where's my independence? My backbone? My capacity to live life fully every day is required. You'd think he's the only reason I can exist.

Then she went back into the dining room, emptied the rest of her things into the big hall closet, and cleaned the room…until the smell of disinfectant was so strong it made her dizzy. Grabbing her keys and purse, she unlocked the front door, opened it wide, and there stood Hammer Cody's wife, Hannah.

"Hi, Aria. Sorry to intrude… When you didn't answer, I got concerned." She held a casserole dish in her hands. "This is homemade macaroni and cheese. It's pretty basic. I used Cheddar, Swiss, and Gruyère." Hannah gestured to the bag hanging from her arm. "There's a small sliced ham—you just need to heat it up whenever you're ready. Oh, and a bag of fresh apples from Julian. Have you been up there yet? Great pie."

Aria didn't know what to say. She stared at the willowy woman wearing blue jeans, a Life Is Good T-shirt, and sandals and sporting an uncertain-looking smile. Finally, it dawned on her she was being rude. "Come in."

Hannah headed straight for the kitchen. She laid her items down and then immediately put the food in the refrigerator. "You'll want to heat the macaroni at 350 degrees for about twenty to thirty minutes. Whenever the top bubbles, it's done."

"Would you like a cup of tea?"

"That'd be great." Hannah helped herself to a seat at the end of the island. She wiggled on the stool and then looked down. "Michael was right. These are nice looking. Did you find them online?"

Aria nodded. "Please thank him for me. I didn't realize everything…would happen the way it did. Hammer was kind to help out." She took two mugs and her stash of different flavored tea bags out of the cabinet.

Waving a hand in front of her face, Hannah made a derisive noise. "It's what they do. It's what we do." She took a deep breath and said, "I was sorry to hear about your loss. If there is anything I can do. Any of us… We'd like to help."

"I…uh…" Aria wanted to say, "*No, get out and leave me alone.*" But she did need help. She wanted to get a bed for her brother, and she needed to get one for herself and Dan. Her back was aching from sleeping on the air mattress, and she didn't want to wait for Dan to return. He should have been home days ago! "Is there somewhere I can buy furniture? I want to get a desk for my brother, too."

Hannah grinned. "Absolutely! You've asked the right woman. I have a bachelor's degree in shopping. Well, it's really business, and I honestly have two master's degrees—finance and philosophy. But I promised myself I'd add a PhD eventually. Come on. Turn off the hot water. I'm driving. We'll get the beds, the desk, and anything else you need and have some lunch, too."

Aria switched off the stovetop burner and moved the pot of water to the sink. She put away the tea and the mugs. Picking up her purse and keys again, she felt a small part of her lighten up. "Hannah, you're not at all what I expected."

"What did you expect?"

She answered honestly, before she could stop herself. "Someone uptight."

"Yeah, we once lived on base. I know exactly what you mean. Don't get me wrong, not all bases are bad... they are just different from how we operate." Hannah gave her a wicked look. "So, dish. Who is the thorn in your side? Are her boobs lifted up to her earlobes and does she have a plastic-surgery body, or is she only condescending and trite, based on her husband's rank?"

Laughter spontaneously burst from Aria's mouth. "All of the above. Her name is Caybreena Hinnell."

Spending time with Hannah Cody was the best medicine Aria could ever hope for. She had been a miracle, with her wry humor and her love of bargains, showing Aria the most cost-effective stores with the best quality items and how to really make the commissary and exchange work by adding in coupons. Aria had almost forgotten how good it felt to laugh. She'd really needed this.

"Call me if you need anything. Otherwise I'll check in tomorrow." Hannah gave a small wave and a big smile before she pulled away from the curb. *Why was there something so special about spending time with a friend, especially someone that awesome!*

There was lightness to her steps as she entered the house with bags of clothes for Jimmy and herself, and a few additional items for Dan had made her feel useful. After five today, the store where she purchased the bed, dresser, desk including chair, and wardrobe would deliver Jimmy's new bedroom set. The items should fit in her former office, and hopefully give Jimmy a sense of belonging in the new home.

She placed the bags on the couch and began to peruse her purchases when her cell phone sounded. She took it out of her purse and looked at the phone number. A frown lined her lips. It was the high school. Her genius brother was a year ahead of his age, so she had registered him as a sophomore. He hadn't mentioned anything about his classes or teachers. Perhaps this was a "getting to know you" phone call. She hoped it was. If it were another accident, she'd need to be institutionalized. "Hello?"

"Mrs. McCullum, this is Principal Jeffries. We need you to come down to the office," said a soft-spoken man who spoke rather hesitantly. "Immediately."

"Is Jimmy hurt?" Her newfound calm was slipping away…being replaced by flat-out worry. Her hand clutched over her stomach. *Please, please, please let Jimmy be fine*.

Principal Jeffries's tone climbed up an octave. "Ma'am, he isn't hurt. But he has been taken to the police station. If you could come to my office, I will explain what has happened and then you can go there to arrange…the details of his…uh, release."

"What?" Her eyes darted back and forth. What was she supposed to do? Where the hell was Dan? She wished he were home! "I'll be right there."

Touching the speed dial on her phone, she called Dan.

"Hey, I'm out fishing. Leave a message, and I'll ring you when I've caught my limit." *Beep*.

"Dan. I need you. I'm at the school. Jimmy's in trouble and I could use your help." She hung up and then looked at the phone. She didn't want to do it, but she did need someone to help her. Mark's face danced in her mind—in truth she had been trying to distance herself—but she knew if she called, he would come.

She hit speed dial and waited for Mark to pick up. Listening to the phone ring was torture. She should have answered his text messages and not blown him off. Only she didn't know what to say. Distancing herself from Mark a little had seemed right, to let her have more time with Dan. Wasn't that what newlyweds were supposed to do, have time together? Things weren't necessarily unfolding that way. Dan was still gone on his training mission, and she didn't know when he would be back.

As it rolled to voice mail, she hung up and redialed.

Finally, Mark picked up. "About time. I was beginning to wonder if you ditched me for good. How are you feeling? How's Jimmy?"

Relief flooded her. "Not good." She took a deep breath. "Mark, I know I haven't been a very good friend lately, but I need your help. I think Jimmy has been arrested. Could you please meet me at the principal's office at the high school in Coronado?"

"Of course, I'll be right there." He rang off.

She put her phone back in her purse and looked at the items strewn on the couch. "Please, let me be able to handle this…" Fishing out her keys, she put her purse on her shoulder, straightened her spine, and said, "I can do this." Then she headed out the door to face whatever was awaiting her.

Aria spent less than twenty minutes in the principal's office, where she learned that on Jimmy's first day of school he had gotten in a fight. They had let it go, given the extenuating circumstances of the car accident, the death of his uncle, and his new scholastic environment. But on his second day of school when Jimmy had brought a Ka-Bar knife, albeit an unsharpened one, their zero-tolerance policy had been forced into effect. Jimmy was suspended, pending a review of his case by the School Board Committee. There was no way to fight the decision.

She had left the office with Mark, feeling as if she were the one in trouble. Where had Jimmy gotten the knife? With the trident symbol etched into it, she had a pretty good idea.

Thank God, it had been dull! But still, shouldn't Dan put his keepsakes in a better place?

Politely, she thanked the principal for his time and asked him to please advise her in writing concerning this event—including the names of the individuals who had been involved in these proceedings—since her brother had never committed acts of violence before and wouldn't do so unprovoked. She then left his office. It had taken a lot out of her to be that cool when all she wanted to do was scream and shout "Why, why, why!"

Damn! How had she missed this…why hadn't she noticed there was a problem with Jimmy? Shouldn't she have better mom radar for him? As if he could sense her thoughts, Mark said, "We'll work it out. He's a kid who just lost his uncle and is under stress…new environment, et cetera." He kissed the top of her head. "I'll make it better."

She nodded, grateful that he was there. Why was it she always had to depend on a friend? And why lately did she feel her own husband was too hard to find?

They had been asked to sit, to wait until the detective handling their case was free. Aria was a bundle of nerves, and she clasped Mark's hand as if it were a lifeline. He stroked his thumb back and forth over her skin.

"It will be fine. Just relax. This is his first offense and no one was hurt." Mark's words soothed her a little, but she wasn't going to feel better until her brother was in her arms and they were leaving this place for home.

The desk sergeant asked them to go through the door and to down the hall. There was a man waiting there who showed them to two chairs in front of a large desk. Another man, dressed in a suit and tie, stood. "Mrs. McCullum? I'm Detective Calfry."

"Yes." Aria shook his hand. "This is my friend Mark. He's a...lawyer. My husband is out of town."

Detective Calfry opened a file and examined the contents. "Your husband's in the Navy. A SEAL."

"That's correct." Her fingers twisted anxiously in her lap. She squeezed them together, trying to force them to be still.

The folder was closed and Detective Calfry looked up. "I spoke with your brother, James. The knife he acquired is your husband's, correct? There was no sharp edge and, according to James, no intent to harm or kill. But it is still weapons possession on school grounds." He leaned forward, placing his hands on the desk. "Our concern is that situations like this can escalate. Today it's showing off an item, next it's a demonstration. Were you aware that he took the knife to school?"

"Are you kidding me? I didn't even know it was in the house!" Her nerves were raw and she could barely contain her emotion.

Mark patted her arm. "Aria, let me interject, please. The McCullums were just married. The day after their wedding they received an opportunity to move into a house on base and took advantage of the offer. They have barely unpacked, and now this…"

Aria nodded. "And—"

"Please let me continue." He waited until he received a nod from her and then said, "I personally helped them carry their belongings into the house. Daniel McCullum is a very stand-up guy, and I find it unlikely that he left anything lying around. It is more likely that he did have them hidden away and that Jimmy unearthed the knife and was trying to make friends, not realizing what kind of an uproar his choice would make."

Mark uncrossed his legs and scooted forward in his chair. "Now, my question to you, Detective, is…will Jimmy be charged?"

"Before we get to that, please note that Chief McCullum will have to come to the station and pick up the knife when he returns. In addition, he will have to attend one of our safety lectures on weapons safety and the storage of them. But"—holding up his hand, he continued—"there are consequences to Jimmy's actions. You're lucky the judge and police chief were here when it happened. Jimmy will be required to work in Judge Wasa's courtroom as an intern for the entire summer. If you agree to these terms, then he can leave with you today."

Aria could barely contain her relief. *Thank God!*

Mark squeezing her arm for a second time forced her to keep a damper on it.

"If Aria, as Jimmy's legal guardian, doesn't agree, what happens then?" Mark asked.

"He will be brought up on charges and will formally face the judge in his courtroom."

"They want him to learn a lesson," Aria said. "I agree. We'll take the deal."

"Hold on," said Mark. "I could argue there are extenuating circumstances revolving around this case not limited to the fact that his former guardian and uncle has recently died and it contributed to this moment, as well as the undeniable fact this young man was in that car accident that took away his greatest ally and support."

"No offense, Counselor, but this isn't a courtroom. I don't negotiate. I simply follow procedure. The only reason, and I mean the sole motivation, that James Kavanagh is being shown any leeway today is because those two men took it upon themselves to take responsibility for his case and work with him. In my opinion, that kid is getting off easy, and he should probably be on his way to juvenile hall." Detective Calfry sat back in his chair. He steepled his fingers and then looked at Aria. "What's your answer?"

"We'll take the offer. Thank you for your plainspokenness, Detective Calfry. When and where does he need to be for work?" This time she let her emotion show, and her hand shook as she proffered it to him.

He connected with his own meaty palm, and it engulfed hers as if she were a child. "If you'll head over to the desk against the far wall, there's some paperwork you'll need to fill out, and then Jimmy will be released to you."

Mark nodded at the detective, and then they left his desk. "I could have done better."

"No," said Aria flatly. "The offer made to us is generous, and Jimmy needs to learn there are consequences. I couldn't bear to go through a legal battle right now, and I don't think Jimmy could either. This is a gift, Mark. I see it that way, and I want Jimmy to understand it as one, too."

Pulling her to a stop before they reached the desk, he said, "You're admitting that Jimmy did this, that he brought a knife to school. I could fight the whole thing and get it expunged."

She stared at him, incredulous. "He did bring a knife to school. Jimmy screwed up! So did Dan. Both of them need to get that. Either we live in a world with right and wrong—rules—or we live with the chaos."

"SEALs don't live with rules. How naive are you?"

"What do you mean, Mark?" She put up her other hand as a barrier between them. "Be very careful with your next words."

"There is so much you don't understand, Aria. There are always ways to exploit the gray areas—that's why lawyers rock. We know how to deal with the good, because we understand the bad, sometimes intimately," Mark ground out. "You took several law classes. Why don't you get it?"

"I'm not pretending to be some innocent. It's just… I'm a wife now and guardian to Jimmy. I know life isn't perfect, but we have to set an example," she said, her temper simmering. Her voice dropped lower. "And I'm adamant on what I believe. This is my choice. Jimmy will work for Judge Wasa this summer, and I'm going to kick Dan's ass. Let me complete this paperwork and get my brother the hell out of here! Now, move it." She pointed to the spot where he held her arm. She waited until his hand dropped to his side and then she asked, "Are you coming with me or not?"

He nodded his head and followed her to the desk. Her dearest friend did not look happy about it, and it made her wonder...about him and his morals.

The drive home was quiet. Neither she nor Jimmy spoke. Half of her was so angry with Jimmy, she wanted to shout. Every time she looked over at him, the other half of her saw her brother as wide-eyed, pale, and obviously so completely shaken that all she wanted to do was pull the car over and hug him.

As she pulled up in front of the house, she barked at him, "Into the house, now. Hustle."

Jimmy scrambled out of the car and hotfooted to the front door. He used his key to open it, went inside, and positioned himself on a chair at the kitchen counter.

Aria closed the front door behind her, flipped the bolt, and then set her purse and keys in the bedroom. She tried to calm herself as she headed to the kitchen. "Have you eaten?"

"Not since breakfast," he said softly.

"Do you want macaroni and cheese?" She stood in front of him staring daggers, but he wouldn't meet her eyes.

"Yes, please." It was barely a whisper.

She turned the oven to 350 degrees and took the macaroni out of the refrigerator. Taking off the cover, she deposited the large tray in the oven and set the timer. With her back to him, she said, "We need to talk."

There was a long pause. Then he said, "I know."

Walking around the island, she sat down next to him. "Look at me."

When he did, there were tears in his eyes. "I'm so sorry, Aria. I didn't mean to get in trouble. I was trying…trying to…"

"Make friends," she finished. "There has to be more than that. Spill."

"I wanted to prove that I was tough, that the popular guys couldn't boss me around. I read that if you stand up to bullies—a show of strength—then it makes it all go away. I knew taking the knife was wrong…that Dan would be mad…but I didn't think this would happen." Her brother leaned forward, wrapping his smaller arms around her neck, and wept. His whole body convulsed. "I'm sorry, Aria."

She patted his back, trying to comfort him and wanting to lecture him, too.

"I-I-I didn't mean to screw up. Please don't send me away."

Pulling back from the embrace, she wiped the tears off his face with her fingers. "Jimmy, you aren't going anywhere. This is your home now, with me. Wherever I go, whatever I do, you're a part of it, forever. Okay?"

He nodded his head, but she could see the worry still in his eyes. Snot was coming out of his nose, too.

Taking a napkin out of the holder, she wiped at his nose.

He grimaced away from her. "Aria, I'm not five. I can do it."

God, I am treating Jimmy like a child. What do I do?

He blew his nose and then got up to throw the used napkin away. Then he washed his hands.

She'd taught him that. She'd raised him. How could she have thought leaving him with their uncle would be fine while she went off and lived her life somewhere else? Maybe that had been a mistake, too.

Jimmy took a glass out of the cupboard and poured himself some milk. "Do you want some?"

"No, thanks," she replied. She'd taught him those manners, too. Wrestling with herself for a few minutes, her curiosity won out. "Jimmy, were you mad at me when I left?"

He came back around the island and took his seat again. "Uncle David told me I wasn't allowed to get mad about it, because you had worked hard to take care of us and now we had to take care of each other." Wiping his arm across his nose, he removed the rest of the stuff leaking out of his nose.

"Maybe we're both stuck in the past—old roles. You're fourteen and I'm a grown woman. You've got to communicate with me about what's happening, and I've got to stop babying you. Agreed?"

He nodded his head, and his eyes held hers. There was something else happening in there, and she hoped she could get to the bottom of it.

"Jimmy, while the macaroni is heating up, I'd like to talk to you about emotions and better ways to handle them."

Maybe, just maybe, it would help her, too. If they

could both be honest grown-ups, then it would help them move forward on a better footing.

She'd have to remind herself to be a grown-up when it came to handling Dan. She was ready to rip him a new one for not locking up that knife...and for not calling her back when she needed him.

———

She could hear her brother's even breathing. Watching him from the doorway of his room, tucked into his new bed, with clothes hanging up in the wardrobe and his backpack on his desk, was comforting. The talk with Jimmy had gone well. They'd both cleared the air, and she felt better about being a mother, sister, and friend to him.

Lights flashed momentarily through the room and then turned off. A car had just parked in front of the house.

Closing the door to Jimmy's bedroom, she went to the front door, unlocked the bolt, and opened it partway. Dan was getting out of his car and he looked beat.

Opening the door wide, she didn't know if she wanted to hug first or yell at him. It was a toss-up that warred inside of her, so she stayed where she was...waiting for him to come to her.

"Hi," he said as he dropped his gear inside the front door and kissed her.

She kissed him back, and for several seconds her whole world melted away. Amazing, how this man was her solace, her peace, and her pleasure spot. When they pulled apart, the unhappiness and stress slammed back into her head like an ice pick. Her anger at Dan being MIA for the event added another layer of pain to it. "Jimmy's sleeping. I converted my office into his bedroom. The door's closed, but can we go outside... onto the patio to talk?"

"Does that come with beer and food?" He looked so hopeful, she couldn't deny him.

"Yes, go out there and I'll bring a tray." She pointed, and it was hard not to smile at him, but she knew she'd have to admit her anger. Right now it was a wall separating her from him.

In the kitchen she made two plates of macaroni and sliced ham, threw in some apple slices for good measure, and grabbed a beer for Dan and an iced tea for herself from the refrigerator. Placing it on a tray alongside napkins and silverware, she headed outside.

Dan's eyes tracked her movements. She could feel them.

"What happened? I can see the tension in your body." It wasn't easy that her husband could read her like a book—one of the many reasons she'd married him. Right now it was hard to be put on the spot.

"Let's see, I bought furniture for Jimmy's room. Had a great time hanging out with Hannah. I found a darling Tommy Bahama silk shirt for you in the same color as your eyes, with this wonderful embroidered pattern. What else? Oh, yeah, my brother took one of your knives to school, ended up at a police station, and could have been sent to jail if it hadn't been for a compassionate judge and police chief." She inhaled sharply, her temper flaring. "Where the hell are your weapons, and why didn't you tell me they were in the house so I could hide them?"

"Oh, my God! Is he okay?" Dan was out of his chair and moving into the bedroom before she could stop him.

"Dan!" Aria frowned, and then reluctantly followed him. She found him crouched over a duffel.

"Well, your brother must be good at figuring out locks, because I had this combination lock holding the bag closed." Dan held up the open lock.

"My uncle taught him that. He tried getting Jimmy interested in magic tricks, but it never took. Well, most of it didn't." She sat down on the air mattress. She studied her hands and then asked, "Dan, why didn't you tell me…about the weapons? What else don't I know? Are any other things stored here?"

"Phew," he said as he checked the contents of the bag and then locked it back up. "Nothing else is missing. Do I have to go down to the police station to get it?" He lifted the bag and stood. Something about his movements was stiff, and there was a look in his eyes…as if he were hurt…emotionally.

"Yes." She watched him walk to the doorway. "Dan, you need to understand. I'm really mad. We have a major problem here."

"I know." He offered her his hand. She took it and he pulled her to her feet. "I just…I have a story I need to tell you. It's the reason we have weapons in the house. I want you to learn to use them, and Jimmy, too, but with responsibility and an understanding of what they can do."

"I don't want them here. Period." She was adamant. She couldn't imagine a life in which she constantly had to worry about weapons getting into the hands of children.

He sighed. "Aria, hear me out. You might change your mind after I explain why I have them…and who might come looking for us." Dan escorted her outside. They sat down next to each other on the chairs of their new lawn furniture. The cushions were plush, but she couldn't relax and enjoy the comfort. Anger coursed through her body like a wildfire in dry grass, and she couldn't put it out.

Dan laid his hand on hers. "I was wrong. I want you to know that."

She nodded her head, accepting the apology. It eased a little of the frustration but not the bulk of it.

He took his hand back and laid it on the table. "Just so you know, I had intended to order a weapons safe—accessible by fingerprint—and will do so tonight. I also promise to store them at the base until a secured environment arrives." Lifting his beer, Dan took a long draw on the bottle. He stared at the label.

She watched him swallow, waiting as patiently as she could for his story to begin. Her nerves were frazzled and she couldn't stop herself from nudging him. "Dan?"

He nodded. "I was just trying to figure out where to begin." He placed his hand over hers. "I was nine years old…"

Chapter 9

By the time Dan finished his story, Aria had crawled into his lap. He led her to the bedroom, and they gently peeled away each other's clothes. There was a tenderness and closeness to their lovemaking like never before. Dan couldn't get enough of the feel of his wife's skin against his. And Aria was doing everything she could to keep their bodies as close as possible.

With her head tipped back, her hair streaming across the pillow, and her gorgeous breasts just begging for his mouth, he'd never seen anything more beautiful. And she was all his.

He entered her slowly, drawing the moment out, even when she thrust her hips up to take him deeper. Life might not always run smooth, but this moment was perfection. And he didn't want to let it go. No matter what the world might throw at them, here they were protected. Here they were undeniably together.

As their climax surged through them, he'd never felt more loved in his life. Afterward he cuddled Aria in his arms and gently stroked her hair until her breaths evened out, soft and deep.

—∘∘∘—

Dan woke slowly, still holding his wife in his arms. They were both stretched out naked on the air mattress in their bedroom. Making love after their fight had made him feel closer to her, as if he knew more about her soul. His lips brushed her shoulder. *Oh, how I want to wake her*. But the dark circles under her eyes made him want to let her sleep.

He used small movements to shift his body weight. According to Aria, their California-king mattress set would arrive tomorrow. He was looking forward to a real bed. The air mattress had lost its charm.

"Bastard. District attorney, my ass," she whispered in her sleep. "If only…"

He gently shook his head. Aria hadn't taken the story very well, bursting out with angry comments at times against his mother and father and adding a long list of expletives for the intruder.

Long ago he'd gotten over the fact that they weren't the ideal parents, or even halfway decent on a long list of bad mothers and fathers. But life had blessed his sister and him with a remarkably brilliant and loving grandfather who had shown them what the words *joy* and *loyalty* really meant. For that opportunity he was eternally grateful.

After he split away from his parents, he had found true stability. At his grandfather's farm in Louisiana, he could remember, in the winter, sitting in front of a large fireplace as his sister and he roasted marshmallows—pretending it was snowing outside—while his grandfather shared stories of war, falling in love with their grandmother, and the best parts of married life. He'd read Mickey Spillane mysteries, taken them hunting in Vermont and Montana, and taught them how to live off the land. Though Dan had taken to roughing it, his sister preferred pink nail polish and eight-hundred-thread-count sheets. Together, though, they learned how to apologize and share gratitude and were exposed to practical life lessons that added to their common sense.

Anytime they were sick or afraid or upset, he was by their bedside, teaching them how to cope and helping them through the trauma. Everything Dan learned from that wonderful man he took to heart and incorporated into his life, and now into his marriage with Aria.

"I'd be a better mother," she murmured in her sleep.

He kissed the top of her head. "You will be," he whispered.

"Hmph!" she replied, then began to snore. She hadn't liked learning that a few more criminals had gone after his parents, and though they were unsuccessful, there was always a possibility that Caty and he were targets. Another reason Caty's husband watched her like a hawk.

The intruder story had shaken Aria enough that she decided that each member of their household needed to have weapons-safety courses, from gun to knife, with strict understanding and a serious respect. They were a military family, and all of them needed to learn what weapons were about. Though, they agreed his arsenal would be stored on base until the safe arrived, and they would talk about what that meant, the pros and cons. Jimmy was already learning a lesson in consequences, and she gave Dan permission to take that several steps farther. Only Aria and he would have the combination to the safe.

He was relieved the discussion had resolved without a fight. The cold steel felt good in his hands, and it would have been hard to have nothing in the house that reminded him of his grandfather…or for protection for Aria and Jimmy. There would be times he would be away, and it felt good knowing there was protection available to them.

Rubbing his thumbs gently along her arms, he felt Aria rouse. "I'm sorry. I didn't mean to wake you."

She stretched and then snuggled closer. "You didn't. I was only half-asleep."

"I think you were cussing out my dad."

She sucked in her breath. "I *was* dreaming of him… like I was half in this reality and somewhere else, too. That's so funny—you guessed where I was."

"It's not a stretch, given what we were talking about." He whispered, "You were snoring, too."

"Was not!" she denied. She tried to squirm out of his grasp but he held tight.

"Uh-huh!" He loved teasing her and he grinned down at her fierce expression.

She lightly slapped his stomach. "Okay, maybe I snore a little." Pushing herself up on one elbow, she ran her fingers over his abused muscles and asked, "Can you talk about the training mission you were on? Without violating national security and stuff?"

"Sort of. I spent five days in the bushes, waiting for an opportunity to fire two volleys of shots. My legs were cramped and my ass was sore, and I couldn't wait to get home to you." He rolled his eyes. "It happens. We practice when it's peaceful so it's easier, like a reflex, when we're at war."

"Why did it take so long?" She pushed her hair out of her eyes. When it just flopped back into place, he tucked the curls firmly behind her ears…so tiny, those little ears. He leaned forward to nibble on them. She pushed him back. "Please, Dan. I want to know."

"Aye, aye." He grinned at her, but she was serious. "There was another group running the war game, the point of which was to examine the effectiveness of both new strategic techniques and equipment. I was on the equipment end, and overall it was efficient and productive."

Her eyes widened. "You weren't here because of a game."

"Not a game in the way you're thinking of it. This is work, and what I do out there in training could save my life or that of Teammates or other Americans.

"Aria, we talked about this before we got married. You said you could deal with it."

"Yeah, I can deal with it, when you're out saving people's lives. I mean, I worry, but I get it. But when you're twenty minutes away, playing 'war games,' and you can't come when I need you, then yes, I have a problem. I need to know I'm a priority too."

"You are the most important person in the world to me. You should never for a second doubt that. But I have a duty to our country too. And there are going to be times—probably a fair number of them—when the demands of the job prevent me from being here. I can't help it and I can't change it. My Team needs me too." Dan made sure his voice was firm without any hostility or anger. He was sorry he hadn't gotten the gun safe in place or been around to help. Regretting the past wasn't going to change today's resolution. The best he could do…was to incorporate the knowledge of how to move forward.

"I know. And I know we talked about all of this when

you proposed. But I hadn't really seen it until now. I thought it'd be easier. Or that they'd give you other duty, because you're married now. I need you around more." She kissed his stomach. "It was wishful thinking. I'm sorry. I just want us to communicate better."

"Me too." This conversation made him wonder if Aria could handle marriage to him. There were going to be some big obstacles ahead. Maybe they should have lived together first, tried this situation out before they married.

"I'll get better at it. I promise. It's just…with Jimmy and everything, I was suddenly in over my head."

Stroking her curls with his fingers, he said, "You're stronger than you know. But it's true you're going to have to handle a lot on your own. When I'm home, I'll help where I am able. Can you deal with that?"

"Yeah, I get it. I'll have to." Her fingers toyed with his chest hair. She plucked one or two and it stung briefly. He placed his hand on hers. "For the record, I don't like it, but I'll work on it."

"Look at me, please." He waited while she turned toward him. "Always know I'm on your team and I have your back. In terms of the house rules and Jimmy, what you say goes, and I will support it."

"Thanks." She smiled. "That does help some… I can make you the bad guy when I need to do so."

He lifted his eyebrows. "Go for it. I can take the heat." Wrapping his arms around her, he pushed her up in the air and held her in place like a reverse push-up and then wiggled down until he was lying beneath her. Then he lowered her down to him. Giving her his best sexy grin, he asked, "Want to make out?"

"No." She said straight-faced and then began to laugh. "Yes." She collapsed into a riot of giggles.

He rolled her over and blew a "zerbit" on her belly, which made her laugh harder. He tickled her.

"Dan! Stop!" She was laughing so hard, tears were rolling down her cheeks.

"Aye, aye." He stopped and just looked at her. God, he loved her.

———≈≈≈———

"You know what, guys?" Dan said. "We need a day at the beach."

"Chores first," Aria piped up.

Jimmy and Dan groaned simultaneously. But both pitched in to do dusting and vacuuming, and grocery shopping at the commissary, before they headed out for sand and sun.

Dan positioned three kayaks at the water's edge. "You'll have fun," he encouraged Jimmy.

"I've never done this before," Jimmy said, not sounding too eager at the prospect.

"Can you move your arms as if you're pedaling a bicycle?" asked Dan.

"Duh," said Jimmy.

"Watch the mouth," said Aria.

"Sorry." Jimmy kicked the sand and then looked at Dan. "Yes."

"Good," said Dan. "Follow your sister into the water." His eyes tracked his wife's movements as she walked the kayak into the waist-high water, climbed in, and started paddling. Jimmy tried to mimic her action but ended up in the tank a few times.

Aria frowned at Dan as he let Jimmy struggle. Finally, the kid figured out how to balance the kayak and slid in without overturning it. Dan was proud of him—Jimmy didn't give up. If Jimmy had been in danger, he would have stepped in, but failing and figuring stuff out made people stronger. He firmly believed it—a quitter usually shows his true nature, and a winner reveals his intentions by doing something over and over until there is success.

Grabbing his own kayak, he launched it into the waves and hopped aboard. Catching up to his family, he took them farther into the ocean.

They saw lemon sharks and fish, pelicans and seagulls, and two large sea lions.

The three of them kayaked for hours, splashing and laughing. It was the perfect day in many ways. One Dan looked forward to repeating again and again. This was one of the reasons living in Coronado was so amazing— the ability to experience water, nature, and togetherness. He'd hate being landlocked.

As they raced toward shore, riding the waves, he stared at the smile on Aria's face. He just didn't know if he could tell her…what was coming: more missions and more time gone. What would it mean to her? How angry would she be?

His kayak abruptly slid onto the sand, grounding the journey for now. The waves were pulling back, the tide going out and revealing small treasures of shell and seaweed on the beach.

Watching Aria and Jimmy lift their kayaks, he laughed at their antics as both of them landed in the sand. It was just a little more weight than they could handle alone.

Looking up at the sky, he knew he'd have to carry the boats up to the locker. She was motioning to him, wanting him to move faster. But he'd always gone at his own pace.

Reluctantly he stepped out of the kayak and hoisted it onto one shoulder. "I'm coming," he shouted as the wind picked up, tossing grains of sand into the air.

He grabbed the paddle with his free hand and started walking. He'd have to trust that Aria could keep it together…their family. Regardless of what she might think, a lot of the power was in her hands, and he hoped she was careful with it.

———

The next morning, he dressed quickly. Picking up the duffel, he hoisted it over his shoulder and checked to make sure he had his wallet and cell phone before he put his hand on the doorknob. He wished today could be a day off—he wanted so much to spend more time with her—but that wasn't possible.

"Sneaking out?" His wife propped up on one elbow and looked at him. "What time is it?"

He had to get going, or they were going to be late. "Three thirty. I need to pick up JC. I'm taking the weapons, per our agreement. I'll call you later, okay?"

"What? Wait, where are you going?" She placed her hands on her hips and stared at him.

"Work. We're going on the High Altitude jump. Aria, we talked about this."

"I thought you were getting more time off." She was getting angry. He could tell by the way her eyes were narrowing and her words were becoming more terse and clipped.

Shifting the weight to his other shoulder, he said, "I'm sorry, sweetheart. It's a workday. You know how it is—we practice and do more practice and prepare some more and then go on missions. I'm trying to get some time, but it all depends on the Team's schedule. I wish we could be together more too. But this is the life of a SEAL." Why wasn't there a manual—something he could study—so he knew the right thing to say or how to ease her pain? "Hon, I want to help. It's just…I have to go." He walked to her, closing the gap between them. Lowering the bag, he got to his knees and kissed her. "Can we talk about this when I get home?"

"When will that be?" She fanned her face as if she was trying to dry the tears that welled in her eyes.

Crap! This was eating him up inside. He didn't want to leave her like this. She had been through so much. He sighed. "I don't know." Then he stroked her hair, willing his energy into her, attempting to ease her and at the same time bolster her courage. "Bear with me, Aria. Okay? I love you."

Her eyes met his. "Yes." The smile was weak, but it was there. "I'll be fine. I love you, too."

He kissed her once more, so tenderly it tugged his heart, and then pulled out of the embrace. Picking up his gear, he left.

The bedroom door clicked closed. He let himself out of the front and relocked it before he left. Depositing the duffel into his trunk, he stared at it briefly. Filled with knives and guns that lay snugly in their cases, with the ammo locked away separately, he knew it had been as safe as he had been able to make it.

He slammed the trunk and slid behind the wheel. He

knew he should have told Aria about them from the start, but there was never really any harm of anything happening to anyone, unless they got bullets somewhere else or spent a lot of time sharpening the knives. He supposed it could happen, but he was as careful as he knew how to be.

He should have warned her he was leaving the next morning for the jump. But he didn't have the heart. If they were counting strikes between them, he was on strike two, and most likely he was in the doghouse.

As he turned on the ignition and sped away from the house, he prayed things would get easier between them, without this push-and-pull sensation, because this bumpy road—was not doing a lot to ease or improve his mind-set.

Stopping in front of JC's house, he waited. JC was out of his front door and sliding into the passenger side of the Mustang in no time. "You look like someone gave you a sour gummy bear. What's up, coconut?"

"Just stuff…" As Dan sped away from the curb he tried to put his mind in neutral. It felt as if he was getting bombarded with pellets of worry…something that had never happened to him before, and he didn't like it.

"Ah, married life. It's a gem, isn't it?" JC teased, pulling a long sip of coffee into his mouth. "I remember when Jen told me she was pregnant. I was on cloud nine, and that morning while we were diving, I was running low on oxygen, and if you hadn't alerted me, I'd be swimming with the fishes right now. Distractions can kill ya, man."

"It's not like that," Dan said. "Don't get me wrong. I'd be happy if Aria was pregnant. I'm…just not sure how to sort everything out. Parts of each other, we don't know very well. The brother moved in. Being there, and being gone."

"Is the bloom off the rose? Is she ready to dump your sorry ass? You already made it longer than some of our brethren."

Dan's hand gripped the steering wheel tighter. "No. I don't know. Maybe. Maybe not." He sighed. "I'm just frustrated. Don't worry, I'll work it out."

"I know you will." JC toasted him and then chugged down the rest of the coffee. Placing the empty container in the passenger-side cup holder, he said, "Best advice I can give you is to get over it or let it go, because we have some flying to do."

"I'm with you." Even as Dan spoke the words, they felt distant, untrue, and dishonest, but maybe if he repeated them often enough, they would become a reality.

———

At the base they grabbed the necessary gear from their cages…getting psyched up for the HALO jump. Some of the guys were giving each other crap. Dan couldn't quite get into the mood. His mind keep wandering back to Aria, identifying the issues and building strategies to fix them. He was used to attacking issues head-on, making them better, and moving on. The problem was, he wouldn't always be there to help Aria out of a difficult situation or funk.

He leaned into the large metal locker and felt pain rip through his finger. Blood gushed from an inch-long slice. "Damn," he swore softly. When he wasn't focused, sometimes he did dumb shit, and this would be one of those preoccupied moments.

"What's up, Mac?" asked Hammer as he grabbed Dan's finger and looked at. "I can fix that." Digging out a roll of duct tape from his locker, Hammer ripped off a strip and then opened a bag holding hunks of gauze.

"Left over from that knee thing?" asked Dan, who then abruptly sneezed.

JC sneezed, too, and yelled. "Buster, take it easy on the baby powder, you're killing the ambiance in here. I like the fact it smells like feet." He sneezed again. "Come on, give it up!"

People asked him what it was like being a SEAL. They were just a bunch of men, doing what they do. There was no ego. You gave each other a lot of crap, and you made sure everyone was watching the others' backs. Pretty basic stuff, but a lot of the world had visions of grandeur. SEALs didn't. The fact was, overly prideful guys didn't make it in the Teams. This life kept them humble, and that humbleness, in his opinion, kept them alive.

The alarm on Dan's watch beeped. He gave everyone a hand signal. "Grab and go. We need to peel rubber."

The plane climbed up to 35,000 feet. Everyone in the cabin was Team THREE, Platoon 1, and they were a combination of Alfa and Bravo. High Altitude and High Opening, or HAHO, was a "Hop and Pop" 35K jump, and you opened the chute by 34.5K. Today they were doing High Altitude and Low Opening, or HALO, which meant jumping at 35K and opening at 1,200 feet, giving them six seconds to get it right, or "unfuck" and pull reserve in case of failure. Dan knew that most likely there wasn't a man on this plane who hadn't lost a friend in a HALO either in training or on a mission. HALO jumps required split-second timing and full concentration.

Waiting for that moment, most of them were cutting jokes left and right.

"Fly into the arms of your mama, Zankin. Maybe she'll fit you for air wings." Hammer laughed at his own joke so hard, it was punctuated by a loud gaseous fart.

"Oh, man, I want my oxygen. Anything has to be better than that smell," said JC, waving his hand in front of his face.

The jumpmaster gave the signal and they placed the O_2 masks over their faces and strapped them tight. That meant they were five minutes out from the jump site. It was typical, too, for oxygen to be put on in the plane when it exceeded 18,000 feet, if the cabin was depressurized. But for these purposes, the C-130 would stay pressurized until their masks were set and it was close to the time they leaped.

Dan turned to the person next to him and checked his neighbor JC's O_2 flow. It was sound. Hammer was next to him and checked Dan's, and on down the line they all went.

Each of them had packed their own square, as opposed to the round chutes that normal airborne troopers use. Someone else usually packed the safety chutes. The practice was, if the square the SEAL packed failed and the reserve the parachute rigger packed opened, then that safety rigger was owed a case of beer.

The C-130 hit some turbulence, and they bumped around for a few minutes. Finally, the plane steadied out. Dan checked his watch. Three more minutes, then it was time.

He remembered the first time he did a high-altitude jump. It was at 35K and the sky was so dark blue above him, he felt as if he were leaping into outer space. There had been something cosmic about it, as if he had been more scared of staying in the plane than leaping. Back then he'd thought, *if I die, at least I had the courage to do it for something I believe in...SEAL Team.* The best part was, not only did he live, he found he liked to jump.

Spending a few weekends at Trident Field, he had gotten jump-qualified on the civilian side. A few of his friends' wives had parachuted tandem with him. It was strange how none of the ladies would willingly jump out of a plane with their husbands, but they'd allow themselves to be lashed to him. Must have been his Boy Scout exterior or some kind of a marriage thing. He'd once broached the topic with Aria—before their wedding—and she had emphatically said, "No." He still wondered if he should be offended that she didn't want him to jump her.

One of their most recent jumps had been over the ocean, and they had leaped at about five hundred feet over a contested stretch of water and captured four terrorists on an eight-million-dollar yacht. Another jump had been made from 35,000 feet, inserting them behind enemy lines to rescue a diplomat's daughter.

Out of the corner of his eye, Dan saw the light flash red. Those men who weren't already on their feet stood. There were about fourteen of them.

The back of the plane began opening. To anyone

outside the plane, he imagined that when they jumped, it looked like a giant hungry bird feeding its kids. Hammer always said it reminded him of an eagle taking a dump. He had a way with words.

The light changed to green and they ran out, leaping in a giant heap.

Dan cleared the ramp and hit his hard arch. Wind buffeted his body for several seconds. Then he brought his arms to his side and followed JC down in a rapid descent. Checking his altimeter, he was almost there. Dan couldn't hear anything. He'd once described it to Aria as sticking his head out a car window at 120 miles per hour and doubling that experience.

His mind drifted to her. All the issues they were having. "Shit!

He almost missed the signal. JC was the low man, and he had done the wave-off—hand to ears and arms spread—to signal he was about to pull his chute. Low man had the right of way, and he could have flattened JC's chute, killed his swim buddy and himself.

Get it the fuck together! Dan pulled and his square popped. He kept himself focused, his mind clear as he landed about ten feet from JC.

Mentally, he was kicking his own ass! *Crap, Dan! Remember your fucking training!*

His hands shook as he took off his mask and turned off the O_2. He stowed the mask and pulled the tank from his side. The strap had been loose, too. *Why the hell didn't I see that?* If it had dislodged during the landing, it could have blown. *Shit! Where is my brain?*

The jumpmaster landed. As usual, he'd brought up the rear and assured that everyone left the plane safely. Also, he tended to eyeball all of the jumpers. "McCullum, what the hell? That was almost a near miss."

JC was at his side instantly. Putting an arm around Dan's shoulders, he said, "Nah, he just loves me. That was choreographed. We wanted to see how close we could get without smacking face."

Dan started to deny it, but JC had other plans. "I noticed a small tear in my chute. Can you take a look?"

"Really? Let me see." The jumpmaster gave up reaming Dan out and became preoccupied with the tear. "Looks like a tension rip. Make sure you report it when we get back."

JC nodded. "Aye, aye." His swim buddy's gaze tracked his movements. He could feel it on his back.

Dan collected his square and then headed for the truck that was waiting for them. He didn't know what to say to anyone, let alone JC. *Thanks for keeping an eye on me, watching my six. Damn it, I almost fucked up. Let me take my lumps.* Either way, Dan couldn't be more pissed at himself. Later he'd have to figure what was going on with Aria and everything.

Now, well, all he hoped was they'd get to jump again. He wanted to prove to himself that he could keep his mind on track, in the present, and not get waylaid with all the shit his brain thought he had to deal with right now.

Chapter 10

ARIA YAWNED AND SPREAD HER ARMS WIDE. SHE'D fallen asleep after Dan left. Rolling onto her stomach, she wondered if this was what other women went through...missing their husbands and at the same time being frustrated with them, too.

She lifted the pillow on top of her head and buried her nose in the air mattress. She cuddled into the smell, and her mind and body ached for him. She couldn't escape...his scent lingered everywhere.

She remembered the first time she had picked up the sensory cue... Their first meeting had been in Bay Books on Orange Avenue. She'd been searching out Cathy Maxwell's latest historical romance and Nora Roberts's latest contemporary when someone bumped into her, sending her tripping over a small stool and ending up sprawled on the floor.

Looking up, she was prepared to bawl out the jerk who had ruined her day, when her eyes connected with his...a man's gaze so penetrating that she'd hardly remembered being pulled to her feet or the way his hands had brushed over her legs and back.

"Are you hurt?"

"No. I mean, yes."

His hands roamed over her back again, and as they touched her rear...she pulled away.

"I'm fine. Really." Heat rose in her cheeks. *Spice*

and something wild filled her senses. "*You smell good. I mean...I feel good.*"

"*Okay.*" *He stood there, just staring. Finally, he put out his hand and said,* "*I'm Dan.*"

"*Aria.*" *When she took a step, she tripped over her own feet.*

He caught her and held her. "*Maybe we should go get some coffee.*"

Abandoning her book search, she allowed him to escort her from the premises and down to a small bar called Danny's. They both ordered iced teas and in the semidark of the place talked about books and snorkeling, travel and trips... When dinnertime filled the bar, they ate burgers and fries, and still they talked.

As noise made it more difficult to continue the discussion, they left...walking toward the beach. Words left her head when he took her hand. Then silence wrapped its comforting arms around them both as they strolled past the Hotel del Coronado, the Coronado Shores, and onto the Amphibious Base beach.

Dan waved his ID at a security guard and directed her farther down the empty beach. Then he turned her toward him.

Wind whipped her hair in a frenzy of movement as he leaned in and laid his lips on hers. Heat seared her skin where he touched her, and her mouth responded to his as if he were pure oxygen.

Wrapping her arms around his neck, she deepened the kiss, leaning her hips into his. Her heart raced as his hands splayed on her waist. She breathed in his scent... that indefinable Dan smell...and she knew it would be stamped in her brain and on her heart forever.

She sighed. So much for staying in bed.

Swinging her legs off the side of the makeshift bed, she got to her feet. Her phone was making noise from the bowels of her purse. Digging it out, she looked at the message. It was from Hannah. The first message said, "There's a tea this morning. You're invited. No Caybreena types here." The second message said, "It's less than two minutes from your house on the A. Base—on the bay side. Pick you up at 9:00 a.m."

Heading for the bathroom and a shower, she wondered if she could leave Jimmy here alone. Could she trust him, after everything that had happened? Hell, did she even want to go to another military tea? The first one had been such a disaster.

Turning on the water, she put her hand underneath and felt the stream jet, warm and soothing. Stepping beneath the spray, she allowed the heat to relax her muscles. If these wives were anything like Hannah, it might be a relief. The other options for her day were 1) work, 2) gather more frustration toward her brother, or 3) stew about Dan's being gone. She'd take the chance and go with Hannah.

"I can leave a note for Jimmy," she said, thinking out loud. She needed something to get her back on track, and what she was doing now wasn't cutting it. It was time to change her location and her procedure.

—⁂—

"Welcome, Aria, to our little group." A short woman with a rounded figure, glasses, and long blond hair opened the door. She waved them in with a smile. "Hi,

Hannah. Oh! Thanks for bringing the cupcakes and pastry. You can place them over there on the counter."

The entryway was white, and the living room was a brilliant rustic orange. There were books and stacks of magazines in places as well as gorgeous paintings filling the way. Aria was immediately drawn to one of a small boy and girl in a sailboat.

"Do you like it?" asked Francis. Her friend Hannah had shared that their hostess was the CO's wife.

Aria still wasn't sure what that meant or how she should act, but she decided to be honest. "I'm not an expert, but I'm a fan of Impressionism. Whoever painted this…the brushstrokes so delicate and precise and the overall depiction breathtaking…it's amazing. Who's the artist?"

Everyone groaned. Francis shushed them.

"It's me." She took it off the wall and handed it to Aria. "I can't give them away fast enough."

"I couldn't. It's too…much. All of the work that went into—"

"If you like it, then please take it. My husband would be thrilled and I am delighted. Come, take a seat." Francis escorted her to a spot on the couch next to Hannah. "Just give me a minute, ladies." Hurrying to the kitchen, which was visible over the large open counter, Aria watched Francis pop the cork on a bottle of champagne and pull the cork from a bottle of chilled wine that was already beginning to sweat. "We don't need red, right?"

"Too early," said a tall, rather stout-looking woman who looked physically like a linebacker, yet her face had high cheekbones and gorgeous angles. "I'm Judy Parker, the XO's wife," she said from the other side of Hannah. "Don't look so baffled. I didn't know anything when I began this journey either. The XO is the Executive Officer, the second in command, who reports directly to the Commanding Officer or CO."

"Thanks, Judy. Nice to meet you," replied Aria. "I never believed myself to be acronym challenged, but there's a lot to take in."

"You'll get the hang of it soon enough. If you have any questions, call one of us," said Francis, returning to the room. "Our breakfast buffet is ready, ladies." Everyone stood and moved toward the counter. Platters were filled with sausage, bacon, fried eggs, melon slices and assorted berries, oatmeal, and Hannah's pastry and cupcakes. Aria's stomach growled as she looked at the gorgeous food on stunning china. She genuinely liked the vibe of these ladies.

"Ahhh!" A woman in a sundress bent down quickly. "Francis, get a towel. Sorry, I spilled my champers."

"No worries, you know everything has Scotchgard. With three girls and two boys, we usually are in a constant state of chaos. You just got here after the cleaning lady worked on this room. She's still upstairs." Francis laughed. Sniffing the air, she ran into the kitchen. Opening the oven door, she waved away the smoke. Withdrawing a rather burnt egg dish, she laid it on a cooling rack and laughed. "So much for the quiche. Someone hand me the wine."

When everyone had food and drink, they settled back into the living room. Over thirty women chatted enthusiastically. Aria caught pieces here and there.

"How's Jen?" Judy asked Francis as she gave her full

glass of iced tea to a choking neighbor and went to the counter, where she picked up an empty glass and filled it with iced tea and added a lemon wedge.

Francis smiled, "Any day now. Her mother flew in last week, and she's having a marvelous time bossing JC around. She's practically stacked the entire nursery with diapers for the next year." Aria knew those names. JC was Dan's swim buddy, two peas in a pod was how Dan described them…except no one was *actually* peeing. God, that man's sense of humor was bad!

Another woman, dressed in pink shirt, skirt, and shoes said, "Did you hear the awful news about Kelt Haussey, he's from Team SEVEN? He talked to his wife Olivia at 0600 this morning, and two hours later he was shot. They had been planning their tenth-wedding-anniversary party and a second honeymoon in Oahu."

The whole room was quiet. Several ladies wiped their eyes or whisked away silent tears. The tension was so thick, it could have been cut with a knife.

Francis cleared her throat, obviously shaken. She spoke first. "Whose kids have classes with the Haussey children?"

Three women raised their hands.

"Okay, you put together baskets for the kids. Judy and I will make casseroles." A buzz rose from the women. Francis sighed. "Fine. I'll go to Costco instead. After our meeting, I'll call Pamela and see what else we can do to help. Hannah will put the phone tree into effect, if reinforcements are needed."

Hannah nodded. She mouthed a silent prayer and crossed herself. Then she whispered to Aria. "Pamela Johnson is the Commanding Officer's wife of Team

SEVEN. She and Francis are good friends." When Aria didn't reply, she said, "This is what we do…support each other. If one person hurts, we all do. It might still be sinking in for you, but in essence we are one family."

Judy added in a soft voice, "Only some people want to participate and others don't. Just know, the faces or individuals who are involved may change, yet the spirit remains the same."

A chill ran up Aria's spine. She would be devastated if anything happened to Dan. Even with the issues they'd been having, she loved him dearly. Maybe she needed to let him know that more often, instead of sending him out the door with a fight and grumpy attitude.

Voices rose to an anxious pitch as wives sent texts to their husbands.

"Okay, that's enough. Don't get worried if you can't reach your husbands. A bunch of them are jumping and another group is at San Clemente Island," said Francis, raising her hand for silence. "Before we set our minds on helping the Haussey family, let's touch base with everyone here. Gretchen, you start."

"The in vitro took. I'm entering my third trimester. I know a few of you have been guessing…wondering… but we wanted to make certain this would happen before we announced it." The woman named Gretchen couldn't have been more than four-foot-nine, and she looked as if she were wearing a football strapped to her stomach.

Hannah announced, "Yeah, we all knew what was going on, Gretchen. We're having a baby shower for you in two weeks, in case you pop early."

Everyone laughed.

Gretchen blushed.

"Hi to our newest member. Aria, my name is Tristi." She gave a little wave in Aria's direction. "I just wanted to thank everyone who came out to help me when the in-laws descended without notice at the same time the septic system backed up all of the toilets in the house. The smell was horrible, but you helped me get everything in shape—and brought food—and the in-laws didn't even know."

The circle of conversation moved around the room until it landed at Aria.

"Me?" Aria had been listening so intently, she hadn't planned on providing any comments, but how could she refuse, after hearing such personal secrets and comments from the whole room. Denying them would be bad form in her opinion. "I, uh, recently had a death in the family. My uncle passed." She choked up for a few seconds and swallowed the pain down. "I'm left to care for my brother. Makes sense, I suppose, since I raised him from a baby. But he's a tough one. Jimmy didn't speak for the first four years of his life. At first our uncle thought he had special needs, and then one day at an appointment with a new doctor, she mentioned that his diaphragm was small and hadn't finished developing yet. It shocked me completely."

"I've heard of that," said Hannah supportively. "How is he now?"

"Things are getting better. He's fourteen. He can speak, it's just that now he's a teenager—younger and smaller than most of his classmates—and sometimes getting information from him is like pulling teeth." There were murmurs of agreement around Aria.

"Be firm with your brother. 'Toe the line,' in Navy

speak. Don't let him walk away from you. Force him to sit and listen and communicate. You have to be the one making the rules, and those rules should make your life easier, not his." Judy pulled her phone out of her pocket and showed Aria a picture. "I have four teenage boys—all sixteen, and yes, they are quads—and let me tell you, my husband was gone over two hundred and ten days last year, and it is clear to everyone, I rule my house and it is shipshape."

"Wow." Aria absorbed the directions like a sponge. "I might need additional tips on that."

"Anytime," said Judy, replying to a text that had obviously come from her boys. "Your brother is welcome at our house, too. We always seem to have more mouths over for dinner. We put scholastics and sports before games and TV. Also, they will be kind to him, too, or they will answer to me."

"Thanks, Judy, but this might change your mind," Aria continued. "Since we're all being so honest and Hannah has stressed that this is the place to air such things… We recently had a scare; Jimmy took one of Dan's knives to school. Something called a Ka-Bar? No one got hurt, but he got suspended. Luckily, he's going to be working at the courthouse over break as part of his punishment, and I have a feeling it will do him a lot of good."

Kimberly raised a hand. "Is it Judge Wasa?"

"Yes," replied Aria. "How did you know?"

"Laura ran her car into his fence. It was my daughter's first day with a driver's license, and she tried to answer her phone. She broke his fence and wrecked his rosebushes. If you have any questions or problems, call me. I'm friends with his wife now." She patted Aria's knee.

These women amazed her. All of them were SEAL wives, and their desire to offer friendship and a helping hand was extraordinary.

Judy drained her glass of iced tea. "Hit me again, Francis." She gave the hostess her glass and then directed her next comment to Aria. "We don't brook any funny business. I keep a close eye on the boys. As long as your brother plays by our rules, he is welcome anytime, and it will give him a good circle for next year. I heard about Jimmy's story, and I know the person who put him up to it. His name is Falcon Jones, and he has been suspended, too. This is his third suspension, and he won't be returning to our high school."

"How did the principal find out?" Aria was shocked.

"My boys. We take care of our own." Judy lifted up the glass to her lips. "Damn, it's hot today."

"But…you don't even know me." Aria didn't know what to say.

"I know Dan, and the odds were high that you'd be lovely. SEALs tend to marry strong women, ones that have backbone and some get-up-and-go." Judy looked at her watch. She stood and said, "I have to pick the boys up and get them to water-polo practice. They have a session with last year's Olympic team coach. We're going to find out today if they have enough wins and talent to go to training camp."

There was a "good luck" and a "let us know" from the rest of the wives as Judy thanked the hostess, Francis Diggins. She waved at the rest of them and then left.

Hannah whispered, "She's amazing! I know. I want

to be her when I grow up...that is if Hammer and I can ever figure out how to make the baby thing work."

"Let me give you a tip, you need to be in the same room for that to happen," quipped Francis. The rest of the ladies burst out laughing.

"Yep, no secrets in this group. Which is fine, because this is the safest place I know." Hannah took a bite of her pastry and winked at Aria.

Aria had placed two tiny cupcakes on her plate. She took off the wrapper of the first one and ate it. They were delicious. Good heavens, she could eat a hundred of these!

Letting her gaze wander, she looked around at the women. They were all shapes and sizes and of varied ethnicity, dressed in everything from jeans and T-shirts to lovely dresses. Aria liked that. She appreciated the diversity and adored their candor. It was a welcome experience after her last military tea and all of Dan's double-talk.

"Aria, would you like another orange juice?" asked Francis, holding a half-full glass container.

"Sure. Thanks." Aria held her glass in front of her and watched it fill up. Yes, these ladies recharged her battery and took away a large part of the burden she'd been feeling. Aria had learned more than she'd imagined—in some cases, much more than she wanted to know about the realities of being a U.S. Navy SEAL wife.

After hearing some of the stories, she knew she'd have to find a way to appreciate Dan when he was home and not resent him when he was gone. None of that was going to be simple, but maybe she'd make it into something fun. With these women at her back for emergencies and support, perhaps the being-alone thing could get easier.

—◦◦◦—

"Jimmy, can you come in here?" Aria sat down on the couch and waited for her brother to make his way the five feet to their gigantic couch. She was already positioned and had memorized the list she'd written an hour ago. "Jimmy!"

The door opened and her brother sulked his way slowly to the couch. She could feel his reluctance coming toward her in steady waves. He sat down on the very edge without even looking at her.

"Good morning." Even though it was now almost afternoon, she proffered the greeting.

"Morning," he replied flatly.

"Jimmy, look at me." When he did, there were tears in his eyes. She leaned over and hugged him. He let her, and then he cried.

"I don't know what to do," he said.

She stroked his hair. "I know, Jimmy. I know. That's why I'm here. We're going to do this together. Okay?"

His words were thick with vulnerability as he said, "I know we talked about it…but you're sure…you're not going to get rid of me?"

"Never!" She hugged him so tightly, he started to squirm. Relaxing her grip slightly, she waited until his tears had been spent, and then she put an arm's length between them. "We need to set ground rules. First, we talk about everything. If you're sad, frustrated, or upset, I want to know. I'm your sister and I will always be here for you. I need you to talk to me. It is not acceptable to just shrug your shoulders or walk away. Got it?"

"Yes."

"Good. And Dan will be here for you, too. Second, you are never, ever, to take a gun, knife, or any other weapon out of this house. The only time you will be allowed to handle a weapon of any kind is with Dan or me there, understood?" She watched his eyes grow wide. "Yes, you will be taking a gun-safety course, as will I. Dan is in the Navy and they have weapons, so we will learn the ins and outs and *not* touch them other than with him and in the manner he teaches us. Agreed?"

Jimmy nodded his head. "Am I allowed to say... that's sort of cool?"

Aria's tone was purposefully stern. She was looking forward to the gun training, too, but Jimmy had to know the darker side. "Yes, but learning the repercussions may not be, as you will also be going to the VA to meet some people whose lives have been changed by weapons...guns, IEDs, and so much more. Weapons are not toys, and you will learn to respect them."

Her brother swallowed hard several times. She could see his Adam's apple going up and down. He looked more nervous than he seemed willing to admit.

"Third, you must check in with me...during the day and at night. If you decide that you want to go somewhere, you need to ask me first." She waited for his nod. "Lastly, we are going to start our mornings in this house with a walk or run, together. This is going to be one of our quiet times, so no CD players, no iPods, no phones...just you and me. We can talk about whatever you want."

"Thanks, Aria."

She could see the tension leaving his body. If he got on board and lived by these rules, she felt they'd be okay. What she wanted was her happy brother back... and her own ability to handle the responsibility.

"When do we go?"

She lifted her head and smiled. "Go get dressed. I have to make a call, and then we'll get out of here."

He practically bounced out of her arms and off the couch in his race to get to his room. It was hard not to smile as she listened to him throwing stuff about in search of his beach gear. Yes, she told herself, it was the right decision to confront this head-on. Now she just had to pin Dan down and give him a similar talk. Even though he didn't have control of his schedule, they needed some ground rules.

Aria brought Jimmy and Mark down for a picnic and a day of playing in the sand and water. There was a BUD/S training class farther down the beach, so she had positioned them away from the action, closer to the edge of the Amphibious beach and Gator Beach, which ran in front of the condos of Coronado Shores.

The beach was almost deserted, and she liked the quiet. It gave her brother space to work off some steam. She couldn't imagine what it was like to be a fourteen-year-old boy who had lost his only father figure.

Is it time to get you into college classes, something more challenging? she wondered. *Could getting Jimmy to engage his brain more solve these problems?* She made a mental note to check out the policies and procedures of some of the local and online colleges. That kind of planning filled her with a sense of purpose. She didn't feel overwhelmed, just calm and happy.

Does this mean I'm doing it right, living my life the way I'm supposed to and helping those I love? The only sounds were the screech of the seagulls and the slap of the waves as they crashed on the shore.

A little voice in her head shouted, *What's most important…is that you think it's right!*

"I hope so," she murmured to herself.

The sun beat down on her skin. She grabbed her straw bag and hunted inside for her sunblock. Finding it, she placed the SPF 50 on the towel next to her and stretched behind her and adjusted the umbrella so it covered her more effectively. Then she opened the tube, squeezed out a generous dose, and rubbed it into her skin. "Hey, you two, sunscreen."

Her brother looked up and nodded, obediently hurrying toward her. Today he had been on his best behavior. Maybe it had been their talk, or perhaps he had finally accepted the fact that all they had was each other…and they needed to work through the difficult times and enjoy the lighter ones.

Jimmy came in at a dead run, beating Mark back to their little oasis. He sent a spray of sand in her direction and looked very upset by it. "Sorry, Sis." He tried to brush the grains off and it only imbedded them deeper into the sunscreen.

She waved it off. "Jimmy, don't worry. We're at the beach. Sand happens."

He looked so worried. Her brother needed to let go of the past to move forward.

She hated seeing that expression. Wrapping her hands around his, she squeezed them. "Today is about relaxing. Letting go...of expectations, concerns, everything. Today, you're just a California beach bum enjoying the surf, okay?"

"Sure." His eyes held hers.

Abruptly she let go of his hands, located the tube, and tossed it in his direction. "Now slap some on."

"Kids grow up fast, don't they?" asked Mark after Jimmy had lathered up and returned to the shore's edge. He plucked the sunscreen from her lap, squirted a generous amount into his hand, and began rubbing it into her back.

The massage felt good. He pushed his fingers into the knots wedged under her shoulder blades. She tensed briefly as he worked them out, sighing with relief as he finished.

"We haven't done that for a while."

"What?" she asked, leaning her body back so she could look at him.

He pulled her into his arms and hugged her. "You haven't let me touch you, hug you, spend time with you...since you married."

Aria didn't know what to say. She believed Mark hadn't meant that as an accusation, but it had still felt like one. "Hey, I just had stuff to do. We're still..." She fake-punched him on the leg and watched his normally stoic expression grow into a smile. "Besties."

He mirrored her action. "Thanks. You know I love you. I'd do anything for you."

"Yeah, yeah, and I love you, too." She shook her head. Why was Mark always so serious? He needed to

lighten up, too. In all the years she'd known him, he
didn't seem to smile often. Where was Mark's levity—
his laughter and joy? Maybe that was why she was in his
life, to get him to relax. Heaven knows he had helped
her through the tough spots over the years. She hoped
she'd been just as good of a friend to him. "Now, I know
you're just as much of a kid as Jimmy, so go out there
and play too."

"Only if you watch."

"Always," she said. If she was truthful, she had
invited Mark to come with them so that Jimmy would
have a male to bond with, not to make things better
between Mark and her. She considered trying to find
someone for him. Oddly enough, he had never spoken
about liking any one in the entire time they had known
each other.

Mark sprinted down the beach, pumping his arms,
and then he hopped the first wave, the second and the
third. When he reached the spot where Jimmy was hopping them, too, he tackled him into the water. They both
came up sputtering and laughing. She couldn't keep the
grin from her face. This was exactly what both Jimmy
and she needed…a day off from their life…to laugh.

Digging her cell phone out of her bag, she
accessed the camera function and stood. She narrated
as she moved toward the ocean. "Hi, Dan. Here we
are on the beach, not far from where you proposed
and where we were married. We're enjoying a beach
day…and you can see Jimmy and Mark playing in
the water." She zoomed in on them splashing each
other and playing chase.

Jimmy spread his arms wide and waved at her.

Joy radiated from him as he bounced up and down. Happiness bloomed inside of her, just watching him.

Turning the phone toward herself, she looked at it and said, "Wish you were here. We're just playing in the sun, surf, and sand. See you soon! I miss you, Dan." She choked up. "I love you."

She stopped the recording and sent it to Dan's phone. A lump was forming in her throat. She hoped he was safe and sound. Dan McCullum was the one decision she had made for herself. She had never told anyone that he was her greatest wish, her secret desire. On the flip side, he had also brought her pain lately. What she should do with both of those pieces of information was absolutely beyond her...

Spreading the blanket wide, Aria laid out all of their lunch items and called the boys. Granted, it was a little late in the afternoon, but Mark and Jimmy were having so much fun, she hated to interrupt them. When they waved at her, she pointed at her wrist and they acquiesced, making their way toward her.

A man wearing blue shorts and no shirt paused in front of her. An ID was strapped to his arm. Next to him was a leaner man who mopped his face with a yellow T-shirt. They had to be Team guys—with their six-pack abs and large biceps, she couldn't imagine anything else. "Aria? Hey, I'm Declan Swifton and this is Harvey Wilson. We were at your wedding and the reception at the Del. We're Team guys, too."

"Yeah, I went through training with Dan. Same class." Harvey put out his hand and she shook it. Heat emanated from his palm and it engulfed her entire hand. "Sorry, we just came back from a run. Is Dan around?"

"No, he's...uh..." Crap! She didn't know what to say. Was she allowed to mention...anything?

Declan put his hand on her forearm. "Don't worry. We get it. He's somewhere important." He nodded his head. "Looks like a good spread. Do you have extra?"

She didn't...but they could still make do. How could she turn away Dan's friends?

Chapter 11

HIS HEAD THROBBED. DAN HAD NEVER BEEN A PERSON that had headaches, yet today he felt as if his skull was going to explode.

"Big Mac, what's up?" Hammer had been riding his ass since their f'ed-up jump, and Dan wanted nothing more than to smack him upside the brain case and tell him to cool it. Problem was, it would cause more harm than help, so Dan closed his eyes and blocked Hammer.

Leaning against the side of the vehicle, his body moved in rhythm with it until he was lulled asleep.

Aria was moving through the house wearing a clown's nose and those giant red shoes. She was wearing that adorable blue one-piece, the one with the back cut out.

The day was hot and she was fanning herself with a piece of paper. She turned and saw him. Instead of running into his arms, she held up the paper and said, "You see this. It doesn't mean anything. I'd used it to dry the dishes, but it doesn't even do that well. Here, you can have it."

She held it out for him, waiting for him to take it.

Closing the distance between them, he grabbed the paper and read it. His brow furrowed. "It's our marriage license. What do you mean it doesn't mean—?" But he never got to finish his question, as the paper went up in flames. He hurried to the kitchen sink, dropping it in and turning on the water...but he couldn't save it. The page was reduced to a pile of black ash.

"How could you do that?" he asked.

Aria turned her back on him. He could see that beautiful skin, so exposed to his touch, and he wanted to go to her and wrap her in his arms, but anger was pumping through his body.

Looking over her shoulder, she said, "I didn't do it. You did. I was just a participant. You orchestrated this whole thing, and I was the idiot who went along for the ride." She walked toward the patio door.

Suddenly the whole house spun and Aria was really at the front door.

"Wait!" he shouted, but the door was open and she was gone. He fell to his knees and everything around him disappeared until it was he alone in the emptiest place he'd ever been.

"Dan, wake up!" JC's voice pierced Dan's dream like a balloon popping, and he was instantly awake. JC's elbow jamming into his ribs just seemed redundant.

"What?!" asked Dan, staring at his Teammate. He didn't know what to say. He wanted to ask, "Where are we?" but he didn't.

"Come on, we're on North Island. Let's go." JC was standing over him. His pack was strapped on and he was holding Dan's. "I want to get to the car and check on Jen."

Dan nodded. He took his pack from JC and they followed the rest of the Team out onto the tarmac. The headache was stronger now, throbbing under his sinuses. Stopping at the trash can next to the Air Terminal, he quickly laid down his pack and then leaned over the opening and threw up.

A couple of guys stopped, but JC waved them ahead. "Give me your keys."

Dan pointed to the pack. He heard JC rummaging around in there and picking up his pack. Lifting his head, Dan watched him walk away.

A meaty paw on his back told him Hammer was there. "Brother, we have to talk. Back up two feet and sit."

Doing as requested, Dan sat down in a folding chair positioned in the sun. Hammer handed him something to drink and gave him a couple of white pills. He downed them without question and then propped his elbows. His eyes slammed shut. Fuck, he felt horrible!

"Good," said Hammer. "Now, we're going to sit here and have a friendly chat while JC figures out how to turn your alarm system off before it wakes the dead at Rosecrans."

"What?" Dan hadn't even realized the alarm was blaring. He started to rise and Hammer stopped him, forcing him back into the chair.

"Today was probably the worst jump day of your life, including when you were just learning. Am I correct?" Hammer's deep bass voice was like a drum in his ear.

"Yes," replied Dan. Standing up, he raced for the trash can and threw up.

Hammer got up and stood beside him. "Listen, I don't know whether you have the flu and that's why you were positioned above JC when he was about to pull or if you have other shit on your mind, but if I see crap like that again then you're out of the next Op... So fix the shit! Hit medical or whatever needs doing. Got it?"

Bracing his arms on the edge of the trash can, Dan held himself up. "Yes." Having finally emptied the entire contents of his stomach, he stood. A wave of dizziness lightened his head, and then the headache slammed back into place over his temples and at the back of his skull. He didn't blame Hammer; as AOIC, or Assistant Officer in Charge of the Platoon, he helped run the platoon and was responsible for issues that arose. Dan's instincts would force him to do the same thing in Hammer's position. Teammates had to be at a one hundred percent or they couldn't do what needed to be done effectively.

A door opened in front of him, and Dan slid into the passenger's seat.

"You look like hell, my friend," said JC. "What did Hammer want?"

"Just riding my balls, you know how it is." Dan grumbled.

"Want me to drop you off at home? I can pick you up in the morning or drop your car off or whatever?" JC seemed anxious to get home.

"Drop me at the base. I want a shower before I see Aria." Dan took in shallow breaths. Christ, he didn't want to throw up again. "Jen okay?"

"Yeah, she had some false labor. It's going to happen anytime now." JC drove the car through the base, taking a shortcut and heading out a less-traveled gate. Dan looked at the ocean. It was like glass. He longed to swim and float. But it would be cold, and there would be more questions from JC and any other bud he saw than time to relax.

Seeing the Del brought back a whole mass of memories with Aria. His head was close to breaking open. Buildings zipped by and soon enough they were at the Amphib Base. They went through the gate and JC stopped in front of the Platoon Building.

A few vehicles were parked out front, meaning a couple of the guys would be inside. Thank god Hammer wasn't anywhere to be found. He didn't want to have to deal with another confrontation.

"Do you want some company? I could call Jen." JC's message was clear. He was concerned about Dan and at the same time eager to be with his wife.

Dan shook his head. "What? With a stinkpot like you! I've smelled your feet when those boots come off." Withdrawing his pack from the trunk of the car, Dan hefted it onto his back. "Nah, get out of here. Keep the car until I call you."

As he watched JC drive off, he thought, *Perhaps someday I'll learn to do it like you do*. JC and Jen had a rocking chemistry and an easy way of being together. Whenever they hit a speed bump, they'd laugh or hug their way through and enjoy being out the other side.

"I want that," he murmured. If he was honest with himself, that's why he'd gotten married.

Dan walked to the building and keyed in the code. Climbing the stairs felt as if it were taking a million years. When he reached the floor for the cages, the door was propped open and he went inside. A couple of guys were walking out, and they gave him shit about losing his cookies.

The door slammed shut behind them, locking into place. He laid his gear in front of his spot and then stripped his clothes off. Heading to the shower, he kept telling himself he'd be fine.

The tile was cold beneath his feet. He hit the spray

and heat pummeled his body. Slowly his muscles began to relax. Filling his hand with liquid soap, he rubbed it over his head and body, washing away the crappy, frustrating day.

———

Showered, shaved, teeth brushed, and wearing clean clothes, Dan felt better. He'd found a couple of Propels and some vitamins in his locker, and the potassium was helping his body as well as giving him some hydration. Adding in a dark-chocolate granola bar, he was starting to feel human. Grabbing his keys and cell phone, he closed the locker, made sure all of his gear was stowed properly, and then turned to leave.

Stopping at the mirror, he stared at himself. "You've got it pretty good, Dan, my man."

He walked out the door and down the stairs. As he was leaving the building, the cold marine layer bathed his skin with tiny drops of salty mist. Stars were attempting to shine through the cloudy wet layer, and he could see one now and then, but for the most part…it was just him and the darkness.

His phone suddenly vibrated with messages he'd missed during the day. He withdrew it from his pocket and looked at it. Playing the messages from Aria first, he watched the videos of Mark and Jimmy and his wife. There were several. Then he read the messages from Declan and Harvey asking who Big Bird—ah, they remembered Mark from the wedding—was and why he was *so* friendly with Aria.

Dan's gut clenched. He refused to get sick again. He was feeling better, he told himself.

Quickly he answered his buddies, telling them all was well. Mark was just a friend.

They sent a few snide comments back.

In Dan's opinion, it was in his own best interest to ignore them, but there was a seed of doubt there. Several seeds, if he was honest. Was there a man alive who could be friends with a woman without wanting to have sex with her? Unless, of course, the man was dead! The way Mark looked at Aria, it was obvious that Mark Anders was a living, breathing man and his wife was completely unaware of her effect on him.

Chapter 12

NIGHT HAD FALLEN. IT HAD BEEN A LONG DAY, AND Aria was pleasantly exhausted. The tea had been a real eye-opener, and she was happy that she'd gone. She looked forward to getting to know the SEAL wives better. They were different than she'd thought they'd be—funny, relaxed, and very human. There'd been no one-upmanship or cattiness. Instead they felt more like…sisters, or what Aria thought sisters should be like.

One of the stories had astounded her…about a house flooding and the husband being deployed and having three kids under five to keep track of while the wife called the plumber and simultaneously strapped them into a car with a movie to watch and then tried to stop the waterfall coming from her bathroom. These women were remarkable…ingenious. Could she do it, too? Be that on the ball and capable?

Yes, she told herself. Hadn't she raised her brother and helped her stoic uncle as well as gotten herself through school with practically straight As?

Of course, the news that had been toughest to deal with was the Haussey death. Nothing could prepare her for it, she knew it, but she didn't want to lose Dan. Making dinner for him, spending time together… It was the best she could do to tell him stay alive, stay safe, and come home to me—always.

She sliced a cucumber so that the pieces were extra

thin, almost see-through, and then she arranged them on the plate next to the baby carrots, sugar-pea pods, broccoli, and the big bowl of full-fat ranch dressing for the dip.

Checking the clock, she realized it was time to turn off the roasted chicken with homemade corn-bread stuffing and the ears of roasted yellow corn. She knew it was Dan's favorite. It had stretched their food budget a little, but it was worth it.

Breathing in the scent of a home-cooked meal, Aria knew Dan would appreciate it. Things had been a little rocky lately, and she wanted to soothe the sore spots. She missed the calm way they interacted. Where had that gone?

The sound of his key in the lock brought a smile to her face. She walked to the door, feeling the swish of her silk robe against her legs with every step. She hoped he'd like the green silk panty-and-bra set.

The door opened and she beamed at him. She began to move toward him and then froze.

"Aria." The way he said her name was as if he was suspicious, or worse, angry.

"Dan. Welcome home." She smiled, smoothing her wild hair away from her face, trying to figure out what was going on. Had she done something? Her mind ran through a list of activities, and she couldn't imagine a single one that would give him pause. On the contrary, he should be proud of her for getting to know some of his Teammates' wives.

Hanging his jacket on the knob of the front door, he said, "I got your texts. Interesting movies."

Aria turned back toward the kitchen. She wanted to

check that dinner wasn't going to burn. "It was great, wasn't it? We had the best afternoon. A couple of your friends joined us for lunch, too. Declan and Harvey."

"Yeah," he said, his tone flat and cold. "I got a couple of texts from them."

She turned to look at him. Dan seemed off, and she didn't like it.

He spoke again. "So Mark is spending a lot of time with you…"

What was this…was Dan jealous? If he was, should she soothe him or kick his ass for being such a numbskull? "No. Not really. I mean I invited him to spend the afternoon with Jimmy and me. As a matter of fact, Jimmy is staying at Mark's apartment. You know… for a guy's night." Her husband was seriously bursting her bubble. Didn't he notice the home-cooked meal, the sexy nighty, et cetera? She had been happy before he arrived.

Dan crossed his arms and leaned against the wall. "He didn't need to do that. We're a family. We can make it work."

Aria frowned at him. "I know that. I just wanted us to have a little 'alone' time."

"Roger that." He pushed off from the wall and came toward her. "What's all this?"

She looked behind her at the candles and the lovely display of veggies. "I wanted to arrange a treat. A memory."

"Why? What did you do?"

Her formerly pleasant mood melted into a pool of anger. "You think I did this because I've been up to something?" She poked her index finger into his chest like a spear. "You better take that back this instant, Dan McCullum, before I really get angry."

His eyes raced over her face and body. Finally, he brought them back to her own. "It's nice. I like it. Thanks."

"Oh, ho, you are in for a whole lot of trouble, Dan, if you don't take back that crap you're giving me and apologize. Think carefully, my friend." She poked him again, harder.

"Maybe I'm angry, too. I'm not thrilled with your best friend being a man who wants to fuck you."

She sucked in air between her teeth. "Take that back."

"No, it's true. If you'd open your eyes, you'd see it. Aria, can you put your own feelings aside sometimes and look at the world from his perspective? He's waiting for you to see him as your lover. And if that day ever happens, we're through." His words were like a knife.

"Damn it, Dan, how could you ever make such accusations?" She was seriously pissed at him. Her hands were balled into fists.

He seemed to notice them. He put his hands in front of her, palms up. "I'm sorry. You're right, I didn't think before I spoke. I'm not mad at you."

Her temper was already flaring. She always had a hard time getting it to back down. "Today I attended a tea full of SEAL wives, and I did it for you, you jerk!" She tossed a punch in his direction and he caught it. He held it tightly in his fist and then he kissed it.

"Don't you be nice to me after coming in here all jealous and angry!"

His arms came around her. "I wasn't thinking. I had a bad day and took it out on you. I'm sorry, Aria."

"It was amazing." Her breath came out in short

huffs. "Those ladies…their stories made me laugh and some of them broke my heart." Tears suddenly filled her eyes and frustration choked her throat. She spoke through the well of feelings. "Ripped a piece of me, when I learned that Kelt Haussey died suddenly, and I don't even know them!" She couldn't stop herself from weeping, from letting all the strain of the past few days out. Getting married, her uncle's death, becoming a full-time mom, and figuring out a way to talk to her damned husband—it poured from her spirit until she was shaking and hiccupping.

"Shit! Haussey… Damn, that fucking hurts!" He cuddled her closer. "I'm such a bastard. Aria, I'm sorry."

She sniffed. "You can't do that. Come in here and lay all your stress on me. I spent a lot of time to make something special for you—for us—and you're acting like a jerk." Her nails dug into his shoulder. "I hate you sometimes. But I love you, too."

"I know. I'm a jerk."

"Yes, you are." She rubbed her face on his shirt. "Don't die, okay?" She felt her lower lip tremble.

"I won't. I'm here. Please, don't let…this fuckup spoil everything. Let's just start this night over. Deal?" He seemed so earnest, so wishful. "Come on, I really appreciate this beautiful meal and I want to share it with you."

She nodded, hoping the do-over was better. Because right now she just felt hurt and sad that he ever doubted her fidelity.

He leaned down and kissed her. He was tender at first, but soon turned intense—as if he couldn't get enough. After a few minutes she was practically ready to forget dinner and jump his bones right on their new dining room table. She melted into his embrace. God, he felt good.

"How's that for starting anew?" he asked softly.

"It's a beginning," she said. It wasn't hard to admit that she wanted him and was willing. She needed that rock-solid unity that happened when they made love. It made the whole world disappear...made her feel safe and loved. "Dan, I missed you."

Dan seemed reluctant as he said, "Me, too. I've... been dreaming about you." His finger touched her chin. "It's hard...to miss you."

The emotion behind his words set a match to her already-heated body. She arched into his touch as his hands moved over her, peeled back the robe, and explored the sexy underwear set.

"There's food," she murmured, even though she wasn't hungry. He'd been losing weight from all of the training and Ops, and she knew he needed to fuel. And selfishly she wanted him to have a lot of energy tonight.

"I can do both," he said, picking her up and depositing her on the kitchen counter. "I guess I should eat my veggies first..." Stripping off her bra and panties, he picked up a carrot, dipped it in dressing, and swirled it around her nipples. They hardened immediately from the cold. He ate the carrot and then lowered his head, lapping at the taut nub until she was moving into his touch.

He reached for the vegetables, popping several sugar-pea pods into his mouth and then grabbing a cucumber. That he used for a scoop to frost the other nipple.

"Dan," she sighed as he began his ministrations on

her other breast. His heart was racing and he could tell she was on the verge of coming…if only she'd…

"Keep going."

His fingers trailed down her stomach, sliding between her legs and finding her clit, and drew small circles in the same direction his tongue was going.

"Yes," she cried as he pushed her over the edge. Her body convulsed and he could feel the wetness between her legs.

This time he reached for a piece of broccoli, using it to mark her body with patterned strokes all the way to her womanhood. He ate the broccoli and then licked his way down her stomach and up her thighs.

"More!" she cried. His face was buried between her legs now, and his tongue was praising her in ways that made it impossible to issue any sound from her throat other than soft grunts.

He could feel her body climbing, rushing toward the sheer precipice until she reached the end and tumbled in a free-fall decent, crashing toward the ground. "You're safe. Come for me, Aria. Come. For. Me."

And she did, crying out, "Dan. Yes! I love you!"

He held her while her body shook. Willing his warmth to heat her gleaming skin, wet from effort, she clung to him. Aria was his safety, his home, and his peace. Whatever made him doubt their relationship or her? The life they had together was more important than he could put into words. Only she made him this satisfied, and her love could make him feel as if his life were ending and beginning—all at the same time.

Curled up in front of the fake fireplace with its crackling sound, she fed him chicken one piece at a time. The couch was very soft, and she had to lean forward, exposing her cleavage to him, as she placed each morsel in his mouth. Every time he wrapped his lips around her fingers, wiping them clean, she shivered.

"Where did you get the fireplace?" asked Dan, whose eyes were at half-mast. He had already stifled two yawns.

She placed a piece of chicken in her mouth and chewed thoughtfully. "When I dropped Jimmy off, I was detoured down a road I had never been on…and there was this little second-hand shop with this baby in the window. I remembered the stories you told me about your grandfather, and I thought you would get a kick out of it."

"It's cool. Thanks." He leaned down and kissed her. "What did I ever do to deserve you?"

"I'll let you know when you're finished earning the credits toward that goal," she said against his lips.

Dan laughed. "My, my, we are cocky tonight."

"Just aware of my worth," she said with grin as she picked up the chicken and napkins and took them back to the kitchen.

"Do you need any help?" He stretched his arms over his head.

"No. I'm putting everything in the refrigerator and then taking you to bed." She made quick work of the mess in the kitchen, putting the dirty dishes in the dishwasher, covering the food and stowing it away, and then wiping the counters. She washed her hands and dried them on the pretty hand towel with tiny houses on it and a message that read, Believe. It had been a housewarming gift from Hannah, stuffed in with the food from her first visit. Aria wasn't certain what she was supposed to believe in…but she knew she'd get there eventually.

Aria walked around the couch, and she couldn't resist teasing her fingers over Dan's taut stomach and chest. He could have been used as a poster boy for fitness. She loved touching him, being caressed by him, and most of all…being wrapped safely in his arms.

Placing her lips on his forehead, she kissed him. "Hey, you feel hot. Are you okay?"

"Yeah." He pulled out of her embrace and got off the couch. Dan took her hand and led her to the bedroom. "I got sick earlier, but I'm fine now."

She tugged him to a halt. "I don't think so." Cupping his cheeks with her palms, she gauged his temperature. "Wait here."

It was only a few feet to the bathroom. She flipped on the light and rummaged around in a drawer. "Here it is," she said.

"What?" he asked from the doorway. "If that's a rectal thermometer, you can forget it."

"Ha, ha. It's oral. Now open wide." She shook it out, checked to make sure it was at a low point, and then slid it under his tongue. "Close your mouth."

"Mmph pleasure."

"Don't talk," she ordered, shaking her finger at him.

He put both hands up before him and then sighed.

Taking his hand, she led him into the bedroom, flipped on a light, and sat him down on the air mattress. He bounced on it gently and gave her a stern look.

Aria stared right back at him. "Don't give me that look. The mattress company canceled today and is coming tomorrow."

Checking the time on his watch, she pulled the thermometer out. "Dan, it reads 103. That's pretty high. How about if you take a cold shower or some Tylenol?"

"Took some aspirin already." He lay down and stretched his body out in the center of the bed. "I'm fine, Aria. Let's just go to sleep." His eyes were already closed, and she could see worry lines around his mouth and eyes. She stood there watching him as he dropped off to sleep.

Going back into the bathroom, she wiped off the thermometer with some alcohol, put it back in its holder, and stuck it in the drawer. She rinsed her hands, brushed her teeth, and rubbed a soft warm washcloth over her face. Snapping off the light, she went back into the bedroom and found him huddled in a ball in the center of the bed.

She didn't like the look of that. Turning off the light, she lay down next to him and placed her hand on his back. He was shivering. Spooning her body against his, she held him tight until she fell asleep, too.

———

Waking up to the sound of someone retching had her on her feet and running toward the noise.

Aria stood in the bathroom doorway, staring at Dan as he huddled over the toilet, throwing up that wonderful dinner she had made him. She knew it wasn't the cooking and was concerned it was the fever. She searched her mind… What kind of infection could he have?

She wet a washcloth with cool water and waited until he was done. "Dan."

He looked up at her and his face reminded her of a boy's...so young and so hurt. "I'm okay." Then he leaned back over the bowl and threw up. It took a few minutes before he stopped, but this time it was evident his stomach was empty.

She handed him the washcloth and he wiped his face. She took it back and tossed it into the dirty-clothes hamper and then opened the medicine cabinet and took out a small bottle. Breaking the seal, she poured a small amount into a cup. "Drink it."

"Smells sweet. I don't want anything sweet."

Raising her eyebrows, she gave him a stern look. "Do it before you start dry-heaving again."

He did and the grimace that followed made her laugh. "I will never drink Coke again."

"Yes, you will. Cola syrup is magic. Not only will it stop the heaving, but it will also give you a little energy. Now into the bath with you." She stepped over him, put in the stopper, and turned on the water. As she helped him off the floor, she noticed his thumb was swollen and there was a small red line leading up his wrist. After settling him in the tub, she picked up the injured digit and examined it. "Why didn't I notice this before?"

"It's nothing." He waved her off.

She went to the kitchen and got a small knife, matches, a metal pan, some bottled water, Palmolive green soap, and salt. Going back into the bathroom, she unpacked her collection and said, "Don't give me that crap. Now give me your thumb and tell me what happened."

Dan let out a long breath. "Can't we add some heat to this water?"

"No. Man, you're fussy when you're sick."

"My grandfather would read to me. Will you read to me?" Dan's eyes beseeched her.

She laughed. "Yes, but only if you answer my question."

"Good." He splashed water on his face and then stuck his hand out for her to look at. "I cut it on the cage. So much crap in there. I wasn't thinking, and look what happened. Hammer fixed it, so it's okay."

She lit a match and heated the end of the knife. Then she put the spent match aside and laid the sharp point of the knife over the wound. Pushing it deeply, she kept going until blood welled out. "Does that hurt?"

"I guess," he said as he used his feet to turn on the water.

"Stop messing around," she said, and he immediately turned it off. "Now watch this."

He leaned his head over the side of the tub, doing as she asked.

Aria filled the small pan with water, salt, and a few drops of soap. Then she put his finger into it. The blood seeped into the pan, turning the water a color.

"Pretty color…like roses."

"Shush. Watch." The wound oozed thick pus.

"What's that?" asked Dan, whose interest seemed much more sober.

"Infection. Whatever was lingering in that cage! You guys need to clean them. Get some bleach and really scrub 'em down." Aria waited until the puss had completely oozed out, and then she dumped the contaminated water, rinsed the bowl with hot soap and water, and performed the whole process over again.

"I have Cipro. I'm going to give you 1000 mg now, and tomorrow you're going to the doctor." Aria worked, making sure the septic line was gone before she stopped.

"Where did you learn to do this?"

Aria helped Dan out of the tub, rubbed a towel briskly over his body, and brought him his robe. "I want to change the sheets." She pulled off the wet linens, wiped the mattress with a spray cleaner, and put on another set, grabbing a clean blanket from the closet. "Two good friends of mine from high school, Liz Palmer and Augusta Shaw, were first responders. They dragged me to wilderness training school, a place called SOLO—Stonehearth Open Learning Opportunities—where I ended up earning my emergency medical technician's wilderness certification. They teach you stuff to do using what you have…and how to manage when you're far away from home or medical professionals."

"I didn't know that about you."

"There's a lot you don't know about me." Aria smoothed out the wrinkles and then pointed at the bed. "At one point, I thought about being a doctor."

"Why didn't you?"

"Too many other things took precedence." Aria peeled off her T-shirt and took another one out of the drawer. She put it on and took the other one to the bathroom.

When she got back, Dan had sunk to his knees and was crawling onto the bed. "I feel better. Thanks."

"Yeah, I bet you do. Sepsis can knock the shit out of you. Dan, for future reference, you should have checked the wound again."

"I had other stuff on my mind." Dan rolled away from her, pulling the blanket under his chin. "Shit like that happens all the time. I can't always stop and take a time-out for a boo-boo."

"Understood. I'm just saying people die from sepsis. Your body is so primed that the infection spread fast and you need to keep an eye on..." She stopped speaking. The man was breathing like a train, and he had definitely fallen asleep on her again.

Chapter 13

SO RARE WAS THE CIRCUMSTANCE OF WAKING UP WITH
the sun already in the sky that it often disoriented
Dan. The voices raised in high emotion woke him
from his heavy sleep and forced him into alert mode.
Unfortunately his head, his body—everything—felt as
if he'd been hit with a ton of bricks, and there was a
throbbing in his finger, too. *Probably for the best if I
get moving.*

He stood and stretched, and his joints popped and
resettled. He could hear Aria and Jimmy arguing.
Nothing that seemed dire or urgent…she just sounded
very frustrated.

He checked his thumb. The septic line had completely
disappeared. Pulling back the bandage, he saw the cut
was still deep and angry. When he pushed on it, blood
welled up slowly. It looked clean otherwise.

Grabbing the rubbing alcohol off the floor, he
ignored the cotton balls, peroxide, and bandages and
poured it straight on the wound. It burned! "Mother—"
He didn't finish the statement as the door opened and
Aria walked in.

"Oh, good, you're up. How are you feeling?"

She came around to his side of the bed, picked up
a cotton ball, added some peroxide to it, and held it to
the wound. Then she put a butterfly bandage over it to
close the gaping hole, added antibiotic ointment, and

wrapped a dressing around it. His wife looked at him and then placed her hand on his forehead. "No fever, and the wound's clean. I think you're going to survive it."

"Good, I have today off and I'd hate to spend it in bed."

"Really? Off." Her face brightened. "Then after a trip to the doctor's…"

"Aria, I don't need the doctor. I'm good." He took her hands in his. "What I need…is to spend the day with my family, Jimmy and you." Bringing her fingers to his lips, he kissed each one tenderly.

"Fine," she said, withdrawing her hand. "At least let me see if they'll call in a prescription for your own antibiotics, though."

He pulled her into his arms and kissed her nose. "What? You don't think I had food poisoning?"

"Daniel Gregg McCullum, don't you dare say that or I'll never make another home-cooked meal." Aria's eyes were wide and her chin jutted out defiantly.

"Just kidding," he said, hugging her.

"Ahem," came a voice from the door.

He looked up to see Jimmy.

"Dan has the day off and wants to spend it…with you. So go get ready."

Dan looked over at the sullen teen. Oh, yes, this is precisely how he wanted to spend the day off…with a pissed-off teenager. He'd prefer that Aria were with them, but he was up to a challenge. Besides, whether Jimmy liked it or not, they were all family now. Perhaps the teen would be better off getting that fact through his head sooner rather than later, and without the attitude. "What did you want to do today?"

Jimmy shrugged and went down the hall to his room.

When he disappeared inside, Dan looked at Aria. "Are you sure you don't want to come?"

"Hell, no. I'm staying home. I'm at the end of my coping scale. He's *all* yours."

———

Dan put the Mustang into high gear and passed the slow-moving camper van. He wasn't quite sure what activity he should do with Jimmy, and getting him to talk was like pulling quills out of a pup that had surprised a porcupine—unpleasant. The fact was, Jimmy was more likely to talk to another guy when they were alone than with his "mom" close by. It was hard to admit that Aria was right to suggest that they make an outing without her. The problem was...this was one cranky kid.

"Since none of my suggestions seem to suit you, is there somewhere you'd like me to drop you off?"

Jimmy said the words quickly. "I want to go back to Mark's house."

Works for me, Dan thought as he turned the car in the direction of San Diego.

"You were just there last night, but I can have you there in less than five minutes. Ten, if there's traffic." Dan pulled onto Orange Avenue and headed for the bridge.

"You better not." Jimmy looked at his feet. "Aria will get mad."

"Is that what you two were arguing about this morning?"

"We weren't arguing...just disagreeing strongly," said Jimmy.

"Hate to break it you, dawg, but that *was* arguing. Dressing it up and making it sound pretty doesn't change the fact." Dan was comfortable calling anyone on his shit, because in the Teams that's what they did every day—owned emotions and reactions—and worked their asses off to be better.

Jimmy turned in his seat. "Why aren't you more like Mark? He loves her! You ruined everything."

Dan drove over the bridge and took the first exit off. The street was clear of traffic, and he pulled the car over next to a small park. "Get out."

"W-what?" Jimmy held his gaze, and despite the fact that it was a rather sketchy area, he got out of the car. Holding the door open, he said, "If I get killed, my sister is never going to forgive you."

"That, my young ward-to-be, is *not* going to happen." Dan got out of his car and beeped the alarm on. "Come on. We're going to have a talk."

The boy hesitated and then followed him. When they got to a picnic table, Dan sat down. Jimmy was reluctant but eventually sat in front of him.

The birds were chirping and someone was yelling at a house close by. The smell of grilled meat permeated the air, and the rush of traffic on I-5 and the bridge gave off sporadic waves of air movement. None of it was pleasant.

"Okay, I get it…I was wrong…I apologize." Jimmy shoved his hands into his pockets, refusing to meet Dan's stare.

"Jimmy, look at me. I married your sister. I'm family. Mark isn't. You can trust me." Dan's jaw clenched. He forced himself to relax, but the muscle throbbed with unexpressed emotion.

The teen's gaze lifted slowly.

"I want you to tell me why Mark is supposed to be with Aria." Dan used his softest tone so that Jimmy would lean forward to hear him.

"You're not going to punch me?"

"No," said Dan, startled by the question.

Withdrawing his hand long enough to rub his sleeve over his nose, Jimmy looked at him with a dubious expression, a cross between shock and awe. "Mark came to our house in Vermont a couple of times. He told me how he was going to marry Aria someday and that we'd all live together in a castle. He has a lot of money and this whole wall of pictures from the time my sister was little through this month. Mark told me how he watches her and knows what she needs and wants. I asked him questions, and he really knows her, too."

"Did he take the photographs?"

"Some of them…" Jimmy squirmed in his seat and then stilled.

"Where did he get the pictures?" Dan didn't move. He kept his outside very calm and relaxed, but inside he was contemplating the various ways he could get rid of Mark and bury the evidence. The man was becoming a major hassle.

"I gave them to him. It was a secret between him and me. I thought because he would be her husband… it was okay."

"What did you get in return?

Jimmy's fingers twisted the string on his hoodie, making a giant knot out of the end. "None of your business."

"Tell me," said Dan, leaning forward. He didn't succeed in keeping the hardness out of his eyes this time.

Looking at the table, Jimmy's fingers laid flat—spread

wide. When he looked up, there was something dark there. "He gave me money. Nothing you do is going to make me tell you how much."

"Really?"

Tears welled in the corners of Jimmy's eyes as Dan stared at him. "A hundred dollars a picture." The kid looked away and then wiped his eyes. He laid his head on the table. With his face covered, he asked, "My uncle and I needed the money. Did I...did I do a bad thing?"

Dan resisted the urge to tell the kid it would be okay, because he wasn't sure yet. He'd never say something unless it was true.

Patting Jimmy's back and comforting him wasn't going to get the lesson across, and this was going to be a major issue. Dan didn't know where to begin. Mark had not been honest with Aria, who was operating on a completely different understanding of what their friendship was about. Christ, he needed help on this one! "What do you think, Jimmy?"

The teenager shook his head and wouldn't lift it up to meet Dan's eye.

"Time to get moving."

Jimmy pulled away instantly as if he'd been struck. He scrambled away from the table and crossed his arms over his chest. "Where are you taking me?" asked the kid, on the verge of crying.

"To meet a friend of mine who owns a climbing gym and is one helluva good guy." Dan beeped the car open and watched Jimmy climb in and secure his seat belt. Then he walked around the car and got inside. As he started the engine, he wondered what Aria would do when she learned the truth about Mark. For now, his job was clear…to work with the kid and help him find his footing. What better way to get the process moving then to climb—reaching for increasingly higher handholds and footholds—even if it was in a gym?

———

"That's it, Jimmy, keep going." Dan explained the issue to his friend and mentor Pete Anson, whom he'd met years ago when he was a lowly tadpole going through BUD/S training and assisting at one of the West Coast Navy SEAL reunions. The man had a bevy of girlfriends vying for his attention, but the retired frogman seemed happiest when he was working.

Pete had imparted an excellent piece of wisdom: "Anything can taste like honey if you think it is." The phrase had stuck with him through survival training and some rather awful Ops where he had to eat dirt and bark just to stay alive. The basic premise was sound. He had changed the way he looked at things and made the experiences more pleasant. Now he was a master at turning stuff around and making it into something better than it actually was.

He hoped Pete could give him some advice about what to do with Jimmy. As the teenager climbed, Dan filled him in.

"Son, that's why I'm a bachelor…I never could stomach handling complications with relatives." Pete scratched his ear. "But if he were mine, I guess I'd tackle the honesty thing first…about him coming clean to his sister. Next I'd get him to understand that no one has a right to mess with his personal space."

Dan nodded his head. "Yeah, I'm hoping there isn't

an issue. Regardless of the answer, I have to help him move forward in a way that can be peaceful to his heart and soul. No one needs to move through life with the weights of regret attached to his every step." His eyes tracked Jimmy's movements on the wall.

"Help!" Jimmy yelled as he lost his footing and was hanging by his hands.

"Don't panic," said Dan. "There's a foothold to your right at four o'clock and one to your left at seven. Remember, you have a safety line. Be fearless."

The teen nodded and then found the spots Dan had directed him to. There was a huge grin on the kid's face.

"I got it! I did it!" Jimmy yelled and then was moving up the wall again. Even fourteen-year-olds could lose their cool and get centered again. The best part was watching the achievement happen.

Pete came up behind Dan and put a hand on his shoulder. "Take some friendly advice. Don't bury that Mark dude. Let the police in on it. Handle what's on your plate."

A woman came up and asked Pete to come answer a call. His friend nodded to him and then left.

Dan's eyes went back to the kid clinging to the wall, whose fingers were white-knuckled and whose face was an expression of pure concentration. The posture was tense and his body was almost contorted as he made his way forward. Muscles would be screaming in protest at this point, shaking with the strain and beginning to ache with the sheer pain of holding.

Under his breath Dan said, "The police can't put him away long enough. Someday everyone gets free."

"I never knew I was good at climbing. Thanks for taking me, Dan. Can we do it again…soon?" Jimmy had eaten his way through two bacon cheeseburgers and was opening his third. If he kept eating this way, a growth spurt was going to occur—either up or out.

"Slow down," said Dan. "We have food at home."

"Yeah, but there are vegetables involved."

Oh man, that will be a whole other thing to tackle— good eating habits. Dan finished his salad and drew a large gulp out of his fruit smoothie. "Listen, I know we talked about it in the car and you agreed to tell your sister the truth, but this can't be a one-time thing. Anyone who asks you to do anything who isn't either your sister or me—you have to tell us. I don't care if your teacher asks you to jump up and down while you hum the alphabet song, you have to tell us. Keeping secrets screws with your brain, and it ultimately hurts you and your family. Do you understand?"

"You keep secrets all the time." Jimmy challenged.

"If I reveal information that needs to stay secret, people die. Anything having to do with my job that I can share, I do. But I won't intentionally put people in harm's way—that's my rule." He scratched his chin. "If information is vital for someone's safety, then I figure out a way to talk. Do you have any rules you live by?"

"Like what?" Jimmy stuffed the rest of the burger into his mouth, chewed, and swallowed, and went after the last of his French fries. Drowning it all down with a chocolate shake, this skinny kid was looking around for more.

Dan pushed his apple slices toward him. The kid ripped into the bag and scarfed them down. *Mental note…buy more food.*

"If people don't communicate with each other—share the stuff that hurts, scares, or brings pain—how can life get better? I'm not saying you have to do it with every-body, just the people who are closest to you," said Dan.

"Like Aria…and you." Jimmy wiped his mouth on the sleeve of sweatshirt. "I guess I never thought of stuff that way before."

"Did you have a girlfriend, or was there someone you liked?" asked Dan. He was curious—was fourteen old enough to be interested in dating? Thinking back to his own experience, he decided it was probably right on track.

Jimmy's cheeks pinked. He rolled his eyes and then dropped his hands to his lap. "Maybe."

"Come on, dude. I get that we're just getting to know each other. But we need to have a dialogue of some kind. I can be your friend, your brother, or"—he paused and scratched his chin—"whatever you want."

Jimmy heaved a long, slow sigh and then he said very quickly, "There was one girl that mattered. I dated her a couple of times and had sort of settled on Sara, when…I came out here for the wedding."

"Sorry, man, do you want us to fly her out here some-time?" He knew he could arrange the visit. Maybe it would help Jimmy feel better about his life in California, too. Of course, they'd have her mother come out with her. *Shit! Will I have to give "the talk" to the kid? Oh, man, that isn't going to be fun. Better to do it now than wait.* As a matter of fact, he could tackle the whole subject while they did another activity—make it a "guy talk" experience. "Let's dump the trash and get going."

"Wait...I, uh..." Jimmy looked up at him, his face going through several contortions. "I have something to say to you, and I don't know where to start."

"Just go for it," said Dan, encouraging him.

Jimmy pulled his hood up over his head. The kid's eyes were so wide, Dan felt as if he could gaze into his soul. "I didn't know...that it could be like this."

Dan was at the door and he held it until Jimmy caught up with him. "Like what?"

"What the other kids talked about...what it's like to have a dad?" The kid smiled up at him, and every protective instinct in Dan's body stood on end. He knew it...he'd move mountains for this kid. Whether Jimmy was officially his or not, that kid had made a spot for himself in his heart.

He followed the teenager outside, and they both got into the car. There was still a lot more foundation to be built beneath them, but Dan knew personally what it's like to feel alone in the world and how to find a path that fits how a person's spirit is supposed to thrive. Perhaps he could guide Jimmy, help him find his way, and learn what a different life it could be when an individual could one hundred percent like who he is and what he does with his life.

Turning on the ignition, Dan headed for the base.

"This isn't the way home," said Jimmy, perking up.

"No, it isn't," said Dan. "We're going to pick up some firearms and have that gun-safety lesson Aria talked to you about. Then we're going to do some target practice. I admit it will be fun, but I want you to take it seriously."

"I will! I promise! This is awesome. This has to be the best day of my life," said the teen as he started dancing in his seat. "Thanks, Dan, this is too cool!"

Squeezing the steering wheel for the count of three, Dan paced his words as well as his speed. Coronado had pricey speed traps, and this next path with Jimmy might be costly, too. "Jimmy, if we do it right, this is just the beginning of many wonderful things to come."

Chapter 14

STANDING IN THE COMMISSARY—THE NAS NORTH Island grocery store—Aria stared at the tuna cans. Being in the store instead of spending time with Dan and Jimmy had seemed like a good idea at first. She wanted the guys to bond, but she missed being with them. There were so many layers to her emotions, she didn't how to satisfy all of them at the same time.

Picking up a package, she examined it. There were many shapes and sizes. Did Dan like tuna packed in water or oil? Or did he prefer the flat package, with nothing on it?

She sighed. She didn't know what to buy him, other than the few foods she knew he ordered all the time: turkey, chicken, fish, steak, and vegetables. Personally she hated tuna, but Jimmy adored it. Should she purchase the items she knew her brother and she liked to eat and wait for Dan to speak up? That didn't seem right, yet she didn't know where to begin either.

Aria hung her head. She was discouraged and disillusioned and seriously had no idea where to go from here. Looking at her grocery cart, she could see a theme—chocolate, cupcakes, wine, and fruit. That wasn't even close to a balanced diet. Turning her cart around, she literally ran into Francis Diggins, the XO's wife and the hostess of the last Team THREE wives party. "Francis, I'm so sorry."

Broken egg yolks seeped from Francis's cart and landed on the floor with teeny, tiny splats.

Francis beamed, seeming to find the occurrence amusing rather than alarming. "No harm. Probably better if they land on the floor than I cook them."

Aria burst into tears. She felt she couldn't do anything right, and those layers peeled back like an onion in hot water until all she felt was the raw, acrid core.

Francis walked around the cart and hugged her. "Oh, Aria. It's fine. Really. Come on, I think you need a break. Let's get out of here for a while."

Aria allowed herself to be led away, and they walked to the front and stopped at the office. Francis explained to the manager that they would be back and asked if someone could watch their carts—also, there was a huge mess in the tuna aisle. Then the XO's wife linked her arm with Aria's and led her through the facility until they reached the food-court area with vending machines and cafeteria-style restaurants. "Are you allergic to anything?"

"No," sniffed Aria as she dug in purse for a tissue, blew her nose, and then tucked it back inside. She withdrew hand sanitizer and rubbed it on her fingers and palms for good measure. Damn, when would things start getting easier?

"Good, take a seat and I'll join you in a minute." Francis placed an order at the smoothie bar and in just a few minutes returned to the table with two giant concoctions. "I love these things…the pineapple fruit smoothie. Probably more calories than anyone should consume in one day, but they taste great."

"Thank you." Aria accepted the drink and took a

polite sip. The creamy drink soothed her throat and she drew another—longer—sip. "This is good."

"Isn't it? The kids enjoy shopping with me because we always stop for one of these and split it." She smiled. "I guess I'll have to enjoy this one all by myself."

"Where are the kids?"

"At Judy's. The boys are going for some kind of badge and needed to do work with different ages of kids. I offered mine as the guinea pigs, though I've had them watch our little ones plenty of times." Francis drew heavily on her straw and pulled away suddenly. "Oh! Brain-freeze." She patted Aria's hand. "What's happening in your world?"

Aria couldn't stop herself from blurting everything out. "Besides the fact my uncle died leaving me with my little brother to raise, who is good one minute and obstinate the next, and my husband is here and then gone, and I don't know who to lean on or how to handle any of this…"

Francis tilted her head to the side. She looked at Aria for a time, then said, "Well, you have us—the rest of the SEAL wives—if you want anyone to help you, accompany you somewhere, or if you just need to let loose. Also, believe it or not, while your circumstances have been tough, a lot of the wives have a tough time adjusting in the beginning of marriage.

"SEALs tend to be attracted to strong, independent, and put-together women who don't go gently into a relationship where all of a sudden they have to take on someone else's schedule, existence, and focus with a minimum of hassle. I don't tell many people this…but I was pregnant when we married, and I was the one that was reluctant to get hitched. Ox had to do some fancy footwork to land me."

"Weren't you worried about losing your identity?" Aria looked at the table and shook her head. "I don't want to lose my goals and dreams. I think that's what I'm most afraid of…that one day I'll wake up and everything I wanted for my life will be gone."

"Then don't let that happen. Be yourself in everything you do. Don't hold yourself back."

"How do I do that?"

"Live." Francis smiled. "I'm happy. I love Ox with all my heart. He's constantly telling me he'll support me in whatever I want to do. Before we married, I was a chocolatier. But it was only *one* of my wishes. On that list was also being a wife and mother, which in many ways fulfills me in a manner my career could not." Francis leaned forward. "When I'm ready, I'll create tasty confections again. But the trick I've learned about marriage is…dedicate yourself each day to falling in love with yourself, your husband, and your world."

"I'm sure some days are easier than others."

"Very true. Our men have one of the most dangerous jobs on the planet. The reality of our lives is significantly scarier than any of us are willing to face, so we move on with our days, living ordinary existences, waiting for our men to retire—praying and hoping they get there. SEAL Team, the kids, and me—that's all Ox wants out of life. It's that basic to him, and I'm going to give him everything I have to make it work, even though some mornings I wake up with a nervous feeling in my stomach so painful I want to cry. So then I'll cry and move on with a smile. Did Mac talk to you about any of this before you married?"

"Not really. We only dated for a month." She paused, thinking. "What should I do? I feel like I've lost my strength. I don't recognize the person in the mirror anymore."

"Ask yourself who you can live with and without? Remember there's rarely an opportunity to go back, once you close the door. If you aren't willing to be there day in and day out for Mac and his challenges, tell him. Be honest about it. Face it head-on. Being a military spouse isn't for everyone. It takes a daily dedication to the person you love and a commitment to stick it out and stay the course," said Francis. "But it is never easy. Most of us celebrate what we have when it is in our hands and stay the course—hold the rudder—when we're going it alone.

"Being happy or not being happy—that's a choice you make on a moment-by-moment basis. Flip a switch, you're happy. Flip the switch again, you're sad. Decide what you want, Aria, and go for it, but don't let your fear of being alone take away love. Remember, we're all here because we want to be."

The XO's wife's purse vibrated. It was a tiny Rioni purse. Aria couldn't imagine how she could hold anything in there. It was pretty adorable. Francis took her phone out and answered it. "Okay. Sure. Usual stuff. Yes, I can be home in an hour." Pocketing the cellular device, she stood. "We need to get moving. Our men are going out for a while and will need provisions. Come on, I'll help you." She paused and placed her hand on Aria's arm. "Whatever you have to say to him, you might want to wait until he returns. Just a small piece of advice. Don't want him distracted in the middle of an Op."

"What? Wait, they're leaving again? They just got back from jump practice or whatever it's called." Couldn't the Navy give her a break?

"Yes. I don't have any details, but for now I can help you put items together for him. Judy and I have shopped for Mac before. We often do it for a bunch of the men…when they are single." Francis led the way back to the commissary. Boy, that small woman could move quickly. Aria had to speed up her steps until she was almost running behind Francis.

———

Aria turned the knob. As she suspected, the door was open and Dan had piles laid out all over the couch. She walked inside and closed the door. Watching him, she waited for him to acknowledge her. It didn't take long before he was standing in front of her and giving her a peck on the forehead. "Hi."

"Hi, Mac!" she said sarcastically. She grabbed his arm and showed him her phone. "Do you see this? I didn't hear it ring, because you never called to tell me you were going away. If I hadn't run into Francis Diggins, I never would have known you were leaving *or* what to buy you for your trip. How come she knows more about your diet than me?"

"Babe, do we really have to do this now?" Dan walked away from her, entering the bedroom, banging around in there, and returning with a handful of T-shirts.

"Really, you're walking away…in the middle of an

argument." Aria was furious! She didn't know where to start. All she wanted was to spew her frustration.

He dropped the T-shirts on a stack and then came back to stand in front of her. "If you want to talk to me while I pack, go for it. But what would really help me is for you to take a seat, let me finish, and then I can give you my full attention." His eyes held hers, and they were friendly but focused. She didn't want to screw him up, have him leave without the items he needed. If the shoe were on the other foot, she'd want to be able to get her life together, too.

She'd give him this one. "Fine. Pack. I'll wait over here." Sitting down on a chair next to the counter, she placed her purse on the top and tucked her phone inside. Watching him seemed lame, so she went outside to her car and brought in the groceries. She filled the kitchen. Looking into the top of each one, she found the three bags for him and placed them on the couch next to his gear.

When he came out of the bathroom with his travel kit, he smiled at her and then placed the items into his duffel. Placing her hand over her heart, she felt it tightening. Shit, was Francis right? Was she so upset with Dan because she was afraid he was going to get hurt, or worse yet, die? A wave of dizziness slammed through her and she sat down. "Make sure you bring the antibiotics with you…just in case that finger acts up."

"I already saw the Corpsman—he was at the gun range—and he said it was clean and healing well. He complimented your technique." Dan moved quickly and she was sure he had done this many times.

"How many missions have you been on?"

He looked up. "A lot."

"When do you have to go?" She held her breath. Please, please, please let them have time to…to just be together a little longer.

"Can't say… Soon. It's easier to pack early and see if there is anything I need. I'm not fond of waiting till the last minute." He nodded at the now-empty grocery bags. "Thanks for the provisions. It was exactly what I needed."

"Francis helped me. I'm married to you. How come you didn't call me?" Aria pursed her lips. "I think that hurt most."

"We're not supposed to. My guess is that Ox has a code word he uses with Francis and that's how they communicate. We could do the same thing…have a set of words that mean other stuff." Dan picked up his duffel and placed it by the front door. On top he placed another, smaller bag.

"Where are you going?" She crossed her arms over her chest. Her ire was rising again, and she had to keep herself in check so she didn't tap her foot.

He shook his head. "I can't tell you."

How could Dan look so peaceful? He had the countenance of a man about to go take a run or a swim, definitely at ease. Was he crazy? He was going to war! A small part of her kicked up—this is what he did, put his life on the line. What was wrong with her?

She asked her next question quickly. "How long will you be gone?"

"Don't know." His short answers were getting on her nerves. She wanted to shout, *Give me something, anything, to reassure me you'll be safe…and come back soon!* But she didn't. She held herself in check.

Gesturing to the items at the door, she said, "Long enough to need a couple changes of clothes and provisions…"

"Yes." He walked toward her. "I'm ready to talk now."

She put up her hands. "Well, I'm not ready to talk to *you*." She hated that look on his face—the one that said she was being a shrew. She sighed. "Just…give me a few minutes." Turning her back on him, she walked the long way around the counter and through the kitchen, stepping over the bags of groceries. Heading for the bathroom, she closed the door and turned on the light and fan. Sitting down on the toilet, she put her head in her hands and cried, weeping for her dream of what life together was going to be like and for the fear she couldn't voice to the man she loved more than her own sanity.

When she came back out, she could hear Dan talking on the phone. His voice was low, a murmur. When he saw her, he waved and she walked outside to the patio to join him.

"Yeah, man, thanks for leapfrogging." Dan closed his phone and pocketed it.

"Who was that on the phone?" she asked, then kicked herself for asking that question. She'd have to learn to roll with things without the need to take control. "I mean…you don't have to tell me if you can't."

"Declan. He and a few of the guys are going to stop by while I'm gone. In case Wall Boy gets a little jumpy." Dan pointed behind her.

"Huh? I don't get it. Who's Wall Boy?"

"Jimmy. I took him to the climbing gym today and he was remarkable. I'm proud of him. You would have been, too. I've arranged a yearlong pass so you or even Declan can take him down there for some exercise. Who knows? You might like it, too." Dan seemed as if he were hiding behind a facade. Why was he acting that way? What was wrong?

As he took a seat next to her at the table, she asked, "Is there something you want to say to me?"

"Yes," he said. "But I'd prefer that we went for a walk. I don't want to talk where Jimmy can hear us. Want to take the walking path around the neighborhood? It's important, Aria."

"Sure." She went inside, grabbed her cell phone out of her purse, and scrawled a note to Jimmy and left it on the table.

They walked outside and she watched Dan lock the door behind them. "You locked the patio door, too, didn't you?"

"Yeah," he said. "I think we should do that every night. Okay?"

"Why?"

His hand took her elbow, escorting her farther from the house. "Dan, you're making me nervous."

"Sorry, that's not my intention. We have to talk about your brother."

She turned back, looking at the house. "Is he okay? Should I go back and talk to him?"

"Not right now. He was exhausted after our day. Last time I checked on him, he was sound asleep. Given everything that's happened…we should let him sleep."

She shook out of his grasp. "Talk, McCullum, and quickly." She kept pace with him, walking farther down the road and heading for the path.

Once they were on it, he began. "If you knew some-one was using Jimmy, even if it was someone you trusted, would you believe him if he told you?"

"Yes, of course!" She dragged him to a halt. "What happened?"

Dan opened a gate, and they sat down on some rocks. "Aria, how long had you known Mark when you brought him to Vermont for the first time?"

"It was Christmas of my freshman year. I met him in my prelaw class. He was the teaching assistant, and I was flunking the class until he started working with me."

The expression on Dan's face contorted, and then as quickly as it arrived, it disappeared…replaced by a neutral mask.

"Don't do this. Just talk to me. Straight out." She bit her bottom lip. Her heart was racing, and she didn't like this one bit.

"During the first visit to Vermont, Mark convinced Jimmy to spy for him. He's been stalking you since your freshman year of college."

"What?" Disbelief was written on her face.

Dan wrapped an arm around her.

Aria was shaking so hard, she could barely stop her teeth from chattering. "No. It can't… He couldn't…" Her mind was running through every memory and inter-action with her brother, looking for clues. Yes, there were times she would be in Vermont and Jimmy would ask if she'd called Mark or some kind of strange ques-tion, but she'd thought he was just being a weirdo kid.

"No," she said softly. "I don't believe it." She looked at him, begging him with her eyes to deny it.

"I wouldn't walk down this path unless it was true." Dan held her gaze and the firmness made her quiver inside. "I asked Jimmy…casually…as we progressed through the day about his relationship with Mark, and every answer got more disturbing. I know you don't want to hear any of this or believe it, but I need you to face the truth so we can prepare."

She pushed his hands away and stood. "Prepare for what?"

"To keep Mark out of our lives. He is obsessed with you." Dan stood across from her. The muscle in his jaw was flexing, and she knew that meant he was either frustrated or angry. She'd put her money on anger, but she didn't really care. Her husband was accusing her best friend of being a stalker. She didn't believe it, couldn't. Mark had been too good to her over the years.

Starting back for the house, she felt Dan's hands catch her and spin her around. "Let me go."

"No. Tell me what you're going to do, first." He held tight to her.

For the first time in her life, she considered kicking a man between the legs. "I'm going to wake Jimmy and ask him to tell me the truth."

"Which truth? Mark's or his?" Dan's comment didn't make any sense to her.

"I don't understand." She knocked his hands away and crossed her arms over her chest.

"Exactly. You're going to accuse your brother of lying, just because you don't want to be wrong about the person you chose as a friend." Dan's comment hit like a ton of bricks.

"I…I'm not wrong." The wind was knocked out of

her. She went through the gate and started walking back to the house.

She picked up her pace until she was running. Her legs pumped as she ran toward home, frantic, with tears streaking down her face and her legs burning.

No! No! No! Mentally she said the word again and again, unwilling to accept Dan's logic. But if she really looked at the track record, Mark lied all the time. She'd seen him do it with his clients and everyone around her…though her bullshit meter usually picked up on it.

Shit!

She got to the house and sat down on the front step. She didn't know how to go in and face Jimmy. It seemed like only a couple of years ago that she'd been changing his diapers. It was hard enough to survive the deaths of her parents and the most recent loss of Uncle David. Now she had to deal with losing a friend, too.

Dan sat down beside her.

She noticed he didn't try to touch her. He didn't say one word.

Tears streamed down her face. Looking at her husband, she said, "I could never let anyone hurt Jimmy. I'd kill him first."

"That's my Aria." His words were soft, gentle.

The next day was packed with activity. First they woke Jimmy at the crack of dawn and took him into Coronado for breakfast, and then they spent the morning walking around town.

"I'd really like a dog," said Jimmy with a tremendous amount of animation in his voice. "Can we get one?"

"Well, we do have a fenced-in yard, but I think this is something you might have to earn," said Dan. Turning to Aria, he asked, "What are your thoughts?"

Catching on, she said, "You'll have to do your chores every day, no more trouble at school, and keep your grades up for one month, and then we'll talk."

"That's a long time." Jimmy's enthusiasm waned.

"You'll have to keep all of that going, if you want the pup to stay, too."

"Deal," said Jimmy, quickly putting out his hand.

Aria shook his hand and so did Dan. She took it as a sign of hope that things were improving…for all them. Spending time with Dan was blissful, and somehow the irritations and problems that had grown so frustrating and disheartening slipped away in his presence. There was a calm pace and a peacefulness to her world when he was beside her.

Dan checked his watch. "Good, we still have time."

"For what?" Aria was puzzled. What could be better than this?

"To get in some target practice."

"Cool!" said Jimmy immediately.

A lump formed in her throat. "Yeah," she said. "Cool." Inside she was downright icy with anticipation.

———

Bam! Bam! Bam!

"Great job," said Dan, patting Jimmy on the back and taking the spent sidearm from his hands. "Now for Aria."

Bam! Bam! Bam!

Her shots were grouped closely together in the center

of the target. They were at the shooting range on NAS North Island. According to Dan, there were only a couple of officers practicing with their 9 mm's. They didn't stick around...and soon enough they had the place to themselves.

Oddly, Aria could honestly say it was serene here. Above was blue sky and in front of them the ocean slapped on the shore; she felt herself relaxing by degrees. She was surprised at herself. *I didn't think I'd like this... but I do. I have to concentrate in order to hit the target, and it forces my concerns to go away.*

Feeling a tap on her shoulder, she put down the gun and removed her earplugs. "Yes?"

"Impressive," said Dan, holding his own plugs. "What were you thinking?"

"That nobody is allowed to hurt us," she said candidly. Somehow it felt good to say it out loud, but she still couldn't believe the news about Mark. Whether it was true or not, she was doubtful she could ever hold a gun on him or anyone else.

"I want you to try the .44 and .45, too. They're heavy and have a recoil, but I like them better than the .38." Dan put his earplugs back in.

Jimmy sat down on the bench and watched.

She picked up the .45. An image came into her head of lifting the double-barreled shotgun with her dad. He'd wanted her to shoot game so badly, but the kick from the gun had dumped her on her ass the first time, and the shot had gone wild and high, bringing down a duck instead of a buck. Her response had been to cry, while her father laughed and brought it home for dinner. It had been impossible for her to eat it, mainly because she'd shot it, but her parents had enjoyed it. "Don't think of the killing, think of the purpose."

Steadying her hand, she thought, *Safety*, and pulled the trigger. Again and again, she fired until there was nothing left. Putting it down, she looked at the target. The bullets had gone straight through the outline of the head.

"You're good at this. I'm proud of you."

"So are you," she said.

"I'm trained in handling weapons. You aren't but you've kept an open mind and performed well." He touched his hand to her hair. "It's one of many things I admire about you."

She grinned. "Well, I like the way you communicate with me. Compliments don't spill from your mouth like trite offerings. Your comments have meaning, depth, and I have to earn them."

He kissed her lips tenderly.

"Somehow, by doing this…I think I understand you more."

He pulled back, glancing over at Jimmy, who was playing a game on Aria's iPhone. "How so?"

"You're very disciplined and determined. I don't think I understood what kind of dedication you needed to have to do what you do. Learning about weapons has shown me the type of concentration needed, but also how to compartmentalize things in my brain. It gives me distance and perspective, if I allow it, to see things more clearly. Also, when I allow other stuff to interfere in what I'm doing, I mess up." She sighed. "I get it now—why the SEAL wives group was explaining how important it is that we handle stuff at home so you don't have to think about it, can perform your missions, and be safe."

Tension eased out of Dan's shoulders in one giant movement. "That's a mouthful." He leaned his head against hers. "Yes. Thank you."

"I'm not saying that I'm going to be good at all of this, but I'll do my best."

"That's all I ask. I love you."

"I love you, too."

"Do you want me to go wait in the car?" asked Jimmy.

"No," said Dan.

Getting in the spirit of things, Aria turned to Dan and asked, "What else do you have?"

"Time to learn about knives."

———

The rest of the afternoon was spent firing and talking. She learned a lot about weapons in general: safety, loading and unloading, cleaning and storing, stance, and the best way to hold a position. It was an eye-opening experience.

On the way home, they picked up pizza and salads.

Pulling up in front of their house, Aria felt her stomach roll.

"I'm right behind you," said Dan, bringing up the rear.

"Yeah! Pizza! I'm so hungry I could eat a whole one myself," said Jimmy, voracious as always. "I'll get the plates."

She watched her brother hurry into the kitchen and set the counter with plates, napkins, forks, and knives. A grin was plastered to his face, and he couldn't hide his elation. The time with Dan had been good for them both.

———

As she cleaned up, she listened to Jimmy's interaction with Dan. She had never seen her brother so animated. It was as if a giant weight had been lifted off of him.

"Hey, guys, before we have dessert, can we talk?" Aria kept her tone light. "Come sit down at the counter with me."

She put hot water on for tea and laid out fruit salad and chocolate-chip cookies.

"Are these homemade? I love these, Sis." Jimmy ate three of them before she could even answer. Dan wasn't much better; he'd stuffed four of them into his mouth.

"Yes. Slow down, guys. I want to have a meeting of the minds."

"What does that mean?" asked Jimmy with a full mouth, spitting crumbs in all directions. "Sorry."

"Use a napkin," she said, pushing one in his direction. She made three cups of peppermint tea and sat down with them. "Jimmy, it sounds like you had a great time at the gym yesterday."

"I did. Dan's amazing! We're going again, too." Jimmy blew on his tea. "Can I have sugar?"

Aria nodded. "You know where it is."

Jimmy got up, walked around the island, and took the sugar out of the cabinet. When he faced her again, she asked, "Can you talk to me, Jimmy, about Mark? I've been wanting to find out…about the talks you've had with him."

He put the sugar on the counter and stepped back from it. His whole body stiffened, and he looked down at the floor. "Do I have to?"

"Yes, I need to know what's been going on, from the very first time he spoke to you." Purposefully keeping her tone light, she tried to make her comment easygoing. "It's just you and me and Dan. We're a family, and we're here for each other."

"That's what he said, except there was no Dan. It was you and Mark and me, and he said the pictures were just to help us get closer. I didn't think it was bad. I'm so sorry." Tears welled in his eyes. "I didn't even want to do it anymore, but Mark got so mad when I told him no. He said you'd be safer if he could keep an eye on you." He hiccupped. "I just didn't want you to get hurt…"

Aria was off her stool and around the counter instantly. She wrapped her arms around Jimmy and held him as his thin body shook. She looked over at Dan, and the expression on his face was grim. God love him, he never looked away…just sent his strength to her, and she never wavered as she held tight to Jimmy.

Chapter 15

THE EVENING HAD BEEN A STRUGGLE. IT HAD TAKEN A long time to walk through Jimmy's story and then to calm Aria. He didn't want either of them to be upset, but he was sure that purging the pain and clearing the air had helped them both.

He hated leaving now, but the Op was happening. There were personal stakes in this event, too.

No doubt his buddies would be stopping in to check on Aria and Jimmy while he was gone, but it didn't make it easier to leave. If this Op weren't the one mission he'd been waiting for, he would have tried to pull out for family reasons.

His wife…she was so strong. It amazed him how she handled things. *Does she know how remarkable she is?*

Lying down next to her, he pulled her into his arms. She fit perfectly into the grooves of his body as if she had been made for him. Together they were one being with multiple appendages that only moved in synchronicity.

"Have I told you…that you're amazing?"

"No. Why?" She asked, rubbing her cheeks along his arm, beckoning him.

"The way you handle things. Life says, 'Hey, this is a hard mountain to climb,' and you figure out how to conquer it. You've done that and so much more with the hurdles thrown in your way."

"I'm not perfect."

"Neither am I, but you live boldly, Aria. You try, you do, and you succeed."

He kissed her neck. "I admire those qualities in you."

"I feel I owe you an apology."

"For what?"

"For Mark. In truth, not only for my blind spot with him, but also for the fact you're my husband and you deserve the chance to become my best friend. I think I held that opportunity away from you for a while, because I was scared to put too many emotions in one place."

"Apology accepted."

"But I owe you more!"

"Then give it to me." He hugged her close. "Your actions have always spoken volumes. Your loving nature—the way you care for your brother, you, and me—is terrific. Not many people are as conscientious as you. Give yourself a break. Just be you, Aria. That's exactly the person I want to be married to."

"Thanks," she said, smiling up at him. Naked and stretched out alongside him, she whispered, "Stop thinking and make love to me."

"Gee, I don't know. That's so hard to do," he teased.

His hands stroked along her flesh, changing her breathing to short gasps. When she was moving into his touch, he kissed her. The passion so electric it made her forget everything but him...this kiss...this moment.

As he braced himself above and slowly...inch by inch...slid inside, she climaxed. Her whole body was alive with delighted pleasure.

Her Dan. He was always so in control. She was going to change that...

Aria thrust her hips, changing their rhythm from something slow and steady to one that was fast and breathtaking.

"Wait, Aria. I like watching you," he said, trying to slow her down.

"I like coming better," she said, tossing her head back and climaxing. "My turn to be in control." Her sheath squeezed over his cock, and he had to hold back. He wasn't ready to release...not yet.

"I'm...not...ready," he panted...holding on.

Her nails scraped gently along his chest. Reaching his nipples, she teased them...sending him out of control. "I love you, my husband. My lover. My friend."

"I love you, too," he sighed as she lay her head on his chest. "More than you'll ever know."

Dan dozed. When he awoke, they were still cuddled close together.

Aria lay quietly in his arms and he hugged her close, smelling the sweet scent of her hair. He could stay this way forever.

Feeling moisture on his bicep, he rocked her gently. "Hey, what's up, Aria?"

Wiping at her eyes, she said, "I'm going to miss you."

"I'll miss you, too." He took a deep breath. "Think of my being gone this way—instead of actively missing me, go live. Go out and do all the things that make you happy, knowing that I'm applauding your ability, your guts and ingenuity. Truly, it is so much easier to live now and enjoy the present than to wait for a future date when the living begins."

"Puts less pressure on you, too," Aria commented.

"True. When husbands deploy a lot, they are told by their command staff not to upset the harmony at home—not to establish dominance and change the schedule or natural course of things. But coming home always does change things. My greatest wish is that whether I'm coming or going, you'll be experiencing and expressing who you are."

Aria nodded her head slowly. "Dan, why…did you pick me?"

"What do you mean?" he asked. "I knew from the first moment I kissed you, Aria, that you were special. There was something so unique about you—the way you thought, expressed yourself, moved, and lived. Just know I'm not planning on dying any time soon. I won't make guarantees that I can't keep, so I'll tell it to you this way—I love you now and forever, and every day we can share our happiness is all I want, as long as you're joyful, too."

"Thanks." She leaned up and kissed him. "Just tell me this, though, now that you see all the complications…do you regret any part of this marriage?"

"No, of course not. Why would you ask that?" She baffled Dan sometimes. Did she think he would go through all of these difficulties because he wanted to dump her?

"Don't look at me like that. I was so shocked when you proposed that I never went into the reasoning." His wife's eyes bored into him. "Don't say 'I love you.' I know that, and I love you, too." She put her chin on his chest. "I want to know what happened on that mission, the one that led you to the proposal. Whatever you can tell me. Please."

Dan sat up, dislodging Aria from his chest. Man, he did not want to tackle this question. In many ways, though, she had the right to know. Having bitten the bullet thus far...today was as good a day as any to give it to her straight.

"I was in South Korea. JC and I had a few hours of liberty and were walking around town. A guy I'd gone through BUD/S with named George Gould, who we called GG and had been a rock star for his ability to run and do pull-ups but had rung out the first time the instructors got in his face, had become a sniper. When his time was up, he became a sniper for the FBI. It was pretty strange, seeing him abroad, since the FBI's territory was in the USA, but we had a beer to trade news anyway. When we left the bar, JC was pretty wasted and I was feeling a buzz. But I noticed these suspicious looking guys entering the establishment, behind us. After we heard several shots, JC and I went back in and found GG bleeding out on the floor. He gave us this name and address and told us to help her out. She was his fiancée.

"Well, GG was dead and the authorities wouldn't have taken kindly to us hanging around there, so we left. The address was tough to find, but we managed it and introduced ourselves to the woman inside. Her name was Sandra. She lived in South Korea, but her family was originally from up north. While we were talking, some nasty guys came to her door, so we took her back to the ranch.

"Command had a bit of a scuffle about it, and the CIA

came in and took over. It wasn't until years later that I was on an Op to meet an informant in territory we're not supposed to be in—please don't guess—that I saw her. I had no idea that the CIA had turned her into an asset and forced her to work for them. She told me that she only had to work five years and then she'd be free to become a U.S. citizen and receive a salary for the time she worked…up north.

"Sandra needed me to meet her the next day, to give me information about an operative who had been planted and had turned traitor. Already the traitor had been responsible for eleven American deaths, and he was promising more to the high echelon of the government. I was pissed when I got back, and I talked to the Team about it. We weren't cleared to take her out, but we were going to. It was my fault she was in this situation. I should have followed up, done something.

"The next day, when we went to meet her, Sandra was followed and shot. She died in my arms, giving us the information we needed. She was more of an American, a patriot, than the man who had betrayed us, even though she wasn't actually a citizen. If my friend GG had managed to marry her before this all began, it would have been a different story. But he didn't." Dan let out a ragged breath.

"I'm not a priest, Aria. I've killed people—a lot of them—but Sandra's death hit me so hard, I couldn't recover. I started thinking about you and the future, my swim buddy JC and his wife Jen, and the things I wanted for my own life. It horrified me to think I could wake up one day and never have taken a risk in my personal life. Here it was I could walk into a firefight, but I couldn't say 'I love you' to the one woman I can never get out of my mind." He shook his head. "I couldn't live like that. I needed closure to live my life fully, go for the grandest wish of all...for those friends who didn't get to do it and for myself."

His chest shook. There were no tears, but he could feel the pain in his chest. "Christ! How could she live and die that way, being forced to spy for what was 'almost' hers?"

His wife came into his arms and wrapped herself around him. She held tight as his body shook and he gave himself over to the emotion that had held him for so long.

When the brunt of the pain subsided, he gently pushed her away. "I know, I said I'd be here...to help with Jimmy and spend time with you, too. But I have a chance to avenge Sandra, to actually get the head-quarters of the terrorist cell that's been going after our people." He cupped his hands around Aria's cheeks. "I volunteered to do this. I hope you understand what it means to me. To us."

The emotion was plainly written on his wife's face, a fierceness that meant she was on his side. She nodded and then turned her head and kissed his palms. "We'll be fine. I promise not to say anything to anyone."

"Thanks." He kissed her lips...so tender, and mighty sweet.

"Kill those bastards!" she said against his lips.

He laughed. She was his, and she seemed to under-stand what was at stake for him. "So, we're good."

"Almost," she said with a wicked gleam in her eye. "It depends if you've recovered enough to satisfy your wife before you leave. She'd love to send you off…with a bang."

The next morning came too quickly. He'd barely caught any sleep, but it was time to get up and get moving. "Hey, are you going to drive me, or should I have Hannah pick us up?"

"Us?" Aria was barely awake and her words were slurred and groggy. "Why Hannah?"

"We're not supposed to leave our cars at the airport, if we can help it." He stretched his arms over his head and groaned. His body craved a workout and run, but it wasn't happening this a.m. unless they could figure out a way to do it on the plane. "Me and JC. Jen's on bed rest, with the babies."

"Right, of course, I forgot. I'll do it. I'll drive you. Just let me get my purse." His wife stood up and headed for the door. She padded around the bed and he had the perfect view. Damn, but she had the cutest ass!

"Maybe you should put some clothes on," he offered.

With her fingers on the door handle, she looked down. "Crap! I'm out of it. Good idea."

Dan grabbed his clothes and went into the bathroom. He brushed his teeth and took a quick shower and then went into the kitchen to make coffee. The fresh brew woke his senses even more, and he took a few sips before pouring it into a travel mug. He also made a cup of tea for Aria, who was standing at the door watching him. "Why don't I drive?"

"Stellar thought." She gave him a half smile and then stopped him from moving past her, demanding a good-morning kiss. He complied, it being his duty and all.

Looking down at his curvy red-haired vixen, he said, "I just ask one thing—that there are no tears. It isn't done."

"Roger that," she said with a salute.

"Where did you learn that? Your salute needs work, by the way."

"You didn't complain when I was saluting you last night," she teased.

"Ha, ha." His memory replayed her appreciation, and his body was already responding. "Aria…" he warned, wishing he could take her back to bed.

She hugged him. "Seriously, I'm learning stuff from you. You're rubbing off on me, Chief McCullum." She whispered. "Or should I say, Big Mac."

"Too sexy, when you say it." He grinned. "Well, hopefully I'm rubbing you the right way with my attentions."

Her laughter came out in a spurt of joviality. "Yes. Again and again."

He flipped on the outside light and then held the door for her. Aria took their hot beverages, and he hoisted his gear onto his shoulders. They locked up and left. "Check through the window before you open the doors, okay?"

"I will," said Aria.

"Keep a log of his calls, and if he threatens you, call the police." Dan felt uneasy about leaving them. "You and Jimmy could go stay at Caty's house. Maybe it'd help your bonding."

"I'll keep it in mind," said Aria. "She doesn't know any of this, does she?"

"No, she's been giving us space…the whole newly-wed thing." Dan beeped the unlocking system, triggered the trunk button, and laid his bags inside. "Might be nice if you touched base sometime this week or next."

He turned on the ignition and buckled his seat belt. He waited while Aria did hers.

"Will you be gone that long?" His wife's face looked so young and vulnerable.

Leaning over, he kissed her again. So worth it! Her kisses were wonderful.

"I don't know." Putting the car in drive, he pulled away from the curb. "Trust me, I will come home as soon as I can. I want to be with you. Got it?"

She laid her hand over his as he drove to pick up his swim buddy, the other best friend he now had. Aria, through all of the hardships she'd endured, trusted him, honored him, and believed him when he asked it of her. His wife was remarkable.

———

As they pulled into the parking lot of the NAS North Island Air Terminal, JC was quick to get out of the car. He got his bag out of the trunk and hotfooted it to the group gathering by the fence.

"Guess JC wanted to give us some privacy." Aria leaned over and gave him a big grin. "Could we get away with something sexy happening in the car before you leave?"

He smiled. "No, but thanks for the thought. Listen, JC's pretty stressed about leaving, with his wife so close to going into labor. Could you go over there, maybe say hi or something?" Dan got out of the car and went to the trunk to get his gear.

She followed him and took the keys from his

outstretched hand. "Sure, though isn't it sort of strange…
given that I've never met her before?"

"Actually, Jen is the one female associated with
SEAL Team that I did talk to…about you." Dan kissed
her nose and then planted one on her lips. "She's the
best egg of the bunch. If you like Hannah, you're going
to love Jen."

"That's quite a list of social interaction you're giving
me, Dan." She only looked slightly perturbed. When she
smiled, he knew everything was all right.

"Wouldn't want you to miss me or anything…"

"Never," she said, entwining her hands behind his
neck and kissing him with a punch that practically tented
his trousers. "Get those bastards."

"Roger that."

"I love you." She leaned her body against him briefly
and then broke the contact. She stood tall. *That's my lady!*

"You, too." He took one last quick look and walked
away. His mind was already gearing up, focusing on
what was to come… Kicking ass.

~

They stowed their gear and took their seats. Ah, yes,
nothing more fun than riding all day in an airplane. Well,
maybe a root canal was more satisfying, as something
actually got fixed. Dan knew he shouldn't be complaining, even in his own head, because their flight was as
direct as it got, flying to Asia. The C-17 was hauling
ass! They wouldn't be riding the usual big birds with the
multiple stopovers in Oahu and the Philippines. They
could zip over the ocean, stop in Guam for a quick refu-
eling, and their next stop was South Korea.

Turbulence bounced the plane. The ride might be fast, but no one said it would be smooth.

Closing his eyes, he thought of Sandra Niang and the circumstances surrounding her life. At the bar, GG had spoken of a woman who had changed his life. Why GG had traveled halfway around the world to get her, he understood. Love mattered. If only GG had gotten her out of the country faster…well, she probably wouldn't be dead. Damn it, why had the CIA made Sandra into an asset in exchange for a crappy deal? Hadn't they realized she would have had to commit a criminal act, probably several, to be accepted into the terrorist group? He wondered what she had done.

A meaty palm landing on his shoulder startled him. Dan's eyes sprang open and his sight was filled with Hammer, leaning down. The man's breath smelled like egg salad. "Listen, I heard…about the sepsis. I shouldn't have ridden you. I thought you were hungover or some kind of crap like that. I should have known you wouldn't go up and jump unless you were in top form." He rubbed his chin. "Are you good to go?"

Dan looked at JC, who shrugged. His swim buddy had probably spilled the beans defending him. How could he fault the guy? Damn it, secrets were *so easy* to keep in the Teams. You practically couldn't take a leak without everyone knowing how much and what color.

Whatever. Dan nodded. There wasn't much he had to say to Hammer. He understood the reason that his Teammate called him on the crap surrounding the HALO jump. This shit is dangerous!

"Mac, I'm not good at this stuff. Sorry about the—"

Hammer looked as if he were in pain, as if someone had stabbed the soft tissue between his legs with a tack.

Raising a hand, Dan stopped the CPO. "It's fine. You did a good thing. I would have called you on the same shit. We're good."

Hammer stared at him.

JC said in a mocking voice, "I love you, Hammer. I love you, too, Mac." He yawned. "Aw, shucks, thanks! Can you two kiss and make up later? I'm trying to get some shut-eye." JC shifted in his seat, obviously trying to ignore them both. But JC wasn't done. When he began making kissing sounds, all of them laughed.

Hammer swatted JC on the top of his head and retreated to the front of the plane. Dan watched him go. If a friend can't call it like it is…that wasn't someone who honored your energies. The Hammer, he was definitely a bud.

JC shoved his elbows under Dan's ribs. "Never enough space on these things. I'd like to see a plane with beds on it."

"I heard they had that kind of thing in first class."

"No way!" JC kicked his legs out and then crossed them again. "My knees feel as if there are pins in them. I hate the flying part."

"But you love to jump," said Dan, teasing his buddy. "Maybe you should have feathers instead of all that hair on your back."

JC sniffed.

"What?" Dan looked over his shoulder at his swim buddy.

"I feel like you have a new boyfriend." JC scratched his balls. "It hurts me, my brother."

"Give it a rest. I'm going to get some shut-eye." Dan murmured, "Fuck you, JC."

JC sighed, "If only I could fuck... I miss my wife."

I second that, thought Dan. *I miss Aria already, too*.

——◦◦◦——

The jet touched down smoothly.

Everyone on board was prepped and ready to go. Two hours from their destination, the Team had chowed down and gone over the strategy. The part that stuck in Dan's head was the lack of options. Usually they had a few alternatives if the shit went sideways or all out hit the fan. In this case, there weren't a whole hell of a lot of options.

Dan pursed his lips. One of Gich's preferred quotes—the British Army adage "Proper planning and preparation prevents piss-poor performance"—kept coming to mind, and that little gem raised an instant red flag for him. He brought up to the Team those things that didn't set right. "What if our path is blocked?"

"We wait," replied LT.

"For how long...forever? It's like being stuck in a bottleneck." Dan was not thrilled.

They'd looked at the map, but there was only one other option, because there were known minefields on either side, all around the compound.

"What happens if we run into booby traps or IEDs and over half the Team is wounded? No helos can enter the area without starting a war." Hammer pointed out those lovely problems.

Anyway they laid it out, it was a crapshoot. Nope! Dan wasn't thrilled with this plan—at all. Felt like a suicide mission, unless they were very, very smart.

Resigned to some degree, they hashed it out among themselves—the eight of them—and settled on who was taking what position as they patrolled in and out.

The plane door opened and they grabbed their kits and put boots on the ground. Vehicles were waiting to take them to their quarters. It was an old Quonset hut with a stack of cots and a couple of hammocks. They dumped their duffels and went through their packs, making their kits as light as possible.

No one spoke. If someone was listening, all they'd hear were men scuffling about. Nothing would be said to give anything away, but that was just SOP—standard operating procedure.

Hearing a single honk, the XO nodded to them, and Dan's Team grabbed their gear and exited the building. The second Team, an Intel Officer, and the XO stayed behind. That was the backup option. If things went sideways, the sailors who handled the crap took the fall. The whole Charlie Foxtrot—or Cluster Fuck in civilian parlance—is transitioned to those higher up the food chain, if it turned into an international incident.

Who else knows? Are the Navy brass the only ones, or does it go all the way up to the president? It was hard to judge what the consequences of this mission would be…but they were committed now. According to their protocol, there were some points where they could bug out, but personally Dan wanted to go all the way. Seeing the image of Sandra in his head one more time, he relished the anger pumping in his system. Turning that heat into fuel, he smiled.

Bastards, he said to himself. *We're coming for you.*

—◦◦◦—

Taking half a day to reach their location wasn't bad. The trucks had dropped them off at a heavily wooded location close to the border. The driver had made sure no one was looking and nothing was in the area when he stopped, and he'd made a show of looking under the hood and cleaning his windshield.

The Team slipped out of the vehicle and took cover in and around the bushes and trees, waiting in the thick foliage until the truck left…making sure there was no one and nothing going on. Then they ghosted their way over the border, past the guard patrols to the planned destination.

The SEALs watched the guard outpost building for an entire day. With its number and decal, it was easy to identify, and nothing had occurred. No one went in and nothing came out.

This is where the Intel led us! How could this crappy place have anything to do with Sandra's killing? It has to be hoax.

Their mics were silent. If necessary, they communicated with hand signals.

Finally, they began to move. As they neared the small guard building, Hammer held the Team as he inspected something suspicious. Sure enough…it was a bomb.

Pointing to the entrance and exit of the building, Hammer and Dirks defused them quickly using an easy-to-find dismantling point outside. Those guys had been EOD, or Explosive Ordnance Disposal, before they joined the Teams, and they had a knack for playing with C-4 and shit like that. It was a skill Dan wished he had.

"Whoever set the charges was planning on returning. More like they were keeping something in, rather than

someone out." Hammer spoke softly to Dan. They had
been able to ascertain from the windows that no one was
inside, and as they entered the building, Dirks took up
a spot at the door and JC was farther out in the bushes,
keeping lookout. The rest of the Team had taken positions elsewhere, in case this was an ambush.

Dan's eyes scanned the room. An old table, cracked
and scarred, sat in the center of the room with two
mended chairs. A stool sat next to an ancient wood-
burning stove, and a teapot was on top of it with the
lid ajar.

Dust matted the molding around the ceiling and floor.

Three mugs were sitting on a drying rack next to a
large jug of murky water. There were jars of loose tea
and something that smelled foul, some kind of root, next
to it.

The place looked abandoned, but only for a couple of
days. There was no telling when someone would return.
Hammer paced the length of the room and frowned.

Dan nodded. His eyes scanned the molding again.
Yes! There was a clean spot. How had he missed that
the first time? He spotted a paneled portion of the wall
toward the back of the room and walked over to examine
the worn edges.

He pointed it out to Hammer. The EOD genius examined it, gave it a thumbs-up, and then they pulled the
panel. It was a closet with a darkened hole at the bottom.

Dan shined his flashlight down into the darkness,
and American faces looked up at him. "Damn," he said.
Touching his throat, he said, "LT, we've got hostages."

The Team switched positions as LT made his way
into the building. They lowered ropes and hoisted the

four men out of the hole. They'd been tortured. They were dehydrated, and a couple of them were badly hurt. Their Corpsman, Zankin, was itching to come in, but there was no way the room could hold any more people. And, Dan and Hammer were getting more antsy and spooked by the minute. "We need to 'shit and git'..." said Hammer, hefting one of the men onto his shoulder.

Dan agreed and the others complied. They lifted the other men and moved out, leaving Dirks to hook up the trigger for the explosives again, and then made their way back to their hiding spots. Darkness fell as they hightailed it off of the small exit road seconds before two trucks came over the horizon.

In the clear, they double-timed it up a small incline, where Dirks offered to bring up the rear. LT agreed and Dan hung back with him.

He gave the EOD Specialist a questioning look, and Dirks pointed at his eyes with two fingers and then at the small guard-outpost building below. Three guards dressed in local patrol attire were on the ground, bowing to someone obviously higher up the ranks. The man standing in front of them was yelling, if Dan's Korean was correct, about his time being wasted.

The smallest one undid the explosive device, and the higher-ranked man entered along with two others, then closed the door.

Dirks counted on his fingers. One...two...three...

The building exploded, taking over half the group with it.

The others—only two or three—were shouting and pointing. It was obvious they thought the local guards had screwed up with their explosive entrances.

"Now, that's art," said Dirks.

Dan nodded, and they double-timed it to catch up with the rest of the group.

About twenty miles away from the guard building, or more accurately, what was left of it, they'd found a good place to stop briefly. Zankin gave the wounded men a once-over, added some pressure bandages for wounds that had opened, policed the garbage, and they were on their way again.

They traded off carrying the wounded men.

Circling around one of those country patrols, they slipped over the border and were safe on the South Korean side. Thomas radioed for the truck. Brock was on his six, as usual.

They waited, hidden, for the pickup and watched the traffic pass by.

JC and Dan were hunkered down next to the Marine who was the most alert of the bunch. Unable to resist the opportunity, Dan asked, "Did you learn anything…"

"Buck Brandwinde. Yeah. They talked about the number-three leader of the party coming from the lake-side, somewhere only a few hours away. I think…they mentioned mountains and a hot spring." The Marine's whisper was soft but hoarse.

Dan handed him a non-scented cough drop, keeping his hand out for the wrapper. He pocketed the waste and then closed his eyes. He could see the path clearly…how to get to the described location. There were only three like it in North Korea. The one he was thinking of was the single hot spring in the southern part.

Brandwinde sucked his candy quietly, enjoying the opportunity to relish it. Every now and then he twitched, his muscles obviously still cramped from his imprisonment.

A wizened man holding a staff took goats down the road. The sound of the goats' discontent at being herded filled the woods.

Dan took the opportunity to whisper with JC. "I know the place…there's only one possibility near mountains and a hot spring. I can get us there." He had spent hours studying the topography of the area. His mind could visualize every bump and hill.

"That's crazy. We're not prepped." JC wasn't buying into it.

"This might be our only chance. What if the terrorist cell moves?" His body was alive with anticipation. He was already making mental notes of the best direction to take and all of the options available to them.

For a time the sound of bleating goats was all they heard. It eventually faded.

A man in white pants and a shirt with a traditional straw hat led eight children of various ages past their position. They sang a song about butterflies in the sky. Before they made it all the way past, several scooter-type motor-cycles buzzed by with couples perched on top. One child came dangerously close to Dan, JC, and Brandwinde.

Clapping a hand over Brandwinde's mouth and nose, Dan held tight as the child paused and then ran to catch up with the rest.

When the threat was gone, Brandwinde said, "What gives?"

"Even though those are unscented and unflavored, there's still some odor. I didn't think anyone would come that close."

"I thought we were safe in South Korea?"

"We are," said Dan. "But you never know who's watching. The DMZ is unmonitored in places."

Time ticked by slowly. Dan had to stop Brandwinde from fidgeting several times. The man's body had a mind of its own, and Dan could only imagine what was happening on the other side of the road with the rest of the Team.

Finally, they heard the gearbox grinding that signaled the approach of the truck. Just as before, the truck pulled over and the driver got out to inspect the front of his vehicle and look under the hood. The men loaded in, and Dan moved quickly to the rear. He had an earful for the LT about this lakeside terrorist headquarters, and he knew some of his brethren would want to join in on the fun, too. In Dan's opinion, Operation White Hawk wasn't complete, not until those responsible were made accountable. He wanted the headquarters of the terrorist cell.

JC stifled a sneeze. It was bad planning to stick him in that field, but there hadn't been much choice. All the enemy had to do was walk about ten feet to their right and his swim buddy would be revealed. Splitting the Team—sending half to South Korea and the rest of them heading north—meant they would be moving faster. Being caught here would mean a slow death.

Dan held his knife at the ready. He could take two of them instantly and sink his weapon into the others fairly quickly. They'd stripped down to the bare essentials so they could move faster. Dan held himself poised to pounce.

There were four North Korean men patrolling together,

just like the SEAL Team. Yet the tangos were all smoking cigarettes with their rifles slung over a shoulder. They were chatting amicably about a new girl at a bar, and nothing changed in their demeanor…as if they hadn't heard or seen anything. The enemy continued down the road without even noticing them. *Hallelujah!*

Dan let his breath out slowly and slid the knife back into the holder on his belt.

JC moved quickly, getting out of the field and standing by his side within only a few moments.

"I changed my mind. I want to go home," JC joked. "Where are my pretty red shoes?"

"Too late. Wear the dirty diaper and like it. Ain't no magic going to get us anywhere faster," said Hammer. Both he and Dirks had caught up to them, too.

The rest of the Team stayed below the border accompanying the Marines, who were in pretty bad shape, back to base. It seemed likely the biggest guy would lose his leg.

"I want a beer," said Dirks.

"I want a cheeseburger," replied JC.

Dan ignored them, instead thinking about their course. Once they were on the other side of the border, he was the only directional genius keeping them on track. Though the LT had argued briefly about Dan's plan, he understood its value. The Team, then, was split down the middle: Brock, Thomas, Zankin, and LT went to base and the rest of them followed Dan. In times like this, when his buddies trusted his instinct as the "human compass," it made him feel good and reminded him of the US Navy SEAL motto, "Ready to lead, ready to follow, never quit."

Hammer, Dirks, and JC were on his six. Everyone in the Teams had the same type of training in terms of compass reading, using the stars, and how to read plant clues such as moss, and so on. But Dan had a special gift, and his Teammates had seen it in action. He just hoped they weren't going to run into a whole pack of trouble.

He'd asked JC to stay behind. He'd never forgive himself if something happened to him, especially with those baby boys on their way, but JC was stubborn, saying, "I came on this mission because there's work to do. Besides, you're still here, and I'm sticking for the same reason. So shut the fuck up and hop to it, frog."

They were heading along the border, going back and forth, as it was beneficial until they reached a good spot to head north. Along the way, they discovered a kimchi pot and stopped for a quick feast. The pickled cabbage had the acidic flavor of garlic, peppers, and brine. They ate silently, only eating about half the pot, and then they put it back the way they had found it. Heading into territory where they wanted to blend in, the local cuisine would help them. Not everyone in the Teams agreed with what they were doing—adding to the smells that would come out of their pores—but Dan and his present Teammates had found it made all the difference.

They learned the technique from a Vietnam-era frogman who'd run missions throughout the region. Anyone who could survive that deadly and chaotic shit had their respect, and so far the advice had paid off for them—they were still alive.

Along the way, when he could, Hammer snapped photos to add to their database on the region. They knew how bad the risks were, but it wasn't going to stop them. It was a day-and-a-half hike in and who knew how long out, depending on which path they took. But this score wasn't private anymore; both Hammer and Dirks had been Marines before making it through BUD/S training and becoming SEALs. They were pissed at what had happened to those hostages—members of the Corps. With JC and Dan feeling connected to Sandra's death and everyone wanting this terrorist group—which had been a major pain in the ass for all of them—dead, the stakes in this game were pretty high.

They stuck to what they knew…running when it was feasible and staying silently still when it called for it. Hiking up through communist country was dicey at best. They often had to stop and stay tucked away while troops marched by or citizens ambled past their positions. The city slickers didn't appear very aware of possible intruders, but the country ones knew their terrain, and that made things trickier at times. Luckily the Intel placed the headquarters of the terrorist cell at the base of a mountain, tucked back into the mouth of one of the ravines. A scan of the region showed a lake, and that was their favorite kind of mapped feature. Dan was point man most of the way.

Finally, they reached the heights just above their goal. The waning smell of cooking gejang filled the air. The pot was abandoned, being stalked and eaten now not by human beings but local critters. The SEALs grabbed a few of the pieces and ate them, tossing the shells as the animals did before heading downward. Taking advantage of the starless nightfall, they headed down the mountain.

Dan had secured his night-vision goggles and took point. If there was an IED, he wanted to make sure he was the one who found it and the Team got over it safely. He wasn't eager to get hurt or die, but this was his idea and he didn't want anyone going down on his watch.

The hairs on the back of his neck rose. Something was up!

Dan held his fist in the air, giving the signal to stop, and they all froze like deer in headlights but with a small difference—the SEALs sank to one knee, becoming indistinguishable from the rocks around them.

They listened as a man and woman walked by. Dan knew enough of the language to understand the conversation. When the couple was out of earshot and eyesight, they continued.

"What was it, Mac?" Hammer's voice was a throaty whisper over the comm.

"He's trying to get her into bed...but they're from rival families and it's forbidden." Dan's reply was so soft, even a dog would wonder what he heard.

Spotting some sophisticated radar and listening equipment on top of the building, Dan knew they were in the right place. With the threat past them, Dan signaled to the rest of the group to move.

A shed was in their rather circular path to the building, and inside Hammer found the same kind of explosives as before. They loaded up and headed to their goal.

Amazingly, there were no guards. Either these terrorists were so confident in their ability and the security of their establishment or just horribly complacent. Dan didn't care which it was; the lack of guards to be eliminated was in their favor.

Dirks and Hammer were the experts, so they planted explosives around the outside of the house and set up a remote trigger. If someone didn't know better, it would look like little kids had decorated for a surprise birthday party. But these streamers were laced into the foundation and up the corners of the building with some rather unique explosives attached. Anyone would be hard put to locate the stuff, as it was underneath layers and layers of foliage. Though if someone did find it before the Team left the area, because it was their own stuff, the most likely thought would be that they had a traitor in their midst.

Excellent! See, two can play at that game, you bastards, mused Dan as he thought of Ru and what he had told the government's party officials.

Dan kept examining the doors and windows. He was eager to get inside. But there were people in there, too, and it was risky. He could hear them moving about.

Finally, someone opened a shade and then a window. A woman who looked as if she had just had sex smoked a cigarette and dumped the ash through the opening. She was complaining about the supplies they were lacking.

The ash fell an inch from Dan's nose before the wind whisked it away.

She spoke quickly, talking about the electricity going out intermittently and that they needed to have a better generator. Yesterday the ancient thing had almost started a fire. Then she asked that a message be sent to that effect…that this place was a firetrap.

When Dan heard her footsteps and those of another person leave the room, he knew this was his chance.

Removing his goggles, Dan looked into a window.

He could see several computers and a map of the USA with pins, and lists under the cities. Withdrawing a small camera, a high-tech one, he used the scope to focus in and then he snapped close-ups and one wide angle of the map. On the wall next to it were pictures of people's faces. Sandra's was up there, and it was x-ed out. He shot photos of that wall, too.

At last! Here are the bastards who killed Sandra.

There was no telling what else was in there. His fingers itched to pull the hard drives and take them home, but it had taken longer to get over the mountaintop than they had planned.

JC got his attention and pointed to his watch. Dan looked at the sky. Shit! There was no way they'd make it over the mountain before they were revealed by daylight.

Hammer was thinking the same thing, and he signaled for them to tuck into the water for the day. They all agreed and headed for the place with the best cover... the lake.

Their steps were cautious, though they encountered no personnel or IEDs on the way. If there had been, their SOP—practicing in peacetime so fighting was a reflex—would have aided them. Knowing how to operate instinctively as well as make decisions on the fly made it easier to reach a goal effectively.

Silently Dan moved into position first. He squatted down and duck-walked into a great hiding spot. There was a minimal amount of dried leaves and twigs, and he'd stay covered as long as they were concealed.

Beetles moved around his body, some scattering out of the way and others nudging him, unsure of what he was. As long as no one took a bite, he wouldn't need to reduce it to dinner. If there were any centipedes in here, he'd never hear the end of it from JC. The man had a serious aversion to them, and though he'd stand there all day covered in them and not say a word, later when they were alone it would be an endless tirade on how he hated all those legs and what they made him think about.

JC's foot got caught in a rock. It took him a few seconds to dislodge it, but not before a ripple moved out over the lake. His swim buddy slowly stilled his movements…waiting for the wave to dissipate before going any farther.

Soon enough he was only a couple of inches from excellent cover. Among the plant life, this is where he would be hidden, and yet he could see around all sides if he must. Even in full daylight, the weeping trees bent mightily over them and grew so close to the reeds, they would shade them from view and even allow them to fashion a breathing tube, if they had to go for a dip. There were a couple of spots like that around the lake, and with them split into two Teams, if they got into a pinch, they'd be able to handle it.

Hammer and Dirks signaled they were all set.

Dan and JC responded in the same manner.

Unless they were discovered, which they had worked their asses off to make sure didn't happen, their strategy meant…it was going to be a long fucking day.

Chapter 16

AT HOME, ARIA WAS ATTEMPTING TO HOLD UP HER END of the agreement. She was tired, though. SEALs had been stopping by her house at all hours of the day and night. First it was Declan, and then Jack Roaker and his wife Laurie. The one that had amused her the most was Commander Gich. He'd stayed for two days and drunk the house dry of liquor. Jimmy couldn't get enough of Gich's stories, and she was thrilled when the two of them went running on the Strand together. If Jimmy stuck to the positive side of his behaviors, she'd welcome Gich back anytime.

Yawning for the third time in ten minutes, Aria thought about turning Dan's car around and going back home. But she'd promised to check on JC's wife, and that was exactly what she was going to do. Besides, she had to thank Jen for talking to the high school. She was the former vice principal and had talked the school board and staff into allowing Jimmy to do his work from home and finish up the first semester of his sophomore school year. Aria was grateful beyond words for the assistance and was bringing an overloaded gift basket that weighed almost as much as her brother, who was sitting in the front seat next to her. He had written a thank-you card and several paragraphs on what this opportunity meant to him.

During the next school break, Jimmy would be working

in Judge Wasa's courtroom. She had spoken to the judge and learned that her brother would be taking on the role of unpaid intern: getting coffee, doing filing, looking up precedents—if he had a knack for it—and attending court when the judge was presiding. It was a good way to spend the school break.

Aria had been concerned that Jimmy might run into Mark, but so far her former best friend had not contacted either of them. There were many times she'd thought of contacting him to get his side of the story, but then she looked at her brother and couldn't do it. She was the only line of defense for him, the one barrier between someone harming him or protecting him, and she needed to be his superhero.

Keeping that in the forefront of her mind, she allowed him to use her computer for homework only, and he had to ask her to log in before he was able to use the Web.

"I think that's the house," said Jimmy, pointing. "Wow, that lady's big."

She looked at where her brother indicated and she smiled. "It's the correct house number. Now remember, don't tell her she's big. Pregnant women are sensitive about such things. If you have to comment, tell her she's pretty, but only if it's the truth. Otherwise, say nothing but 'Thank you for your help.'"

"Aye, Master Chief." Her brother saluted.

"What's that about?" Aria looked at her brother, puzzled.

"Dan told me women are a rank higher than their husbands, because they are in charge. I am to respect you and listen to you."

She raised her eyebrows. "Really? How long is that going to last?" Not that she was complaining…

"I like Dan better, and I'm a lot more scared of Dan than I am of Mark. I don't know why I ever listened to that tool! I should have known better." Jimmy kicked at the floor with the toe of his tennis shoe.

Aria pulled the car into the driveway and put it in park. "I don't like you talking that way. Can you get rid of the recriminations and the judgment for a little while?"

"Yes. Hey, she's walking over." Jimmy waved at the short woman with the huge belly.

Turning quickly, Aria almost wrenched her neck. "Get out of the car. I don't want her to have to walk all the way over here. Get the basket, too."

Opening her door, she hurried over to the wobbling lady. "Hi, I'm Aria, and that's my brother Jimmy. We wanted to introduce ourselves and thank you for the wonderful things you've done."

"Hi, Aria. I've heard so much about you. Hi, Jimmy. Come on in." Jen stopped moving forward, though she was still holding her belly. She bent over for a few moments and then she stood. "I swear they are having a fistfight in there." Sure enough, her shirt was moving. Directing her voice to her belly, Jen said, "Stop it this instant, or I'm calling your father." It worked.

"That was amazing! Can you really contact JC?" Aria asked.

Jen shook her head. "But they don't know that," she mouthed. "Those two seem to be calm only when JC is around. It's seriously frustrating. Better not be like that when they're born. Let's go in."

Walking slowly beside her, Aria admired the yard. "This is gorgeous. Did you do it?"

Waddling more slowly as she walked up the steep

bank, Jen said, "No, JC has the green thumb. He doesn't even trust me to water any of it. There are sprinklers hidden everywhere." Pointing to a line of rosebushes, she said, "He gave me that one for our first wedding anniversary and on down the line, except for the last two—those represent our sons."

"Are you sure you don't need any help? Your face is getting a little red." Aria couldn't stop herself from having her hands at the ready in case the woman fell or toppled or needed a push. Did women really get that big? From the back she looked like she was a small lady with a shapely backside. From the front, you just wanted to wrap your hands around her stomach and help her out.

"No. The exercise...is good...for me. My doctor wants me...to move around...some." Shifting both of her hands to her back, Jen huffed her way upward. "I'm sorry...I didn't make it to your wedding. JC takes...this bed-rest thing seriously. I've never been...so bored in my whole life. Though it is a weird break...not to have him singing dirty songs to the babies. My headphones and I have become good friends."

"Seriously? Like Navy songs?" Aria laughed. "I could see that. How's his voice?"

"Like a cat having kittens." Finally reaching the porch, Jen yelled, "Mom. Dad. We have company. Come meet Aria and her brother Jimmy! You remember me telling you about them."

Aria put her hand on Jen's arm. In a hushed voice, she said, "What did you tell them? Jimmy's sensitive about the whole school thing."

"I told them that you were going to be my new friend and Dan has never gone gooey in his life, except when he talks about you. Any woman who can melt him like that deserves my praise and support." Jen patted her hand and turned toward the door as it squeaked open.

There was nothing Aria could say. Never in her life had someone ever said anything so kind to her. Emotion squeezed her heart. *I should have come here sooner, a lot sooner.*

Visiting with Jen was incredibly heartwarming. Aria had never felt so at ease with someone as she did with JC's wife. Dan was correct in his prediction that they would become fast-and-furious friends. When Jen's parents took Jimmy out for ice cream, she told Jen the whole story, and for some reason trusted her completely, maybe because Dan did, too.

Aria took a sip of her iced tea. "Did I tell you I contacted one of my old roommates? Lulu knew Mark in college. When I asked her about him, she told me he was creepy and used to follow her around, asking questions. She considered getting a restraining order at one point, and then suddenly he lost interest. Lulu said she never understood how I could be friends with him."

"Why didn't she warn you?" Jen looked shocked. "If you were my friend, I would have said something."

"Yeah, I asked her. The rest of our roommates talked her out of it." That knowledge made Aria feel sick. "You know…the three of them were really close. They dropped out together, were in each other's weddings, and had babies at the same time. I didn't follow that path, so we didn't stay…close."

"No offense meant by this…but I think you can do better, friendwise." Jen sucked on the lemon slice before she dropped it into her unsweetened tea.

"Me, too." Aria smiled at her.

"I don't think I would have had your restraint. I would have found the son of a bitch and kicked the crap out of him. A woman's lower body, especially her legs, are often stronger than a man's." Jen kicked out a leg, demonstrating her technique. "One quick kick and that would end his lust."

"I don't know that it's that simple," said Aria. "He knows everything about me. I had to change every one of my passwords…because I shared them too. I feel absolutely violated, and I don't know how to make it up to Jimmy. Do you have any ideas?"

"I've worked with a lot of abused kids. It's a complicated situation. But there are actions you can take that are effective. Be open. Have a space for talking…a time away from your normal environment."

"Yes," said Aria. "We've been walking around the neighborhood every day. It's been pretty good. Sometimes I talk. Other times he does. The silence is harmonious, too. I just want to make sure I'm doing it right. I don't know who to ask questions of."

"Me! Please ask me. I'd love to have something else to concentrate on." Jen trailed her fingers over her belly. "Aria, remember, kids are resilient. Don't keep bringing it up or trying to make it up to him. Let him come to you…unless you see a problem, and if you do, call him on the issue immediately. Pretend he is a canine— reward him when he's good and say no when he's bad."

"Oh my gosh, I can't believe you just told me to train my brother like a dog." Aria laughed. "That's so not politically correct."

"Well, crap," said Jen. "Practically every baby book

says the same thing on training and guidance…it all feels like dog training to me. In my opinion, it's a compliment. Our old treasure, Chilly, who was a boxer, ate better than us, slept on our bed, we picked up her poop, bathed her, and wiped her butt. She watched movies with us, got to go to the beach to run and play, took doggy-training classes, and generally had an awesome life. If I ever die, I'd want to come back as her. Wouldn't you?"

Aria wasn't sure about the dog/kid training stuff, but Jen did seem to have a generous heart. The whole house was baby-proofed, and there were two baby every things everywhere, from high chairs to infant swings. "Are you going to get another dog?"

"Yes. When the twins are two years old… We want them to have something to howl with besides us." Jen waved her hands. "Just kidding. You are so easy to tease. I'm sorry, I'll have to restrain myself. Honestly, we're waiting for the terrible twos to arrive, because my sister-in-law will be going to college at that time and living with us. Part of her rent-free arrangement is to help out in the afternoons and a couple nights a week. I have visions of taking a nap or a bath and perhaps even having a date night with JC, but the reality will probably be all of us chasing the munchkins throughout the house. I'm sure the babes will be running."

"You're looking forward to it, aren't you?"

"Yes, I've always wanted to be a mom…just like my own. It took me a long time to get pregnant, and I'm going to treasure these little guys like the crown jewels." Jen tensed and then relaxed. "Are you going to…have children?"

"Yes…someday." Aria looked around this house. Photographs of JC and Jen filled the walls, and every corner looked lived-in and enjoyed. She wanted that type of home, where people could visit and be comfortable, where she could be happy welcoming another stage of her life. She wasn't sure how she would get her life into that position, but she felt it would come. Dan was the key—their joy together, communicating, loving, and enjoying every moment. Could she be as strong as Jen? In all likelihood, yes, she could. Regardless of any concerns, she wanted to try.

"I miss having a dog," said Jen, staring off into space. "Excellent protection. You might consider getting one…given your situation." She fanned herself with her hands. "I cannot wait for these kids to get out here so I can love on them. Though…" She paused and crooked her head to the side as if listening to something Aria couldn't hear, and then she returned to the conversation with a smile. "I really, really want JC to be home for it. Maybe if I cross my legs…well, if I could cross them…"

—◆◆—

Aria drove down the road, admiring the view of the ocean. It was a beautiful day! She found herself humming and enjoying the memory of meeting Jen. Jimmy had had a great time, too. He ate an entire ten-scoop sundae all by himself and then played touch football in the park with Jen's dad. Her brother looked tired as he leaned back against the headrest and he yawned.

"So what do you want to do when we get home?"

"Veg out in front of the TV or play a video game."

Jimmy's voice was getting sleepier. He cuddled his chest with his arms, a habit which he had done since he was a baby. There were so many times over the past few days she had been reminded of his childhood. Jimmy was a teen and growing up, almost a man, but it was hard to look at him without seeing his start in life.

"According to our agreed-upon schedule you have an hour of TV and forty-five minutes of gaming time. Are you sure you want to waste it now rather than save it for tonight?" She glanced at him, and his eyes were slowly closing. "We can watch *Fletch*. I know how you love that movie."

"Fine. I'll wait."

She pulled into the turning lane and then into the Silver Strand neighborhood. There was a crowd of people at a house near hers.

"What happened?" asked Aria as she joined the group.

Several neighbors nodded at her as they looked in, too. In the arms of many of them were baskets or canned hams. Aria had a sudden impression of being at the zoo during feeding time, and she wasn't sure who were the exhibits and who was the audience.

When she looked in the window, all at once it hit… making her stomach clench. Inside the house Eve was crying. Her triplets were sitting on the couch, dressed in matching blue sailor suits and holding their teddy bears. They looked miserable and their faces were streaked with tears.

She watched the hated Mrs. Hiney fetch and carry and comfort Eve. Standing there for ten minutes, it amazed Aria…seeing the ice queen's warmth. Maybe she shouldn't have judged that book by its cover. Filing that nugget away for future thought, she backed away from the window.

She knew what had happened, and the fact that no one had said it confirmed that terrible fear. Eve's husband had been killed. There was no way to make it gentle. This was the ice pick of all outcomes. Everything changed from there. The death of a loved one was the devastation that would never heal, and the loss would never go away.

She shivered. *Oh, God, please…*

Looking up, she could see there were dark clouds overhead and the wind was picking up. She said a silent prayer, hoping her husband was safe. Then she went inside to escape the cold air blowing in from the ocean and locked the door securely behind her.

Chapter 17

DAN AND JC TOOK TURNS DOZING. FOR YEARS THEY had performed this type of task together, and Dan knew keeping himself hyper-vigilant was one of the ways that kept him from giving into the cold. His core temperature was low after spending all day undercover so close to the frigid water. Sure, he'd chugged a couple of thumb-sized energy drinks and downed about ten power bars, but he was still fucking cold and cramped.

He wondered how things were going with Aria. He missed her.

Hammer signaled that it was time to leave as full dark blanketed the area. The moon was just beginning to show a sliver of light, but there was still a ton of cover. Hammer and Dirks left the safety of their cover first. Dan and JC hiked around the lake to their side, keeping to the shadows and the bank. When they reached the edge of the foliage, they silently left the reeds and greenery behind and followed their brethren, acting as rear guard.

A smile formed on Dan's lips as Hammer detoured them through the hot spring and then up the mountain. Pretty nice to be moving, warming the body up…even for a short time!

The terrain was rough as they worked their way up to the rocky plateau. When they were at the top, Hammer triggered the explosives. The building fell in on itself, killing everyone inside, and they watched until they knew everyone was gone in the fiery wreckage. If the enemy did an investigation, it should all lead back to a traitor in their midst.

That's for you, Sandra, and all the innocents these bastards have crushed! Dan felt the emotion rock his gut.

The Team disappeared over the ridge and made its way down into another valley and up the other side. Dan's memory for terrain images was eidetic. He never forgot a layout once he saw it, and actually enjoyed being teased about being Bravo's human compass, especially when he remembered a pass between two large mountains that was only a half mile to their right.

Dan led them in the direction they needed to go. It would have been impossible to traverse some of the mountains—the sheer cliffs were dead ends that couldn't be handled without the proper gear. Regardless, he was glad they traveled light, having left their larger packs behind in the truck.

They were making better time taking the straightforward path, and it would have been a bitch to heft everything through this area, especially for the last part of the escape he had in mind.

"I'd rather go caving than bouldering," said JC at one point as he sliced his calf on a sharp outcropping. The cut wasn't too bad, but if they didn't do anything, the blood might leave a trail behind.

Hammer had threatened to use duct tape, but luckily for JC, he didn't have any on him. It was in his kit. It was too funny, watching him gesture that info.

Dan gave Hammer a wry look, then split JC's pants wide and sprayed his injured leg with nonscented hand sanitizer before holding the skin together and slapping superglue on the cut. It worked! The handy items were smaller than a penlight. His amazing wife had given him both of these treasures, pointing out that they'd fit snugly in his pocket, where she'd tucked them. Damned if they hadn't come in handy! He'd have to thank her…personally.

Catching a few stray sounds, they got moving again. They couldn't stop for long, as lingering would only provide a target for the enemy, so they scrambled down a hillside and up a different side of the mountain. It would take them longer to go this way, but it was a cleaner escape, in Dan's opinion.

The stress and exhaustion was starting to hit him. Dan knew he had about eight hours, tops, before he needed to catch at least twenty minutes of catnap and get a serious meal. He'd eaten all of his stash and had even grabbed food from JC, but he could tell the rest of the Team was tiring, too. Luckily, he had a plan that should be a minimal risk and take very little energy to get them to safety.

Avoiding villages and the occasional cluster of houses, they made their way to a cliff overlooking the Sea of Japan. The view was stunning. The smell of the salt air was welcome…like coming home.

The four men took cover under the trees and reviewed the plan. Farther down from them was a rather busy town, even for 0400. Chances were this was the best spot they could pick, and given the footprints, they'd have to go soon or risk being discovered.

"Really? Did you really have to pick a cliff this high? See that spot, the one over there? It's shorter and leads down to the ocean. You know…walking." Dirks spat out his comments. He was pissed off; he was not a fan of heights but always managed to deal with them. There was nothing they could do to change the plan at this point. They either leaped into the water or risked getting captured. "I'm not objecting to the whole plan... just how we get into the water."

Hammer gave Dirks a frustrated look. "By the time we hike over there and climb down the cliff, it will be full daylight and the window will be closed. Sorry, my friend. Suck it up!"

"Damn." Dirks frowned and then rolled his shoulders and shrugged.

Dan studied the scene below the cliff, finding the landmarks and catching the rhythm of the water. This was the deepest water and the safest jumping point. With the tide going out and the currents pulling south, if they were smart about it, they could catch a ride all the way down to a safe zone. They could practically float their way there, too.

Dan wondered, *How many people have escaped this country using this spot?* Standing on his toes, he looked down even farther without losing his balance. *How many have been impaled and died on the rocks below?* He wasn't sure he wanted to know.

Hammer was looking at the sky and checking his watch. "Come on, let's move. Sun's going to be up in a few hours—we've got to hit it if we're going."

"Agreed," said Dan. Giving his most serious face to JC, he said, "JC, do you want to hold my hand?"

"Ew, I might get cooties!" His swim buddy laughed softly and then checked the area one more time. "All clear. Dan, it's your idea, so you're first up."

Dan nodded. "Remember. Jump to your left—the waves will pull you straight out into the sea without you getting stuck on a rock." Then Dan took a breath and ran as far and fast as his legs would carry him until he was pumping the air and falling down, down, down, into the ocean below.

Chapter 18

ARIA'S HOUSE SEEMED TO HAVE A REVOLVING DOOR. The minute it closed, another person opened it and came through. They didn't even bother knocking anymore. It was a strange sensation to know that people felt that comfortable with her and Jimmy.

Exhausted after a day with Judy's boys, Aria left Jimmy playing video games with a bunch of Dan's SEAL buddies. She was hoping she could catch a little shut-eye. But sleep was a long time coming. She dozed for maybe an hour, caught up in a string of frustrations and nightmares. She didn't know what to expect in the fallout with Mark, because she hadn't talked to him and because everyone was taking the possibility of an incident with him so seriously. Her worry factor was through the roof, and what she really needed was for everyone to go home and give her some space.

After rolling over for the fourth time in five minutes, she gave up, threw back the covers, and left the bedroom. Flipping on the hall light and another one in the kitchen, she felt better.

Night had enveloped their small neighborhood. The sounds of children playing had been replaced with those of dogs barking to come in for the night and ships sounding their horns as they came into the bay. The air was salty and fresh, beginning to turn crisp, and the wind picked up.

She checked the lock on the patio door then laid her forehead against the window, longing for Dan to be home as she stared outside into the darkness beyond her fence. Her nerves were drawn so tightly, she could practically feel them twanging inside of her. She shivered. Her fingers grasped tightly together at the thought of someone out there watching her and Jimmy.

Harvey came up behind and placed a hand on her back.

She jumped a mile and spun on him. "Oh, hi! Sorry." She wrapped her arms around the front of her body and hugged herself.

"Are you okay?" he asked. Concern wrinkled Harvey's forehead and eyes, a strange look for someone that usually seemed so carefree. "Is there something outside? Do you want me to check?"

"N-n-no. I'm fine." She did, but couldn't tell him yes. How could she admit to being afraid of a bogeyman, when it was Mark who had betrayed her trust. It was confusing and disconcerting at the same time.

"It's pretty stuffy in here. Let's get a little air, okay?"

"Sure."

Harvey unlocked the door and stepped out on the patio. He grabbed the sides of the fences and peeked over them and then walked the perimeter of her patio and backyard again.

She wanted to scream, *No! Come back! There might be someone out there…* But Harvey was a Navy SEAL. She didn't think he was scared of the unknown…not the way she was. She shivered. Something felt off tonight. She couldn't put her finger on it. Maybe she was too wound-up. Paranoia was making her crazed with worry.

Her eyes followed him as he circled the back and then stood at the back fence. He stared out for a long time. When he came in, he shrugged. "Nothing out there that I can see."

Going back into the kitchen, he took out two beers, opened them, and handled one to her. "Here."

She shook her head. She didn't want anything clouding her brain, at least until Dan was home and the whole Mark issue was settled. Her phone buzzed again. She gazed at it, unwilling to answer it herself...knowing whose buzzer pattern that was.

"Do you want me to get that?" asked Miller, who was watching the video game that Jimmy and Hayes were playing. "No sweat off my back."

"No. Let it ring." She walked over to the couch. "If it's Dan, the phone dances a different rhythm and plays 'Does Your Mother Know' by ABBA. We love that song. It makes us laugh."

"Aw, man, I can't wait to tease him about that." said Hayes, who blew up a zombie. "Does he do the Johnny English dance to it? Man, just thinking about it makes me split a gut."

"Uh, I don't think we've seen that movie, but we'll check it out." Aria felt distracted, and though the guys meant well, she was on sensory overload. She checked the clock. "Jimmy, five more minutes. You played for eight hours today, two of which were on that gaming console with Judy and Duckie's boys, and it's almost time to get ready for bed."

"Twenty more minutes. Please, Aria, I can play less tomorrow." Jimmy's voice whined higher, but she didn't care. She'd give anything to keep seeing that smile on his face and the peacefulness in his eyes. Besides, she could be a soft touch…upon occasion.

"Five. That's final."

"Yes!" squealed Jimmy as he blasted a door and shot into the horde of ghouls. "Got 'em. Got 'em. Got them all! I am the conqueror!"

"Pup pile," said Hayes as he dropped the controller and turned to Jimmy and started tickling him. Harvey joined in until tears were running down Jimmy's face and he had squirmed away.

"I laughed so hard, I'm going to pee," he shouted as he ran to the bathroom and slammed the door behind him. The fan snapped on, so Aria knew she could talk freely for a minute or two.

She turned to Dan's friends. "It's been great having you here. But I need some space. I'm fine. We're fine. We can handle it tonight…on our own."

Harvey finished his beer and placed the bottle on the table. "We can stay. The couch will do fine. We don't mind spending another night."

"Really, it's sweet of you, but I need breathing room. You've given up a lot of your free time, all of it probably, and nothing has happened. Maybe Dan overreacted. Nothing's going to happen. We'll be okay without babysitters. Promise you won't stick around." Aria was adamant. "Promise me."

The men looked at each other as if they were exchanging silent messages. Finally Miller said, "We get it. You have our numbers. But if you change your mind, day or night, we're around. And, uh, don't be surprised if we stop by unannounced."

"Thanks." She hugged them each briefly. "You

promised you wouldn't hang around, so don't. I take that kind of agreement seriously."

"Understood," said Miller.

"I'm ready for round two," announced Jimmy, returning from the bathroom and displaying his freshly brushed pearly white teeth.

"They look clean, but you were hardly in there for a minute. But if you're ready for bed…"

"I don't want to go to bed now." Jimmy frowned at her.

"Listen to your sister, man. Talking back is very uncool," Miller pointed out.

"Fine. Then I'm ready," said Jimmy petulantly. "But can I talk to them privately before they go?"

"Yes," said Aria, going into the kitchen and loading the dishes into the dishwasher. She wiped the counters, keeping one eye on the men as they talked to her brother. Seeing Hayes enter her brother's bedroom, she gathered the empty beer bottles into her arms and could see that Hayes tucked him in and said something.

Then the men waved at her and left. They'd been super, but she was seriously craving quiet.

Throwing the bolt into place, she had only one more thing to do. Call Dan's sister.

Picking up the phone, she hit Ignore to the long line of texts without even looking at the ones from Mark and accessed her address book, tapping the box with Caty's number in it.

She picked up on the first ring. "Hello."

"Hi, Caty. It's Aria. Your…sister-in-law." That sounded weird, even to Aria. In theory, if she wanted to embrace it, she had a sister to do things with. "I just called to thank you for being a part of the wedding."

"My pleasure." Her sister-in-law's answer was definitely on the short-and-sweet side.

"What's new with you?"

There was a long pause.

"Well, if you really want to know…"

"I do," said Aria, slipping into her patient voice. Maybe she shouldn't have called.

"I just finished learning to shoot a shotgun. Did Dan ever tell you about our grandfather's collection? Well, my hubby and I went to Louisiana and visited the old house. The caretaker, Doc Franks, took us on an old-fashioned hunt, and I shot a feral pig. He took it back to the house and showed us how to skin it, slice it, and cook it. Isn't that amazing?" Caty's excitement was evident. "Best meal I ever ate. Do you like to hunt? Being married to Dan…oh, you must! We'll need to plan a trip…maybe at Christmas, if Dan is free. He loves that old house. What do you think?"

Aria swallowed the acrid bile that had risen in her throat and went to the kitchen. She took out a cold bottle of water and rinsed her mouth. She'd been able to eat game and had for most of her young life, but the one bird she shot had been impossible to palate. "Sounds interesting. I'd enjoy going on a trip with you. We'd have to bring my brother. My uncle passed away, and he's my responsibility now. He's a terrific kid!"

"Sorry to hear that. If you need me for any anything, please let me know. You and Jimmy are welcome at our home anytime." Caty's voice was sincere—the strident quality was gone—and the sentiment was so genuine, it made Aria feel good about being totally honest.

"What?" Caty called out. When she got back on the line, she said, "Aria, that's my husband. I have to go. Bye-bye."

"Thanks, Caty. Good night." Aria rang off. She laid her phone on the counter and propped her head up with her elbows. It had been a long few days. Getting a good night's rest would make a tremendous difference. Even when Dan's SEAL buddies were here, she couldn't completely let go for very long because she always remembered why they were here. It could be the extra energy in the house buzzing about, too, or her upbringing…her need to be polite and entertain guests. Life was so different when it was just Dan, Jimmy, and her. She wondered how long it would be until Dan was home again. If she didn't get some real "sleep through the night" rest very soon, she was going to lose her mind.

"Hello, Aria." Two wet shoes dropped onto the floor. "So convenient that you're close to the bay. I just rowed right over from the San Diego side."

Aria's head snapped up. Standing in the door was Mark. Her breath froze in her lungs.

"No!" she said, racing around the counter, out of the kitchen, and heading for the front door. *No, no, no! Why did I send the SEALs home?* She moved, but her body was working in slow motion as he caught her around the waist and yanked her down on the floor, bringing his weight down on top of her.

"You're not going anywhere, Aria, my angel." He petted her hair with his long fingers, and when his nails scraped her scalp, she couldn't stop the shivers from racing up and down her spine.

Oh, God, help me, please! She opened her mouth to

scream, but he clamped his hand around it, and when she struggled, he cut off her air. When she relaxed, he let her breathe through his fingers.

"All I'm asking…is that you to listen to my argument. Don't convict me until you have a chance to hear my side." He moved his fingers, stroking her cheek.

Revulsion swept her. She didn't want him anywhere near her or her brother. "Did you ask Jimmy to spy on me and threaten him to stay silent?"

"Yes." His grin was evil, and so delighted with himself.

Why didn't I see this side of him…before?

"Bastard! Go to hell, Mark!" She spat.

His hands gripped her shoulders and slammed her down hard. "Don't say that to me."

Her head hit into the floor. Pain split her skull as the world slowly faded to nothing…but darkness.

Chapter 19

Touching down on the NAS tarmac would be a relief. Dan looked forward to heading home.

With their verbal reports given, the official situation report was put off until they were home. So Hammer, Dirks, JC, and Danny headed for chow. Piling their plates with food, they ate until their bellies couldn't hold anymore.

Arriving back at the barracks, their lovely Quonset hut, which had probably been there since the war, the XO told JC word had come down that his wife had gone into labor. "Get on the next hop out of here."

JC looked so overwhelmed, Dan said, "Ox, I'm going to catch it with him. Can our gear ride out with the Team?"

"Like the fucking Bobbsey Twins," said the XO. "Fine, get out of here."

Dan escorted JC away before the XO changed his mind. "Nice job looking pathetic back there."

"Who's acting? I want to puke!" said JC as he pointed to a C-130 being loaded with gear. "Do you think they're heading home?"

They jogged to the edge of the tarmac and got the loadmaster's attention. Dan asked, "Is that plane heading to San Diego? Are there any empty seats?"

"Going to be mostly equipment, but the pilot might squeeze you in. His name is Lyons. Don't tell him I sent you." He nodded in the direction of a taller, thinner man who was walking around the plane, inspecting it. They thanked him and headed over.

"What do you want?" The pilot was studying the tires. His voice was terse.

"Could you give a couple of frogs a hop?"

"Maybe." He ran his fingers along the underbelly of the plane. "No seats. Equipment only! With a stop-over in Oahu." He looked them up and down. "It's a weight thing."

"I just lost five pounds," said JC, rubbing his stomach. "Listen, it's an emergency. My wife's having a baby."

The pilot rolled his eyes. "Seriously! Labor—like I haven't heard that one before."

JC withdrew a picture from his pocket and showed it to the pilot. "There's even a date stamp. C'mon, see… it's twins. Help me out here. Please…"

The pilot rolled his eyes. "For the record, I didn't see a thing. And if you piss all over the back of my plane, I'll have your heads."

"Understood," said Dan.

They shook the pilot's hand and ran into the terminal for a couple bottles of water and provisions. Then they double-timed it back onto the tarmac, waiting for the right opportunity. When it came—when no one was watching—they walked calmly to the plane, up the ramp, and into the back of a truck, closing the flap behind them.

"I swear I'm lying on stinky cheese," complained JC.

"Fine, I'll take the odorous duffel and you can lie on the lumpy one. This guy had to have bricks in here."

"Ah, this sucks! It's like Army-green hell," said JC, who

made Dan get up and rearrange the duffels. They were still stuck with a ton of luggage and a bunch of extra machine parts, plus equipment and boxes poking them in the wrong places, but Dan didn't give a shit. He was almost home.

Tuning out JC's stream of constant complaining, Dan put his hands behind his head and closed his eyes. To him this was an excellent heavenly respite. It beat trying to get shut-eye in a lake. But the piece of him that had been in pain over the death of Sandra found closure… and wherever her spirit was, he hoped she knew that he had done his best.

The plane's engines fired up. The cabin shook and the vibrations worked through his tired body like a welcome massage. The sound, the drone, was familiar…lulling even. His mind turned off as his body lifted away. Dan didn't feel the plane take off. He'd already fallen asleep, exhausted and ready to be home…to wrap his arms around his beautiful, feisty, and often-ornery wife.

—⁂—

Dan had a bounce in his step. He could hardly wait to surprise her—to show up and see that expression of pure happiness on her face. After he put JC in a cab pointed in the direction of the hospital, he caught a bus heading down Orange Avenue.

Getting off in front of his neighborhood, he ran into his buddies from SEAL Team FIVE. "Hey, Miller, what's up?"

"Your wife kicked us out. We just got something to eat and were on our way back to your house. We thought we'd hide in the bushes and keep vigil." Miller took a long draw on his drink.

"We wouldn't have left in the first place, but I'm pretty sure she would have kicked our asses if we didn't." Hayes put up both hands.

Dan shook hands with Miller. "Thanks for the help. I've got it from here."

"Roger that," Miller acknowledged as he sat down on a bench.

Dan grinned and left the two men to their banter. He took off for home, jogging through the streets and feeling good. He spied his house. Going past it, he circled around to the back and wondered if this plan would work. Would the patio door be open? He was a little concerned it might not be. He'd cautioned Aria on locking it up each night, and he wasn't sure she would unlock it at all during the day.

Spying the door open wide, he hurdled the fence and walked across the yard.

The hairs at the back of his neck rose, signaling trouble. Dan moved into the shadows, the ones cast by the neighbor's fence, and stretched his senses. Someone male was talking.

Dan inched closer. The words became audible, and his blood turned to ice in his veins.

"You bitch! You don't know how great you had it!"

He knew that voice… Mark.

Resisting the urge to charge in to the rescue, he pulled out his phone and texted the police his address and that an assailant—and former friend of the family—by the name of Mark Anders had prisoners and a weapon inside. Making sure it was set to silent, he pocketed it and hugged the shadows as he drew closer to identify where everyone was.

He looked through the back window. Aria was in a chair near the television and tied up, while Jimmy was huddled on the floor, grasping his stomach, in front of his bedroom. The best place to lure this psycho was… lined up with the front door. His mind played over the possibilities and strategies.

Shit! Why, the hell didn't he have his gun?

"Don't you see, Aria Angel, we can travel the world?"

"Mark, that's not going to happen." Aria lifted her chin a few centimeters higher.

Dan could tell Aria was trying to keep calm, but he could hear the tremor in her voice.

Hang in there, baby.

"You love me!" Mark shouted. "And we're meant to be together!" Dan heard the slap as Mark backhanded her.

Son of a bitch! Dan's temper flared and he had to tamp it down. *High emotion is the fastest way to fuck a fight*, his buddy Gich used to say. Quite frankly, Dan agreed.

Dan peered through the window to assess the situation. He caught the flash of a knife in Mark's hand. Jimmy was on the floor, bleeding. Aria had recovered from the blow and was pulling at her bonds. "Mark, please, let me help him," she said. "I'll do anything you want."

"Really?" Mark drew out the word into three syllables and stalked closer to Aria. The tip of his knife slipped across the collar of her blouse.

It was enough of a distraction for Dan to silently slip inside the house. He had Mark disarmed and his own knife at the man's throat before Aria could blink. In that moment, Dan knew he could do it…take Mark's life without a single hesitation. But, he wouldn't go to jail for this scum, so he slid his own knife away and turned the man to face him.

"This is my family. Not yours. No one fucking hurts them." Dan punched Mark in the ribs feeling the bones give way with each hit. Then he moved to the man's kidneys and back, aiming for maximum damage.

A loudspeaker sounded from outside. "This is the police. Come out with your hands up and no one gets hurt."

"You're done," said Dan, his fingers flexing. The satisfaction was sweet, but too short-lived. He ached to hurt this man so much more. No one fucks with a SEAL or his family. "Never come back, or it will be your last act."

"Nooooooo!" shouted Mark as he reached into his waistband.

"We're coming in!" shouted the police. "Throw down your weapons!"

Needing to add a little punctuation to the moment, Dan egged Mark on. "Come and get me, loser boy."

Mark charged him.

Dan stopped him, putting a lock on Mark's arm and sending the gun skittering across the floor. He kicked Mark in the gut, listening to the air explode out of his mouth.

Mark reached around and pulled the knife from Dan's waistband, waving it blindly in Dan's direction.

The front door burst open.

Four officers with guns drawn came barreling through and aimed their guns at the two men.

"This man has attacked me and my family," Dan said.

Mark panted, trying to catch him breath, but his gaze was full of meaning.

The cops grabbed the knife and pulled Mark out of Dan's grasp. In no time, the police had Mark handcuffed and were leading him to the squad car. The monologue finally coming from his mouth was a litany of crazy speak.

In truth Dan seriously wanted a different kind of closure, but he was practicing restraint. Wasn't his XO always saying, it's better to let life take care of things? So the cops were dealing with the justice end, though if Mark ever came back, Dan knew he could easily make this man and his body disappear for good.

Dan turned away from the drama and wasted no time getting to his family. He untied Aria and they both went to Jimmy. Placing a hand on Jimmy's shoulder, he waited for Aria to speak first.

"Are you okay?" Aria asked, frantically checking the cut on her brother's arm.

"Yeah." Jimmy leaned into Dan's arm. The kid had guts. "It hurts, but it's not deep. Harvey taught me how to bluff. It worked. Mostly…" He rubbed his face, wiping away the wetness under his eyes.

Dan could tell Jimmy was stepping up and dealing with the practical side of the incident. The kid was right, though; he doubted the cut would need stitches. His chest swelled with pride.

He kissed Aria and hugged Jimmy.

"Thank you, God!" Aria said. "I'm so glad you're home." She kissed him three more times before she let go.

The officer in charge came back in the house and shook Dan's hand. "Mac."

"Hey, Billy. How's the force treating you?"

"Tonight it's going to make me do a helluva lot of paperwork." Officer Billy O'Connor had gone through BUD/S and been rolled back for medical. His shoulder had never healed properly, and he'd decided on a different path. Their friendship had hung tight. Also, his uncle was the chaplain that had married Aria and him.

"Do you mind if I settle the family and get back to you?"

"Sure. But we'll need to talk to them at some point soon." Billy nodded to the others, letting the family pass through to the bedroom. "Dan, the paramedics will be here in five."

"Thanks." Never in a million years would he have wanted Aria and Jimmy to go through so much trauma. They were strong, though, and they would get through it…together.

In the bedroom, Dan bandaged Jimmy's arm and looked at Aria's eyes to make sure she didn't have a concussion. He knew the paramedics would want to take a look at them, too, but he had to reassure himself that they were going to be fine. When he was satisfied, he waved the paramedics in, and then he went out to deal with the police.

It seemed like hours before he was able to go back to the bedroom. He found Aria waiting up for him. She looked exhausted but relieved. "Dan…"

Gesturing with his head, he invited her out.

She nodded.

He pushed the door wide, picked up Jimmy and placed him in his own bed. Aria pulled the covers over her brother and then he closed the door, only a soft snick sounding in their wake.

Dan led her outside. They stood hand in hand and looked at the stars.

"I'm so sorry. I didn't know. This is all my fault," Aria began, her face twisted in anguish.

"No. It's not your fault" he said, pulling her close.

She clung to him as if he was her life raft and she was at sea.

"Shush. Let out the pain. Release it all, and then be done with it."

When she had finished crying, he lifted her chin with his index finger. "Aria, you can't blame yourself for a psychopath's obsession. No one could control that. Got it?"

She nodded. "Yeah, but it's so much easier said than done." She hugged him tight, and he stroked her curly hair. Her face was hot and wet against his chest.

"In the morning the sun will shine and the sky will be blue and the sunshine will warm your skin. I guarantee it."

"In other words, another day will break and everything will dawn fresh and new. Yeah. That's nice." Aria turned to him. "When did you become so optimistic?"

"It's about reality, not optimism. Bad stuff happens. It's how you rise from it, and move your life forward." He stroked her hair. "None of us blame you, Aria. Love yourself, the way we love you."

She nodded. "I'll try." A smile lifted the corners of her mouth. "I might need you to remind me...about that 'loving' part."

He grinned. "I can do that. A husband's pleasure, indeed."

She ran her hands over his body. "Can I tell you...I

thought I dreamed you? I lay in our bedroom, listening to the police, and I thought it was all my imagination taking that horrible situation and turning it into something my brain could handle." She laid her head on his chest.

"Aria, I'm so sorry. It shouldn't have happened that way. I wish I could have done something more...sent you away, stashed you in a hotel. Something."

"No, you were right. He would have found me eventually. He wasn't ready to let go." She lifted her head a little higher, and there was a gleam in her eye. "We're alive, Dan, and it's because of you. You make us stronger, make us feel empowered." She shook her head. "I know we have more to learn, but I don't know what we would have done if I hadn't trusted you." She stood on her tiptoes and kissed him, and her passion called to him.

He picked her up, crossed the lawn and patio, and carried her inside the house. Laying her down on the couch, he pressed his body on hers. "Let's make a happy memory here. Retake our hill...at the very least, our yard."

Exhausted laughter bubbled out of her.

"Look me in the eyes. See only me. Never take your gaze or heart from what we are experiencing. This room, this house, our world, will be ours again. Let's go to our bedroom and make love."

Nodding her head, she put her hand on his heart. He scooped her up and took her to their haven. Laying her down on their bed, he relished the sight of her.

Gently, carefully, he helped her take off her clothes... and then undressed himself.

This was the moment he needed, and he imagined she needed, too. Then he ran his tongue down her body, kissing her, caressing her, tasting her until she reached up for him…pulling him toward her. Laying himself on top of her, he sunk slowly into her silky depths.

"Dan," she sighed. "My love."

His body pulsed with need, but he couldn't rush. He needed to satisfy her, bring her again and again until her body was spent. Sliding his hand between them, he found her favorite sweet spot and rubbed tiny circles, listening to her soft moans and breathy sighs.

"More," she said as he slid inside her. "More." And her body squeezed and convulsed, begging him to come…to spend his seed inside of her.

When he could take it no longer, he came. "I love you so much."

Reaching behind him, he grabbed the blanket off the foot of the bed and laid it over them.

"Aria?"

She mumbled his name and then drifted off to sleep.

They had done it, retaken a small piece of their home and their sanity. Step-by-step they would conquer their world again. He wasn't going anywhere until it was all theirs again.

Lying there with his wife in his arms and Jimmy safe in his bed, he let himself sigh. This was his world to protect and honor. Strange how he had traveled halfway around the world to fight, when an enemy lurked so close to home. He was glad the Op had gone well; all of them had survived. But never again would he leave his family in such a bad position. A team was only as strong as its members, and he wanted to make sure that his teammates, the ones in this house, were more than "good to go." There was a reason the Navy protected its families, and there was a reason its soldiers and sailors protected this great nation—because we need each other to make the world a safe place.

Chapter 20

THE NEXT DAY THEY LEARNED JC'S WIFE JEN WAS still in the hospital after some complications from her pregnancy. On the plus side, one of the surprises had included a baby sister tucked behind the twin boys. Little Jessica was only four pounds and was being kept in the newborn-intensive-care unit until she gained more weight. Her brothers, Jonas and Jason, were six pounds each, and when Aria spoke to Jen on the phone, Jen said, "I feel like I've given birth to a litter. Is it any wonder I was as big as a house? I can't wait to see you!"

After a little shopping at the Navy Exchange, Aria and Dan brought by a basket of items for Jen, including a huge box of outfits for an infant baby girl. JC hovered over his wife as if she were a fragile flower, and Jen seemed to love every second of it.

They tiptoed over to the boys' bassinets and peeked in. "So tiny," said Dan, waving at the Casey boys. "I'm your Uncle Dan, and this is Aunt Aria."

"What do you think? Do you want one?" Aria cocked an eyebrow at Dan.

"Only one? I was thinking three." His grin was adorable and infectious.

Aria sighed melodramatically. "Only if they come out of your uterus." She winked at him, and he hugged her.

"Let's see how it goes." He kissed the top of her

head. "We'll put it in someone else's hands, how many we have…"

"For now. But I reserve the right to say stop!" she said, looking up at him and kissing his lips.

"Don't do it," said Jen. "This is how I got into this position. In vitro, my ass."

"Shush… You'll wake the babies." JC warned his wife.

"Really? I just gave birth, and you're actually going to tell me to be quiet," Jen teased. "Fine. I'll be quiet. Just so you know, they're all yours, sweetheart! I'm not allowed to lift anything for two weeks." She grinned at them over JC's head and closed her eyes. She'd secretly told Aria it was one week, but she wasn't letting on to JC, and the doctor agreed. How many times in a woman's life did her husband totally dote on her and help out? If she was lucky, many times. If she was a military spouse, probably not very often. Usually there was nagging involved.

"Bye," said Aria with a small wave to the darling boys and another in Jen's direction. She looked forward to spending more time with her.

"You can take on an army," said Dan to JC, giving him an encouraging pat on the back.

"I need a bigger Team," said JC with a semi-panicked look in his eyes. "Maybe if we pull both platoons, we can…"

"I'm here anytime you need me."

JC shook his head. "Oh, man. Diaper changes."

"Uh, we've got to go." Dan pointed at the door, and Aria was in agreement. They'd already waded through their own shit storm, and they didn't need to borrow trouble from someone else.

Together they left…walking through the corridors of the hospital hand in hand.

—⁓—

That night a party was in full swing at the McCullum house. Half of Bravo was squished into their house and backyard, including Hammer, Zankin, LT, Dirks, Thomas, Brock, Duckie, Ox, and their families, as well as the rest of the wives group whose husbands were away. The Teams didn't discriminate—they were all one and on the same footing.

Kids of all ages were everywhere, and the minute someone cried, he or she was picked up, tickled, and/or passed around until the child was laughing again. The Team was family.

Aria knew that she still had a long road to go to recover from Mark's betrayal. She was not looking forward to the trial. But right now, she'd never felt safer. Her house was more of a home than she realized it could be…welcoming, easy, and open. No demons remained. The specters were stomped out en masse by SEAL Team THREE, Platoon 1-Bravo.

"How are you doing?" asked Dan as he placed another tray of vegetables and dip on the patio table. Food was stuffed onto every surface, and a keg was sweating next to the fence. Everyone seemed to be having a great time. "Overwhelmed?"

"No," said Aria, and it was true. "It feels like real life…being married and having a home together. Until this moment, life was surreal and it was too hard to enjoy the positive side. Now all of this seems good… organic and natural."

He nodded.

Aria beamed. These men and women, whom she hadn't even known three months ago, had brought her into their lives and saved her sanity through the chaos. She was making peace with her experiences. With them there were no trust issues, worries, or concerns…only an easy feeling that she didn't have to be anything other than what she already was.

Dan put his arm around her. Her husband…what a phenomenal man!

She automatically secured her arm to his waist. Yes, she told herself. She got it! She finally understood a small part of what it meant to be part of a team. It translated to never being alone—even when you felt lonely—and there was always someone to call. The ability to be strong and capable came from your belief in self and watching out for each other…and that love was the strongest gift of all.

Leaning over, she pulled down the back of Ox's T-shirt. Francis looked around her giant husband as Aria read it: "As the U.S. Navy SEALs would say, 'Ready to lead, ready to follow, never quit.'"

"True words," said Dan, noticing his wife's action, and he hauled her gently into his arms.

"Aye, aye, Chief," said Aria as she turned into her husband's embrace. "An excellent saying."

"In the Navy…'Outstanding' is the highest praise." He dipped her for a very dramatic kiss. "You, Mrs. McCullum, are truly outstanding, and I can never seem to get enough of you."

Several people laughed.

Declan, Harvey, Hayes, and Miller said, "Hooyah!"

With these wonderful souls surrounding her, it made Aria feel as if it were her wedding day all over again.

"Me, either," replied Aria as she kissed him again, not caring who was watching. "Life is remarkable. Hooyah!"

Author's Note

I am the wife of a U.S. Navy SEAL (ret.). I wrote this book and the previous one to share some of the more complicated elements of personal life and relationships within the Teams. Being a spouse, whether military or not, is never an easy journey, but it can be a very precious experience…and one of the most rewarding in the world. Thus, I write SEAL romance novels to honor my husband, our friends and families, and our community.

Please note that I attended Stonehearth Open Learning Opportunities (SOLO) for my wilderness rescue EMT certification, and I volunteered for a rescue squad in Manchester, Vermont, for a time—this is true. But my romance stories are fictional. Reality is woven into the tapestry of my books, because many aspects of this journey are very "U.S. Navy SEAL," and they had to be in there.

I am grateful to those individuals who contributed thoughts, read for me, or answered last-minute questions to verify that I was constructing the story and details correctly. Writing is a path of discovery, and there is always more to learn and more to know. If any errors are discovered, they are mine, and unintentional, as I have written the most thoughtful journey I could.

I am often asked what it is like to be married to a SEAL. In my opinion, it is exciting, humbling, soul touching, and filled with complexities and simplicities that can blow one's mind. Every birth is an outstanding celebration, and every funeral, whether the individual is known intimately or is a distant fallen son or brother, rips our hearts out. Fallen Teammates are embraced and loved for their sacrifice and courage, and those individual sparks are a tragic and horrific loss to the community.

Like the rest of the planet, we are disheartened by age and illnesses that sneak up on those we cherish, and it takes away pieces of our favorite people and family one memory at a time or swallows them in one gulp. The unique spirits of these amazing souls stick with us, and we carry them through our day, month, year, and into the future. We see their smiles in their children and grandchildren, and we laugh about how they would react to something or toast them with a beer. We hold each other, remembering to laugh a lot, to seek fun, and to live with newness like a child's wonder, even when we feel gloomy.

As spouses, when we fight, we make up quickly and easily, especially after misunderstandings, because we're determined to honor our friends by appreciating and celebrating life. Day in and day out, there is always something new on the horizon, yet there are parts of our world that are steadfast—our love and respect for each other and well-wishes for those who fight on.

To me, the best part of marriage is being with my extraordinary man, who chose me to accompany him on this path. My husband makes me feel so well loved as he teases the hell out of me, which I am learning to enjoy but would never tell him, and at the same time is right by my side for every difficult challenge. Being retired, our lives are different than active-duty ones; active duty wives handle a lot more on their own. Yet there are similarities: the missions stay with my husband, and thus with me; PTSD and injuries are unfortunately often part of the combat-related time in the Teams; Teammates make up a large part of our family, and we both remember daily those who died.

What advice would I give those in relationships? Marry your best friend! Don't settle for less. Pick a person who can go toe-to-toe with you, challenge you to be better, and will never quit. There are a lot of paths, some up and some down, but the true winners of the game of life are the ones who live boldly, give generously, and celebrate every day as if it is their last. If you're only as strong as your partner then you both need to be fierce. Remember strength comes from the spirit and a willingness to be courageous, loyal, and determined.

Live life boldly! Dream every dream bigger than the last. And remember, though there is always someone out there to criticize, tease, or remind you of your shortcomings, the fact you stepped up to the experience of living means they can all kiss your ass. Enjoy!

Hooyah & hugs! ~AE

Hannah's Heartfelt Macaroni & Cheese

1 pound of elbow macaroni (or your favorite pasta, keeping in mind that angles allow it to grab the cheese better)
2 cups of milk
3 tablespoons of butter or margarine
A dash of ground pepper and sea salt
¼ teaspoon of parsley
1½ cups of grated cheddar (mild)
1½ cups of grated Gouda or Swiss
8 ounces of cream cheese or Velveeta

Optional:
1 cup of ham or bacon
¼ cup of scallions

1. Boil water in a pan and cook the elbow macaroni until it's tender. Drain the water out using a strainer. Add in the milk, butter, and cheese and place the mixture over a medium-to-low stovetop setting, stirring constantly so it does not burn. When the items are melted and evenly spread, add in the ground pepper and sea salt. If you decide to add in the optional items, do this now. Mix well.
2. Heat the oven to 350 degrees.
3. Butter an oven-safe pan. Pour the mixture into it.

Cook in the oven for 20 to 30 minutes, depending on the oven, or until the top has a nice golden-brown appearance and the edges have pulled away from the sides of the pan.

…and that's the way Hammer likes it!

Aria's Homemade Chocolate-Chip Cookies

Dry Ingredients:
¾ cup of flour
A dash of salt
¼ teaspoon of baking soda
⅓ cup of brown sugar
¼ cup of granulated sugar

Cold Ingredients:
1 large egg
1 teaspoon of vanilla extract
6 tablespoons of margarine or butter (at room temperature)

Add these ingredients last:
1 cup of oats
½ cup of semisweet chocolate or dark-chocolate chips
½ cup of white-chocolate chips

Optional:
¼ cup of crushed pecans (almonds or walnuts are good, too!)

1. Mix the dry ingredients together, and then add in the cold ingredients. Stir with a large spoon until the mixture is doughlike and all one color.
2. Then add in the oats and chocolate, as well as the

optional nuts. Make sure these items are well distributed throughout the dough.

3. Heat the oven to 375 degrees.
4. Place a teaspoon-shaped ball of dough on a greased cookie sheet, leaving room for its neighborhood to grow. Then place in the oven for 10 to 12 minutes, depending on your oven and your altitude. (Those individuals who live above a 4,000' elevation need to add an extra egg.)

Enjoy Jimmy's favorite treat!

Anne Elizabeth has been making these recipes for years.

**Read on for an excerpt from *A SEAL at Heart*
by Anne Elizabeth, the sizzling debut in a series
that shows the personal side of a hero's life…**

If you're not gonna pull the trigger, don't point the gun.
—James Baker

*Operation Sundial, at an undisclosed location deep
in the jungle*

BLOOD DRIPPED DOWN HIS FOREHEAD AND BLURRED HIS
vision. Wiping it away, Jack forced his eyes to focus. He
squinted, but it was useless.

The helicopter downwash whirled mud and dirt into
the air faster than he could blink, and the clouds of grit
stuck to his face. Nothing shielded him from the suf-
focating pelting of the brownout, making him blind as
hell without his protective glasses.

Gathering the five-foot-ten-inch form of his swim
buddy Don into his arms, he duckwalked as low as
he could, heading toward the belly of the helicopter.
Luckily the rain had stopped momentarily as the rotor
blades cut the air, but it made the moment more surreal.

Whup, whup, whup…

He blew air out of his mouth. His nostrils were caked
with grime, but he could still smell the blood seeping
from the bandages he'd fastened around Don's chest. He
squeezed his swim buddy tightly, trying to keep pressure
on the wound.

A stray bullet ricocheted, displacing the air near his face. Where the hell did that shot come from? The helicopter was *so* goddamned loud.

The door of the copter jerked open; the blessed haven was dead ahead. The two door gunners laid down suppressor fire, but it was short-lived aid as enemy bullets took them down. They fell back just within the side door of the helo.

"God help us," Jack muttered under his breath as he finally reached the opening. The men in front of him were practically cut in two by the rounds. There wasn't time to think about them or their families now. With a mighty heave, he lifted his buddy onto the helicopter floor and scrambled in after him.

Coughing the crap out of his lungs, he dragged Don over to the far wall, away from the doorway, and stood up to scan the interior. It took him a minute to take in the carnage. He tried to wipe the image from his eyes as his mind put the gory pieces together. The pilots were shredded. *Damn*.

Making his way to the cockpit, he could see that the glass dome had been compromised and the entire enclosure looked pretty chewed up. "Please let this thing fly." The blades were still turning, so that was a good sign, and neither the cyclic nor collective were hit. But would it be enough to get them out of this hellhole?

He touched his throat to activate the comm mike. It didn't respond. He spoke softly, trying again, "Whiskey. Tango. Foxtrot." *What the fuck!*

Where the hell is everyone?

The rain was starting again, angling into the copter and hitting his face.

Another series of blinding flashes—hard to tell if it

was lightning or shots—from outside, but it forced him to move Don, to stash him deeper in the belly of the copter, and momentarily duck for cover.

Pwing! The bullet bounced off metal.

He was pretty sure it was only a small number of insurgents and one sniper firing wildly. Random shots in the dark. Problem was, even a broken clock was right twice a day, and the dead airmen were horrific evidence of the sniper's success.

A volley of shots. A few rebels cross-fired at one another, sending shouts of anger into the air. *Go to it. Maybe you'll hit each other.*

The only good news was that if he couldn't see them, they couldn't target him directly either.

There was no point in sitting tight. He needed to find his Team. After securing Don and rigging a piece of equipment to hold pressure on his swim buddy's wound, Jack went back to the open door. A glimpse of rag-covered muddy boots to the right let him know that an enemy was approaching. Moving quickly into the disrupted cloud of crud, he positioned himself so his vantage point was optimal.

Two Tangos dressed in frayed pants held Russian 9mms at the ready. Instinctually, Jack withdrew his Sig Sauer, took a breath, and squeezed off several rounds. They dropped instantly.

He checked their pulses. Dead. Now, where were the others? *Here, birdie, birdie, birdie…*

Working his way quickly out of the cloud of dust, he knew he would be vulnerable, but this was his best option. He had to know what was going on. This mission had gone sideways long ago.

Coming up behind a rebel who was caught up in dislodging a jammed gun, Jack holstered his own weapon and, using bare hands, silently broke the enemy's neck. Slowly, he worked his way around the perimeter of the helo. For now, it was clear.

Lightning split the sky, bathing the area better than a floodlight. It was the vantage point he sought.

A noise caught his attention as a door from the factory flew open, banging against the siding. That was them—his Teammates—sprinting from the interior as flames engulfed the structure. They were coughing and several of them appeared to have minor injuries. Jack held his ground, preparing to lay down cover fire, if required. His eyes were desperately searching for a subversive threat, when an explosion lifted him from his feet and threw him to the ground.

Bam!

Thrown backward from the blast, the back of his head smacked something hard. Black spots danced in front of his eyes and bile scored the back of his throat. Swallowing the harsh rush of acid, he lifted his hand—gun gripped tightly in his fingers—trying to focus on the enemy that should have been coming over the large boulders a few feet in front of him.

Nothing. No one.

The smell of C-4, with its acrid ether odor, filled his nostrils even as thunder shook the sky and rain barreled down.

A sharp burning sensation seared the back of his skull, going from ten on the pain scale to numb within seconds. Another wave of nausea made his stomach roll and quake as he deliberately forced his way to his knees and then his feet.

The clock is ticking. Fighting the dark spots, he stood wavering for a few seconds before his sight returned to normal and he could search for them… The enemy: His buddies. Or any signs of life.

His eyes widened.

Giant pieces of seared, cloth-covered flesh were scattered over the ground. It didn't compute at first. Those were his buddies, Teammates from SEAL Team ONE, Platoon 1-Alfa, and only a few of them were moving.

Jack was instantly in motion. Grabbing the body closest to him, he felt for a pulse. The steady thump sent a surge of adrenaline through his system. He gathered the man to his chest, trying to keep his hands on his buddy as he dragged him toward the helicopter. The path was wet with blood and mud, and repeating the task several times, he slipped in the sludge as he loaded the bodies closest to him on board.

Only one Teammate, Gerry Knotts, was left and remained exposed. Jack would be a moving target—a perfect bull's-eye—for the enemy's shoot-'em-up game if he attempted it.

Eyes sought his. His Teammate was alive and signaling him. Jack understood and moved to a rock as far from Knotts as possible. Lifting his 9mm, Jack fired several shots. Bullets peppered around the rock as he quickly belly-crawled back to his original position.

Knotts fired several shots, nailing the Tangos.

Moving up into a dead run, Jack reached Gerry's side and then helped him stand. Together they rushed into the cloud of dirt and grunge, going for the helo.

They left long streaks of mud along the deck as they rolled inside.

Jack checked…seven men loaded, and he was lucky number eight. His life meant nothing without them.

Finally able to close and secure the door, Jack shoved debris aside until it was easier to move around the cockpit. Quickly moving the pilot's body to properly reach the controls, he straddled the chair and checked the instrument panel.

He held his breath, watching the RPM gauges of the turbine and rotor. The helo hovered. The controls required constant small changes to keep the bird in the air. Sweat dripped off his face. "Come on, baby. That's it! Into the storm.

"Now, let's get the hell out of here." As the helo responded, he sighed with relief. He'd only piloted helicopters a couple of times—all his experience was in fixed-wing aircraft—and he was hoping his brief lessons would be enough to get them back to the rendezvous point.

He had to hand it to her—this bird flew, even all shot up. Just as he was beginning to feel okay about the flight, he noticed black spots at the edge of his vision. With the back of his thumb, he rubbed one eye. Nothing prepared him for his sight going, leaving only one eye functioning.

He squinted at the instruments. The radio was blown and there was no luxury of an autopilot. Keeping a helo in the air was a constant struggle against the torque, the wind, and the pilot's ability. "Come on, Jack. Concentrate!"

Wind buffeted his face courtesy of the bullet-shattered windshield. The smell of ozone was heavy and ripe. He hoped the lightning was over.

Wetness dripped down the back of his neck. He

wiped a hand against the warmth, and it came away with fresh blood. His.

Fuck, fuck, fuck!

Looking over his shoulder, he saw the bodies of his Teammates. He didn't know if they were alive or dead. But he could never let them down. He'd get them all to safety—make them secure—even if it was the last thing he ever did.

———

Coronado, California

No other place on the planet was like McP's Pub in October—the seagulls circling and crying overhead, and the women just as raucous. He took a long pull on his beer.

"Welcome home, Jack," said Betsy. The friendly blond waitress with a wide, pearly white smile and a set of 44Ds grinned knowingly at him as she walked by. Hers was the kind of walk that had her hips swinging, and her tight apron full of change played a musical medley to the movement of her sexy saunter.

Some women can move like their hips are on springs.

For those around him—the suntan worshippers—almost any hot spot on the planet would probably suffice. But for Jack, this tiny island town between Glorietta Bay and the Pacific Ocean was uniquely qualified to be his home. Having been assigned to SEAL Team ONE and with an apartment only ten blocks away from the Amphib base, Jack thought this was a snapshot of perfection.

He scratched at the gooey tape mark behind his

ear. The bandage around his head was gone and he was no longer hooked to IVs or being pumped full of fluids and painkillers, but he wished there were an antibiotic or balm for the one place he hurt the most, his soul.

At Balboa Naval Hospital, the medical staff had told him his number one job was to relax until he was fully healed and had his memory back. There were too many holes, too many memories missing from the last Op. The worst part was... his best friend was dead.

Jack couldn't reconcile it and didn't know how to fix the situation.

The rub was... if he didn't take care of himself, fix the recollection issue, he'd be stuck with the label "acute psychological suppression"—forever. That didn't bode well for him.

Do the familiar. Take it easy. Those were the orders from the medical staff.

With those directions rattling around his brain, it meant finding a place to unwind where he could feel the sun's raw heat on his skin, taste the tang of salt on his lips, and have a cold brew sweating in his hand as he savored each sip. Well, maybe not the alcohol part, but everyone had a vice and his was simple: fresh air, exercise, and a bit of the barley.

Ah, beer! The first sip was always sweetest.

At first, being back in Coronado had been difficult. The layers of emotion had punched him in the gut practically every few minutes. Drink in hand, his mind had started to go numb, turn off, and he went whole hog for the break. McP's was the perfect place to just... be. Where men and women interacted, doing a dance as primal and ancient as time itself to attract each other. As the action unfolded in front of him, he saw a few younger brethren had scored, snapping up the curvy and very willing quarry to set off for more serious play somewhere else. Nature's fundamental dance never ceased to intrigue him, though he wasn't looking.

Listening to the slap of the waitresses' tennis shoes against the slate wasn't quite as sexy as the click of a stiletto, but he couldn't complain. Most of them were paragons, Madonnas—look but don't touch—because they were SEAL wives or friends.

A loaded hamburger with a crisp green salad was placed in front of him. Steam rose from the burger and his nostrils flared. Of course, *this* tasty morsel he would be willing to sink his teeth into anytime.

"Just the way you like it, and on the house," said Jules with a wink, another one of McP's waitressing angels. "'In Xanadu did Kubla Khan, a stately pleasure-dome decree…'"

"'Where Alph, the sacred river, ran through caverns measureless to man down to a sunless sea…'" The reference from "Kubla Khan; or, A Vision in a Dream," by Samuel Taylor Coleridge, was a favorite of his and McP's was a home of sorts, his own pleasure-dome. A framed copy of the eighteenth-century poem sat on his nightstand, a birthday gift from Jules and all of the waitstaff at McP's. Even now he could recite each and every line verbatim. His own life was like that poem, a journey, and very much unfinished. He wanted that chance… to explore.

"Thanks, Jules." Jack grinned, unusually grateful for

the human connection. He shifted uncomfortably on the chair. Maybe the incident overseas had shaken him more than he realized. "Hey, how did you know exactly what I wanted?"

Her smile was sweet. "The same way I've known for years that you'd rather drink your calories than eat them. Enjoy lunch, Jack. You're looking skinny." She leaned down and kissed him gently on the cheek.

"Thanks." Part of him wanted to add a sentimental comment about her being a sweetheart or maybe ask about her husband, who was in Team FIVE and probably deployed, but being sappy wasn't his thing. Life was easier with the walls up.

"Don't forget to eat your vegetables." She gave him a big smile before she went back to attending her other customers. Did she know how her aura of bubbling beauty affected men? Probably not.

Releasing the grip on his beer bottle, he placed it on the table and then attacked the salad. It was significantly better than hospital food and MREs. Hooking his fork into the meat, he pulled it out from between the buns. As a SEAL, he was always in training, and he would rather carbo-load with a brew and burn it off running. He wrapped the burger in lettuce and took a bite. The meat was savory and juicy, filling him with welcome satisfaction.

News droned in the background until someone had the good sense to flip on a ball game. There was something peaceful about that… as if it were Saturday and he was a kid again.

Methodically, he ate until the burger and salad were gone. The french fries sat untouched next to the bun halves and a very sad-looking pickle. He lifted his brew, and his lips drew tight, pulling the cold liquid down his throat.

He'd been in the Teams for eight years, and being a SEAL was the basic foundation of his soul. Another enlisted man might state that the military was important, but to Jack it was everything. If he couldn't deploy anymore… well, the concept was too harsh to even contemplate.

His eyes searched, looking for a distraction from his musings. For several seconds his gaze stopped on a large, agile man until his inner gauge dismissed him as a nonthreat. Ever vigilant, there was always a part of him searching for trouble and ready to respond.

At the next table, a dog happily lapped water from his complimentary "pup" bowl. A man in his fifties, probably the owner or an overindulgent dog walker, dropped parts of a hamburger into the water and the dog went crazy—busily fishing pieces out and then chomping, chewing, and swallowing the tasty morsels down as if no one had ever fed him.

Life must be so much easier as a dog. Someone is there to make the meals, walk side-by-side, play, and run. Was that what he wanted? Did he want someone feminine, curvy, and sweet to be there, too?

He'd be better off with a dog. With his schedule he didn't know if either was a realistic wish. His ideal state was being deployed, which didn't leave much time for a home life.

Gripping the cold bottle of beer like a lifeline, he lifted it to his mouth and drank deeply. *God, that tastes good! And it's predictable. Every swallow is the same.*

Off to the side, he could hear the faint buzz of cars

and trucks as they sped down Orange Avenue, confirming that everything was in sync here, normal. That was reassuring to a degree, witnessing the commonplace; this is what "everyday" was supposed to resemble. Calm. Steady. Regular.

Why isn't that me? His mind and body couldn't slow down. Closing his eyes, he forced himself to let this familiar place and a beer soothe him. At least he hoped it would. McP's was a special home for his kind. Owned by one of his brethren, there was Navy SEAL memorabilia on the walls, a trident on the T-shirts, and oftentimes the bar would fill with sightseers and froghogs—women who hopped from frog to frog. In the Underwater Demolition Team, or UDT—the precursor to the SEAL Team—these Navy sailors were called frogmen. Later on, the name was changed to better show their areas of operation: SEAL—SEa Air Land—but the age-old name for the women who pursued them never got updated.

Half his Teammates were in committed relationships, and the rest dicked around almost constantly. Lately, his celibacy walk had turned into a preference. It had begun as a way to concentrate on work, and now...

Maybe he just didn't have what it took—a crap tolerance—to be in a relationship.

The back of his head exploded with a sudden and sharp pain. His hand lifted automatically, rubbing over the healing wound and stubbly blond hair.

"Red Jack!" His eyes whipped open, and for a second, he could have sworn that he'd heard Don. That was impossible. His swim buddy was dead, and there was nothing that could bring him back.

Pain squeezed his neck. His vision blurred and for a moment an image of his friend flashed before his eyes.

The rush of emotions for his swim buddy was the kind of tidal wave that could take out a city, and equally as devastating as it crashed over him again and again. He'd have done anything to have Petty Officer Second Class Donald Dennis Kanoa Donnelly alive and well. Sorrow punched his heart, but he'd never show it, especially not in public.

His phone vibrated. Jack had the cell in his hand before he remembered he was supposed to be on vacation—no one would be calling him for sudden deployment.

Punching a button, he accessed the email. Appointments had been scheduled for him: group therapy and individual sessions. *Can't this Frankenstein wannabe leave me alone? I don't need a doctor.*

He just needed to keep it together long enough to go operational again. Being on medical leave was like swallowing two-inch nails whole: it hurt the entire way down and out. He had way too much time on his hands to think. He needed action.

"Petty Officer First Class John Matthew Roaker."

His name was a command that had Jack sitting up straight in his chair. Any other service would have a guy standing at attention before the rank and name had been completely spoken. Spec Ops was different, more laid-back.

"Taking a trip down memory lane?" commented a gruff man with salt-and-pepper hair and a long bushy mustache. His sideburns were like hairy caterpillars perched on the side of his face. The man took a step closer to Jack and grinned. A fat cigar was clamped

between his lips and his voice had lost the hard edge
and was warming progressively. "Shit, you look like a
newbie jarhead, Jack! We're going to have to mess you
up a bit! So you look like a fucking SEAL."

"Good to see you, Commander," replied Jack, already
proffering his hand to greet his former BUD/S Instructor,
now mentor. With a grin on his lips that spoke volumes
of the man's capacity for jocularity, Commander Gich
didn't appear to be the kind of guy who could teach you
fifty different ways to kill with a knife.

His gaze connected with the Commander's. Jack took
comfort in the stare. Emotion hung like a bad painting
just behind his own eyeballs, but he pushed past the
weight of it. "Sir, it's great to see you."

Jack stood and the men embraced, slapping hands
on each other's backs in heavy smacks and then briskly
separating. There was a tremendous sense of the famil-
ial. Jack needed that right now.

"You too!" said the Commander. "How's the
brain? Is it still swelling? I can think of better things
to make swell."

"Christ! They're not sure. You know docs. Though,
I'm pretty sure the fracture's better." Jack reseated
himself, eager to change the subject. "I was thinking about my first drink here, and then there was the
Hell Week celebration, when you and I drank until
the kitchen opened for the early birds' lunch the next
morning." He could practically taste the stale alcohol.
Bile threatened to rise, but he shoved it down. Yep,
that memory was definitely intact! Why couldn't he
have lost that day, instead of the events from the last
Op? He needed those memories.

"No shit! You were so hungover from those shots that you puked your guts out in the back of my car." Gich signaled the waitress for a beer. "Still doesn't smell right. But it's easy to find Blue Betty in the dark." His grin could have lit up the darkest depths. "So, how's it going, Jack? What's with the shrink-wrap therapy? I may be retired, but I'm still in the loop."

Shaking his head, Jack said, "I don't know. It's been…" He searched his mind for the word, but he couldn't even find that. Who really wanted to know the inner workings of a SEAL? They might not like what they find in there, and then what? SEALs had more layers than an artichoke.

"Hard, complicated, and disillusioning to come back from a mission that's seriously goat-fucked. You're not the first, Roaker, and unfortunately, you won't be the last. Just don't become a poster boy, it's not your gig."

"Yeah, me a poster boy! Could you see me in Ronald McDonald hair?" cracked Jack without missing a beat. It felt good to have someone giving him shit. Everyone had been so "nice" to him lately that it creeped him out. "Sure I can pull off the look, but all those hands to shake, personal appearances, and then there goes your private life."

"Wiseass!" A shapely blond waitress who could easily be a modern-day Marilyn Monroe placed an icy beer in front of Gich. "Thanks, Betsy. I knew you'd remember how I liked it."

"Anything for you, Gich." She winked at him and headed back inside. The bar was pretty empty for a Tuesday afternoon, but it'd pick up tonight and be packed with military personnel on the hunt for hook-ups and single ladies on the quest for the golden ring. That was old hat for him, and he'd rather work out, clean his guns, anything…

"I can make a few recommendations. There are a couple of medical professionals who use unconventional methods. Alternative healing… it might help." Gich looked at him over the top of his beer as he drank. "The person I'm thinking of does acupressure. Did wonders for my knees and lower back."

"Doctors aren't my preference." Jack contemplated getting a pain pill out of his pocket, but he knew it'd be a dicey mix with the alcohol. He preferred to drink, so he left it in his pocket and took another sip.

"Roaker, you can talk to me," said Gich, drawing on his cigar and puffing out a long thin stream of smoke.

Jack sat silently, briefly weighing his thoughts before he shared them. "Six weeks ago when I left here, I was ready for the mission. Even though there were a couple strikes against it. First, Tucker kept getting changing Intel on the location and how it was laid out. Second, the resources seemed underkill for a plan of this magnitude, and whenever I brought it up, they told me to add as much as we needed. So I did, but it never felt like enough. Third, when we got there, nothing was as discussed; the place was a ghost town outside with only a few people inside. Either the information was terrible, or—"

"You were being set up. Seems unlikely, in the Teams," said Gich, softly leaning forward. "What happened next?"

Jack shook his head. "I don't know. I don't remember.

I can see my feet hitting the dirt and watching everyone take position, and then... nothing."

Gich took the cigar from his mouth. "Did you see Don die?"

"I must have..." Pain ripped through his heart as he pushed hard to make it go away. "But I don't remember any of it. What the hell am I supposed to do? I'm beached like a whale until I can remember, and it's ripping me apart to be this still. I need help."

"You need to get out, have some fun. Don't think. Just react and let go of everything." Gich surveyed him with a critical eye before turning his gaze back to watch the shapely blond go through her routine of serving drinks and taking orders. "The watched pot never boils, or in our case, the undrunk beer only gets warm and flat."

Jack gave a half smile. "I'm not really in the mood for socializing."

"Come on, you'd have to be dead not to appreciate that," Gich said, motioning toward the waitress.

He had to admit the bending and reaching of the busty waitress was rather compelling, but he had more important stuff on his mind and couldn't even consider flirting right now. Shifting in his chair, he found a more comfortable position and said, "What I want to know is how do I... get my warrior mentality back?"

Those words captured Gich's attention as his eyes locked on Jack's. The lesson of finding his equilibrium and balance had been the hardest trick for Jack to learn. Gich had worked doubly hard with him on that one. They'd developed all sorts of techniques to help him out, but right now, Jack felt like his skin was crawling off his body and he had to nail himself to a chair to keep still. Did other SEALs feel like an alien in a human body?

With a deliberate and slow movement, Gich brought his hand up and rested it gently on Jack's arm. But no matter how slowly he'd moved, Jack still flinched and had an urge to pull away. Forcing himself to be still took some concentration.

"Give it time. PTSD happens. Ride it out." Gich leaned forward and whispered, "And while you're waiting, go get your whiskers wet and your dick licked. You're a fucking hero; you should take advantage of it." He pulled back his hand, grabbed the neck of his beer, and chugged it down. When it was empty, he waved it in the air. "Tonight, Dick's Last Resort. There are all sorts of SEAL fans there. I'm sure the Naval Special Warfare fund-raiser crowd would benefit from laying eyeballs on you, too. Why not go get your pick of the, uh, ladies? Tour some sweet spots and give your brain some time off."

The idea of being surrounded by that many people made Jack's stomach clench, but he knew Gich was right. He had to get back out there. Going from the Op to the hospital, and now home, had not afforded him the opportunity to decompress, let alone figure out how to socialize with anyone of the fairer sex.

Maybe getting hot and heavy would help. He could love 'em and leave 'em as easily as the rest of them, though it seriously had been a while. Love just wasn't a priority the majority of the time, though sex was almost always welcome.

Acknowledgments

With great thanks to:

My brilliant and loving husband—retired Navy SEAL, EOD, and PRU Advisor—LT Carl E. Swepston; Retired Navy SEAL and EOD LT Commander Thomas C. Rancich, an exceptional soul who answered a ton of questions and provided a great deal of insight, and his amazing Liz; to "O" GOATROPER, John T. Curtis and his Miranda; Retired Navy SEAL LT Jerry Todd—thanks for the HALO help and laughter—and his amazing wife, Pete; former Navy SEAL Dan Peterson, for his humor and inspiration; and much gratitude to the Vietnam-era "Old Frogs and SEALs," who contributed comments and stories; and a shout-out to all of our operational friends—thank you!

To Christine Feehan, thank you for being such an outstanding inspiration and joy. You bring a special gift to our industry and have inspired me greatly.

To Cathy Maxwell, thank you for being so awesome. Faith is the key.

To DC and Charles DeVane—You rock!

Cheers to my friends: Laurie DeSalvo aka Lia DeAngela; Jan Albertie; Alisa Kwitney; Kim Adams Lowe; Christina Skye; Leslie Wainger; Domini Walker; Brian Feehan; Sheila Clover English; Ed English; Barbara Vey; Dianna Love; Denise Coyle; Cathy Mann; Angela Knight; Renee Bernard; Megan Bamford; Mary

Beth Bass; the RWA CoLoNY, RWA-NYC, and RWA-SD chapters; Sam and Diego and Zavier; Maria R., Maria. M., Gini, Maria N., Joao, Frank, and Emanuel; Kim and Paul K.; Jill and Carl H.; Brenda S.S., Mary H., Nonny, Anne M., Kathryn, Erika, Simone, Stephanie H., Ing C., Rose S., Ginger D., Laura L., Cindy, Lynn, Kat, Robyn, Mic, and the entire BB crew; Kathryn Falk, Carol Stacy, Kenneth Rubin, Liz French, Mala Bhattacharjee, Jo Carol Jones, and the *RT Book Reviews* and RT Book Lovers crew.

And to my terrific agent, Eric Ruben.

Thank you to my superhero editor, Leah Hultenschmidt.

To the Sourcebooks team—Kimberly, Beth, Cat, Susie, Skye, and Danielle—and to the fabulous Deb Werksman and amazing Dominique Raccah.

With infinite love and respect to my parents—always!

SEALed with a Ring

by Mary Margret Daughtridge

She's got it all… except the one thing she needs most

Smart, successful businesswoman JJ Caruthers has a year to land a husband or lose the empire she's worked so hard to build. With time running out, romance is not an option, and a military husband who is always on the road begins to look like the perfect solution…

He's a wounded hero with an agenda of his own

Even with the scars of battle, Navy SEAL medic Davy Graziano is gorgeous enough to land any woman he wants, and he's never wanted to be tied down. Now Davy has ulterior motives for accepting JJ's outrageous proposal of marriage, but he only has so long to figure out what JJ doesn't want him to know…

For more Mary Margret Daughtridge, visit:

www.sourcebooks.com

SEALed Forever

by Mary Margret Daughtridge

—⁓—

He's got a living, breathing dilemma...

In the midst of running an undercover CIA mission, Navy SEAL Lt. Garth Vale finds an abandoned baby, and his superiors sure don't want to know about it. The only person who can help him is the beautiful new doctor in town, but she's got another surprise for him...

She's got a solution... at a price...

Dr. Bronwyn Whitescarver has left the frantic pace of big city ER medicine for a small town medical practice. Her bags aren't even unpacked yet when gorgeous, intense Garth Vale shows up on her doorstep in the middle of the night with a sick baby...

But his story somehow doesn't add up, and Bronwyn isn't quite sure who she's saving—the baby, or the man...

—⁓—

"Take two strong characters, throw in some humor and a baby and you've got a perfect combination for a heartwarming romance. The suspense subplot is a bonus in this well-written story." —*RT Book Reviews*, 4.5 Stars

For more Mary Margret Daughtridge, visit:

www.sourcebooks.com

Free Fall

USA Today Bestselling Author

by Catherine Mann

———

On this mission, there are no accidents...

Pararescueman Jose "Cuervo" James is the guy they call for the most dangerous assignments. He lives for his job.

On a high-risk rescue deep in the African jungle, Jose encounters sexy, smart Interpol agent Stella Carson. They'd once had an affair that burned hot and fast, but family is everything to Stella, and Jose just can't go there.

Fate has thrown them into the deadly hot zone together, and sparks will fly...but only if they can live to tell about it.

———

"Mann sweeps readers along with pulse-pounding
suspense, passion, and a full-out frontal assault
of the senses that will keep readers gripping
their seats."—*RT Book Reviews*, 4.5 Stars

"Mann's novel of romantic suspense has everything
she's known for—engaging protagonists, a solid
military background, great sex and sexual tension, and
a ripped-from-the-headlines immediacy."—*Booklist*

For more Catherine Mann, visit:

www.sourcebooks.com

Bad Nights

New York Times Bestselling Author

by Rebecca York

—⁓—

You only get a second chance...

Private operative and former Navy SEAL Jack Brandt barely escapes a disastrous undercover assignment, thanks to the most intriguing woman he's ever met. When his enemies track him to her doorstep, he'll do anything to protect Morgan from the danger closing in on them both...

If you stay alive...

Since her husband's death, Morgan Rains has only been going through the motions. She didn't think anything could shock her—until she finds a gorgeous man stumbling naked and injured through the woods behind her house. He's mysterious, intimidating—and undeniably compelling.

Thrown together into a pressure cooker of danger and intrigue, Jack and Morgan are finding in each other a reason to live—if they can survive.

—⁓—

"Rebecca York delivers page-turning
suspense."—Nora Roberts

"Rebecca York's writing is fast-paced, suspenseful,
and loaded with tension."—Jayne Ann Krentz

For more Rebecca York, visit:

www.sourcebooks.com

About the Author

Anne Elizabeth is a romance author and a comic creator. With a BS in Business and MS in Communications from Boston University, she is a regular presenter at the RT Book Lovers Convention as well as a member of the Authors Guild and Romance Writers of America. Her published credits include stories with Atria/Simon & Schuster, Highland Press, Dynamite Entertainment, Sea Lion Books, and Bravo Zulu Studios, LLC. AE is the recipient of the *RT Book Reviews* LA Banks Warrior Woman Award. She grew up in Greenwich, Connecticut, and now lives in the mountains above San Diego with her husband, a retired Navy SEAL. In her free time, she is also a serious Amelia Earhart who is always on the hunt for a new adventure. Most recently, she jumped from an airplane and flew a glider. Her motto is Live Boldly. Catch AE on the Web at AnneElizabeth.net.